CHRISTIAN HEINRICH SPIESS

THE DWARF OF WESTERBOURG

WITH AN INTRODUCTION BY
DANIEL CORRICK

THE DWARF
OF WESTERBOURG

CHRISTIAN HEINRICH SPIESS (1755–1799) was a German actor and writer. Born the son of a pastor, he abandoned his academic studies for the life of the stage. He wrote numerous plays, but is best remembered for his novels which featured ghosts, robbers and knights, and which were hugely popular during his lifetime. His plays include *Die drei Töchter* (1782), *Maria Stuart* (1783), and *Klara von Hoheneichen* (1792). Noteworthy among his works of fiction are *Der alte Überall and Nirgends* (1792), *Die Löwenritter* (1794), and the great Gothic novel *Das Petermännchen* (1793).

DANIEL CORRICK is an editor, philosopher and writer. From 2010 to 2014 he ran Hieroglyphic Press and edited the journal *Sacrum Regnum*. He has published essays on various nineteenth-century figures including Hugo von Hofmannsthal, Gabriele d'Annunzio and Arthur Machen, as well as contributing articles on philosophy of religion topics to the Ontological Investigations blog. He co-edited *Drowning in Beauty: The Neo-Decadent Anthology* (Snuggly Books, 2018).

SNUGGLY BOOKS

CONTENTS

INTRODUCTION

*T*HE DWARF OF WESTERBOURG, titled *Das Petermännchen* in its native German (literally, *Little Peter*, though the supernatural connotations of this name would be lost on foreign language audiences), represents a pivotal point in European literature. Part medieval romance, part popular shocker and part moral fairy-tale, the novel looks back to the popular dramas of the *Sturm und Drang* period and forward to the Gothic novel. From its appearance in 1791 it exerted an influence on some of the greatest writers of horror and romance in English literature, such as Anne Radcliffe, Matthew Lewis, and Sir Walter Scott.

The current translation was originally published in 1827 and is remarkably faithful to the original, a minor miracle in an age in which translators were apt to bowdlerize, truncate or even add in whole sections of their own invention. Until now, however, it has proved almost impossible to locate; despite the promises of multiple publishers, reprint editions never saw the light of day and the original remains so rare that only a handful of volumes exist in institutions, with the occasional privately owned copy surfacing on the market every few decades for eye-watering sums.

This introduction will endeavour to give a brief sketch of the novel's influence on the Gothic writers and its place in German literature of the time. To begin, though, something must be said about its author.

Christian Heinrich Spiess was born on the 4th of April, 1755 in Freiberg. Like so many of the intellectual and literary figures of the eighteenth century, he came from an ecclesiastical background; his mother was the daughter of an established Evangelical family and his father served as pastor in the nearby mountain town of Helbigsdorf. It might have been expected that the young Spiess, who showed an early aptitude for reading and writing, would follow in his ancestors' devotional footsteps, but the death of his father in 1761 threw the family into financial hardships and obscured any dreams of a set career path they may have had planned for the boy.

He received his preliminary education at a Freiberg grammar school, during which period he developed an interest in poetry and won several prizes for his essays. His teachers and mother had plans for him to enrol at the Gymnasium but in 1770, at the age of sixteen, for reasons known only to himself, Spiess fled Freiberg and the State of Saxony and journeyed to neighbouring Bohemia, where, after some wandering, he took refuge at the Cistercian monastery in Ossegg. This edifice, over the centuries the sight of massacres and clerical conspiracies, with its towering Baroque façade and vaulted interior, ceilings decorated with frescos in the Spanish style and altars curtained in damask and ornamented with precious metals from the mountain mines, quite possibly encapsulated all of the lavish, seemingly over-indulgent ecclesiastical aesthetic later Gothic novelists found so titillating. Here Spiess befriended the abbot and undertook instruction in the Catholic Faith (his motives for conversation were probably financial—in later life he expressed regrets over it to his mother, hastening to reassure her he still held true to the principles of his childhood religion).

Whatever his motives, the young man so impressed his host that the monastery agreed to support him through the course of university education, probably in the hopes he would take up the Cistercian habit himself. He was dispatched to Prague, the then Bohemian capital, there to study at the Karolinum. Over the four years Spiess attended university, he familiarised himself with the contemporary German literary scene and had several of his own pieces accepted for publication in student journals. He also came under the influence of Karl Heinrich Seibt, a philosophy professor who gave influential lectures on morality and aesthetics. Although a Jesuit-educated theologian, Seibt was a central figure in Enlightenment educational reforms, being a tireless champion of German literature and language as a vehicle for high culture and the moral improvement of the nation. His views on the relationship between society and the individual were to influence Spiess's more serious works, such as his studies of insanity and suicide.

The prospect of an academic life did not appeal to Spiess, however, so during the year of 1774, the student once again fled his settled life, and, in a series of moves eerily reminiscence of Goethe's *Wilhelm Meister*, ended up joining a travelling theatre company, the Karl Wahr Ensemble. Its director, Wahr himself, was a self-made man (allegedly a blacksmith's apprentice originally) with strong reformist ideas. The atmosphere of the company, partly due to Wahr, was one of youthful Enlightenment ideals—the theatre as an instrument for the moral health of the nation, romantic patriotism, the brotherhood of man and some Utopian rejuvenation of the social order—combined with that of a wandering bohemian lifestyle which, to established society, was neither ordered nor moral. It was in this environment that Spiess turned his attention from poetry to dramatic writing, mostly melodramas and medieval romances. His own stage debut was enthusiastically received and he was soon appearing in the works of prominent eighteenth-century dramatists such as G.E. Lessing and Goethe himself. He also began a relationship with one of the resident actresses, Sophie Korner, who despite being already married (at least on paper), was to become his mistress and lifelong companion.

The company enjoyed some success touring between Prague and Vienna and sometimes further afield to St. Petersburg. In 1778 it gained a residency with the Kotzen Theatre in Prague; the security of a comparatively permanent venue gave its members far greater control over what performances to stage and the frequency with which they could do so. Spiess saw his own dramatic works performed on a regular basis to favourable audience receptions, which lead Wahr to push him in the direction of writing and directing rather than performing. Around this time he was initiated into a local Masonic order, again at the urgings of Wahr, by all records a positive connoisseur of secret societies and learned brotherhoods, and through this made the acquaintance of a Bohemian nobleman, Count Kaspar Hermann von Künigl, whose patronage was to support Spiess throughout the rest of his life and help facilitate some of his larger dramatic productions.

During the late 1770s and into the beginning of the 1780s Spiess was hard at work on new dramas. At this point he was already turning his hand to the popular *Ritterdramen*, faux-medieval epics of knightly adventure. In 1782 his literary aspirations received a powerful boost with the publication of Friedrich Schiller's great *Sturm und Drang* play, *The Robbers*. As well as appearing in the company's productions of it over the next season (his role was that of the elderly Count von Moor), Spiess joined the slew of young German writers writing verse and prose about noble outlaw figures waging guerrilla warfare against the corrupt society that wronged them. In a bizarre twist of literary fate, that same year Spiess published a tragedy, *Maria Stuart*, which was almost certainly an influence on Schiller's 1800 drama of the same name.

This comfortable arrangement continued until 1784, when the Karl Wahr Ensemble fell to pieces after its leader's long-running feud with another director forced the newly rebuilt theatre's owners to dispense with his services. But if Wahr's literary star had temporarily fallen, Spiess's was on the rise. He retired from the stage and, with Sophie in tow, decamped to the Bohemian estate of Count von Künigl, Bezděkov castle, where he was nominally employed as librarian and accountant to his aristocratic benefactor. In reality he was given unlimited freedom to pursue his literary ambitions. Over the course of the next eight years Spiess completed nearly a dozen plays, including two *ritterdramen* which were to prefigure *The Dwarf of Westerbourg* in style, as well as producing a music-hall adaption of Mozart's *Don Giovanni* which was enthusiastically received in Vienna. He also composed and published a literary work of a rather different tone, his *Lives of the Suicides*, a series of fictional studies purporting to present cases of suicide and the factors that drove the victims to it. Unlike the author's dramatic or novelistic works, in which moral discourse is necessarily off-set by entertainment or shock factors, these stories were intended as serious social commentary. The act of taking one's own life had held a fascination for Romanticism since Goethe's *Sorrows of Young Werther*, and the changes in cultural attitude which gave birth to that movement, the lauding of moral sentiment over rational self-interest, meant that the general public were more sympathetically inclined to those who undertook such tragic courses of action. Spiess (following, one suspects, Seibt) offered a compassionate take on the phenomena, casting his suicides largely as the tragic victims of a cruel and unjust society, normal people caught up in crushing life events, rather than intrinsically deviant or weak-minded individuals.

Again, it was an encounter with Schiller that was to prompt the next stage in Spiess's literary development. Over the last years of the 1780s Schiller had published instalments of his novel *The Ghost-Seer*, a tale of apparent ghostly manifestations and fantastic conspiracies. Although it remained unfinished—Schiller allegedly found it tedious—it triggered a vast public appetite for works of this sort. Soon a new genre, the *Schauerroman* or "terror novel" was born, at first adhering closely to the rationalising formula set forth by Schiller but soon incorporating the robber and knight themes so popular in the theatre over the last decade. Here Spiess was one of the earliest and the most prolific proponents of this genre. In 1791 he published *Das Petermännchen*, which combined the ghost story form with the setting and characters of the *Ritterdramen* he'd grown so apt at writing for the stage. This was closely followed by *The Old Everywhere and Nowhere* (*Der Alte Überall und Nirgends*) which tells of a fallen knight caught up in supernatural intrigues.

These novels proved immensely popular. They were read with guilty pleasure by the intelligentsia, who publically scorned supernatural melodrama, and with open relish by the middle and serving classes able to obtain them from the newly established public libraries. Soon a horde of Spiess imitators sprung up, all eager to capitalise on the *Schauerroman* trend, yet few could match Spiess's own literary vigour. Overnight he became something of a local celebrity, receiving visits from curious parties eager to meet the author of such disreputable but exciting works. Ever theatrical, he wasted no time capitalising on this: out in the forests of his host's estate, near a rocky outcrop local villagers would later dub the "Spiess-Stone" he had constructed a writer's lodge which became the object of pilgrimage for many noblemen and townsfolk from all over Bohemia. This was soon augmented by a fake cemetery complete with grave mounds and artificially aged tombstones. Guests found Spiess a pleasant host, lively and engaging but not pretentious, and he soon received invitations to stay at neighbouring estates, which he enthusiastically took up.

Count von Künigl was happy with his friend's literary success and does not seem to have begrudged funding the eccentric building projects. The two remained close, taking trips together in the mountains and longer journeys over to

Bavaria. Cracks had begun to form in the domestic situation, however. For several years the Count had been engaged in a semi-clandestine relationship with Spiess's on-and-off lover Sophie, who lived with the latter on the estate. More significantly, Spiess had begun his own affair with von Künigl's wife, the Countess Maria Theresia.

The final decade of Spiess's life saw him maintain his prodigal literary output despite problems with physical and mental health. During this period he produced more "terror" novels in ghostly and folkloric veins—*The Twelve Sleeping Maidens* (*Die zwölf schlafenden Jungfrauen*), *The Lion-Knight* (*Die Löwenritter*), *The Secret of the Ancient Egyptian* (*Die Geheimnisse der alten Egipzier*) and *Hans Heiling, the Fourth and Final Prince of the Spirits of Earth, Wind, Fire and Water* (*Hans Heiling, vierter und letzter Regent der Erde-, Luft-, Feuer-, und Wassergeiste*) to name but a few. Sadly, as of the present day, most are still to be translated. In addition to these full-length works he also completed more plays and over a dozen volumes of short fiction, one of which, *My Journeys Through the Caves of Misfortune and Chambers of Sorrow* (*Meine Reisen durch die Höhlen des Unglücks und Gemächer des Jammers*), was partially translated into English under the disappointing title of *The Fallen Minister and Other Tales* and published in 1809. In his private life the burden of the affair with Countess Maria Theresia had begun to take its toll. Whether it was due to jealousy over Sophie, jealousy over Maria, or a general feeling of resentment about being indebted to the Count, Spiess became prone to bouts of extreme melancholy, during which he'd shut himself away in his lodge and see no one for weeks at a time. Perhaps reflecting upon his own internal turmoil he released another moral study, *Lives of the Insane*. As with suicide, insanity is seen as social phenomena and one for which all parties share a degree of responsibility; the sufferers, by giving in to disordered passions which ultimately develop into mania and those around them for their potentially psychologically damaging actions, whether neglectful or overtly malicious. Again, insanity is largely seen as a form of social victimhood (one of the pieces is also notable for including a discussion of what we would know as PTSD in a captive returning from war).

By the summer of 1779 Spiess's health had declined to the point where he found himself bed-ridden for days at a time, suffering from headaches and extreme depression. A final disaster heralded the end: at the beginning of August his secret lover Countess Maria Theresia von Künigl died after a sudden illness. In the decades that followed, scandal-mongers gave credit to a rumour she had taken her own life with poison, something for which there was no evidence at the time (both doctors' records and burial deeds gave the cause as a fever, possibly typhus). On receiving this news Spiess fell into a manic state, experiencing seizures and severe hallucinations, only to return to lucidity briefly before finally following his lover to the grave on August the 17th. Critics and overzealous admirers were keen to link his demise with the macabre nature of his writings, but again, it appears a fever was responsible, although probably in conjunction with underlying conditions.

As Spiess was such a prolific writer he left behind him enough manuscripts to ensure a steady stream of new publications for several years after his death, a process that was supplemented by opportunistic imitators releasing their own work under his name. His fiction remained popular throughout the Romantic period and only disappeared from view when the Gothic novel itself fell out of vogue. He was rediscovered in the mid-twentieth century by psychologists and anthropologists who saw his studies of suicide and madness as historically important records of changes in social perspective regarding mental illness.

Although the *Lives* have thereto attracted the most interest amongst historians of ideas, it was *The Dwarf of Westerbourg* which exerted the greatest literary influence, both in its author's native Germany and in the British Isles. Its original title refers to an actual folkloric entity, a dwarfish house-spirit which is said to serve as a guardian of Schwerin Palace and is honoured by several statutes in that city. The "Little Peter" of the novel is clearly developed from this model; as with its northern proto-type, Spiess's dwarf is introduced as a half-mythical castle guardian and family protector, though the Mephistophelian role he later takes on is original to the novel. Spiess also re-jects the far-northern setting of the original legend and sets his novel in the Rhineland near Speyer, an ancient cathedral city and centre of the Holy Roman Empire more suited as a back-drop for grand medievalism.

As will be clear to the reader, the setting and style of *The Dwarf* owes much to the *Ritterdrama* form Spiess was most familiar with. Tournaments, fallen knights on pilgrimage to the Holy Land in the hopes of regaining their lost honour, and farcical amorous misadventures in Ottoman harems form the basic building blocks of such plays. The novel's theatrical herit-age can be clearly seen in the way in which dialogue is set out as if in a dramatic script (ironically, it was twice adapted back into stage form). Another major influence is that of the *Märchen*, or fairy-tale. Throughout his career, Spiess drew heavily on the rich Germanic tradition of folk and children's tales which was later sampled by the Brothers Grimm and would provide so many fertile motifs for Romantic artists. In this case, the novel's plot follows the course of a moral fable, with a series of trials and a typically folkloric emphasis on the number seven. Indeed, in some scenes, such as the protagonist's encounter with Little Peter's mysterious counter-part Mathilda and her subsequent imprisonment of Clara in an enchanted castle, the reader may divine influences of even familiar fairy-tales such as *Sleeping Beauty* and *Rapunzel.*

For all its traditional packaging, *The Dwarf* is a fully-fledged "terror-novel," complete with the family curses, ancestral spectres, and demon-haunted castle ruins which were soon to become the stock elements of the Gothic novel. It differs though in a major respect from *The Ghost-Seer*, which started the *Schauerroman* craze. Unlike in Schiller's novel and its popular imitations such as Karl Friedrich Kahlert's *Der Geisterbanner* (translated, very badly, as *The Necromancer: a Tale of the Black Forest*), wherein the supposedly supernatural occurrences are ultimately explained away as the result of human trickery, the supernatural is here a very real force, trying at the moral limitation of the characters. Despite being inspired by Schiller, it is thematically closer to that other great *Sturm und Drang* work; Goethe's *Faust*.

The Dwarf is at heart a Faustian narrative, though there are relatively few direct borrowings from Goethe's play—one might cite the race to rescue a seduced lover from execution and the Devil evading contractual obligation due to inability to cross holy ground—which leads one to suspect Spiess drew mainly from older sources, like the original *Faustbuch*. Spiess, more so than Goethe, uses the theme of the Faustian bargain as a way of exploring the personal and social danger of unrestrained passion; not only must the bargainer pay the ultimate price for the ability to get whatever they want, but the unfettered fulfilment of their desires inevitably brings destruction to other parties involved, as is the case here with Rudolph's conquests. Unlike in older stories, complete spiritual ruin does not follow upon the contract signed in blood but from continued exercise of the liberty the devil-bought power gives one (evinced by the way a character continues on to degradation even when released from the contract). Critics attacked the unrepentant supernaturalism of Spiess as socially irresponsible compared to the rationalisations of *The Ghost-Seer*, but, in fact, his novel serves as strong a moral purpose as that of Schiller.

Whereas Schiller's novel pits rationality against deception and conspiracy, those of Spiess pit virtue, particularly the virtue of self-control, against temptation and degeneration. Unlike the author of the original Faust story, or of its subsequent dramatizations, Spiess also attempts to illustrate the Augustinian idea of vice or evil gradually robbing one of one's freedom. Ironically, this relatively sophisticated albeit not particularly original item of moral philosophy was lost on some readers, leading one individual to write an alternative "moral" happy ending much after the manner of that enemy of Goethe who wrote *The Joys of Young Werther*.

Of greater importance, at least for literary history, than the novel's reception in its native Germany was the effect it had on English writers. A translation appeared far too late for it to be included amongst the "horrid novels" pilloried by Jane Austin in *Northhanger Abbey* but none-the-less *The Dwarf of Westerbourg*'s influence can be seen in the works of authors who were to define the Gothic novel. Sir Walter Scott, whose work was to influence the evolution of the Gothic during the Victorian period, consumed Spiess's "terror-novels" with relish alongside the dramas of Schiller and Goethe whilst a student at Edinburgh, reading out whole passages translated impromptu to friends. It was likely the folkloric aspect of Spiess's work and the knightly setting in particular that appealed to him (it should be remembered Scott did much to popularise romantic medievalism in Britain). His biographer recalls him speaking with particular fondness of *The Dwarf*, "a production of *diableri*"—indeed nearly thirty years later in *The Monastery* he adapted an episode from this novel and discussed its merits in a footnote, though misattributing the work to Ludwig Tieck. Closer to home, Anne Radcliffe, one of the main originators of the Gothic novel in English, is reported to have read *The Dwarf* and to have borrowed from it for the funeral scene in *The Mysteries of Udolpho*. Here the influence is limited to more superficial aspects, namely settings and period details, as Radcliffe tended towards the cultivation of atmosphere and mystery rather than the overt moral and supernatural horror focused on by Spiess.

Not so for that other giant of the English Gothic, M.G. Lewis, who probably first encountered the novel during the months he spent amidst Weimar high-society during the summer of 1792, a sojourn his family hoped would prepare him for a diplomatic career but in reality served mainly as an introduction to German literary culture, particularly the *Schauerroman*. It was here he first conceived the idea for his own romance. As is well known, the author of *The Monk* had no qualms about burrowing prodigiously from the works of others and Spiess's novel did not escape his appetites. As with Spiess's *The Dwarf of Westerbourg*, *The Monk* is a novel of demonically assisted seduction in which an initially virtuous protagonist is drawn deeper and deeper into sin, destroying the lives of innocents through their depraved actions (both differ from the eschatological binary of *Faust* by which the character is never virtuous and achieves his ruin at one stroke). Indeed, the influence is so strong that the ending chapter of Lewis's epic can be seen as a fusion of *The Dwarf* with various Faustbuch renditions and a newspaper bagatelle, "The History of Santon Barsisa." Here there is the same final incest plot, the spectral accusal of the protagonist by his victims deployed with greater theatrical flourish by Spiess, and the device of the magic book opened in a certain way to summon the forces of evil. The satirical polemic against French libertinism, that unchecked indulgence of appetite that robs the hedonist of the freedom from constraint that they so prize, that some see in Lewis' novel might well also have its origins in Spiess's Augustinian moralising.

Whilst it would be an exaggeration to say the Gothic genre would not have existed without the works of Spiess and the early terror novelists he inspired, it would certainly have taken a different form. Their background in the *Ritterdrama* helped shape the genre's focus on romantic medievalism, as a counterpoint to the secret society angle of Schiller and his disciples. In addition, the moral fable aspect of their work mollified social demands for rationalisation and gave them greater room for explicitly horrific content. This novel, in particular, is a major source of a moral descent plot that would outlast the Gothic and become a staple of horror fiction, both natural and supernatural. English Romantics may have bemoaned the popularity of such works as the "invasion of Speaking Monsters imported from the banks of the Danube" but we can only hope more of them will be available in translation soon.

—Daniel Corrick

A NOTE ON THE TEXT

THE text of *The Dwarf of Westerbourg* here presented is a reprint of the anonymous translation published in 1827 and offered by subscription.

That translation, though following the original German quite closely, does have many peculiarities of diction and punctuation. For the most part, these have been retained, though occasionally amendments have been made, where errors were obvious. The spelling of a few words has also been regularized, and in a handful of cases, modernized.

The most obvious peculiarity in the present text is that much of the dialogue is presented in play-form. In the edition of 1827, the speaker's name is centred on the page, with the dialogue set below, thus greatly expanding the page count, and making reading somewhat less felicitous. We, therefore, have restored the formatting as it is in the original German, with the dialogue continuing on the same line as the speaker's name, which, we believe, makes the text less confusing, and is certainly how the author intended it to appear.

THE DWARF OF WESTERBOURG

BOOK ONE

CHAP. I.

IN the neighbourhood of the ancient city of Spires, rises on the summit of a rock, a castle, almost as antique as the town itself. The traveller, who ascends one of the sides of the mountain, rising above the ruined dungeon, may behold with astonishment, the Rhine bounding at his feet, in a tremendous abyss, which dizzies his senses. But the exquisite scenery on the opposite side of the mountain, must banish all idea of fear from his mind. There, a gentle descent blends the rocks with the plain, while fertile fields, numerous valleys, and profuse vineyards add to the richness of the whole.

The old castle, which forms a principal feature of this landscape, had, for centuries, been the inheritance of the family of Westerbourg. It had witnessed many illustrious deeds in arms, and splendid tournaments; although its name was never pronounced but with terror, as it was believed, by the whole country, to be the habitation of a supernatural being, whose duty it was to guard the walls, and protect the flocks feeding on its plains against wolves and robbers.

This mysterious phantom was, according to tradition, a little man only two feet high; hair, white as snow, fell over his furrowed forehead, and deeply shaded his hollow cheeks; a beard of similar colour; in his right hand he carried a knotty club, in his left he held the strings of a little wallet, which hung from his shoulders; he wore a brown cloth dress, but never covered his head.

For many years this singular being had been, in a degree, the attendant of the knights of Westerbourg. He was often seen walking in the castle. He appeared dejected when any melancholy event threatened them; but joyful and gay when any brilliant prospects opened before him. Sometimes he passed whole years without conversing with the family. At other times he would cheerfully relate to the knights, assembled in the great hall, the feats of valour achieved by the ancient possessors of the castle. He suffered himself to be ridiculed both by the masters and servants, but severely chastised him with his club who presumed to touch his wallet; and none had the courage to resent his weighty blows. He was universally known by the name of "*Little Peter*," both in the castle and its vicinity; and he devoted his arms and his counsels exclusively to the support of the house.

It was generally believed that this dwarf was a spirit, but nobody could account with any degree of certainty for the singularity of his appearance. When questioned on the subject, he never answered, but cast a melancholy look on his wallet. Each successive possessor of the castle had, from motives of gratitude, endeavoured to render his situation more agreeable. They richly endowed the neighbouring convents, that prayers might be continually read for the deliverance of his soul. But he still continued an inmate of the castle.

Towards the middle of the 13th century, this castle fell to the possession of Rodolphe of Westerbourg, by the premature death of his parents, when he had attained the age of twenty. According to the custom of the times, he lived in the most simple manner possible; hunting in his woods, and collecting the tolls from merchants who descended the Rhine. He had not yet felt the torments or the delights of love so natural at his age. He generally retired extremely fatigued, and rose early in the morning to acquire new strength by pursuing the wolves and bears.

One evening his horn and hounds were heard later than usual, and he roused the badgers from their dens by torch light. When he returned, the moon shone full on all the turret of his castle, and he was so fatigued that he entirely lost his appetite, and left his hunting companions to retire to his apartment. Just as he had taken off his heavy armour Little Peter entered and placed himself near the bed. It was not the first time he had appeared to Rodolphe, as the latter had often amused himself when a boy in deriding his extraordinary figure; but as he had not seen him since the death of his father, he supposed he had forsaken his house forever, and therefore joyfully welcomed the protector of his ancestors; approached him with confidence, and asked him what had occasioned the return after so long an absence?

PETER. I come to offer up my vows for your happiness on the anniversary of your birth

RODOLPHE. The day of my birth?

PETER. Yes, Rodolphe. It is twenty-four years this very night and hour since you first beheld the light. The castle rang with joy; all was festivity and merriments. Have you forgotten the day?

RODOLPHE. No; I remember it with gratitude and will retire to the chapel to pray.

PETER. Stay; I have something to communicate to you. You can pray tomorrow. You are now become a valiant knight.

RODOLPHE. If you think so I congratulate myself.

PETER. I come today from a great distance. More than twenty young ladies, fair as the lilies, slender as the poplars, enquired whether the graceful Rodolphe did not soon intend to lead his bride to his castle.

RODOLPHE. And what did you reply?

PETER. That Rodolphe passed his time in hunting in the forests, and had none to think of the ladies

RODOLPHE. Peter, you expressed my ideas.

PETER. But these young ladies were so beautiful; their eyes sparkled with such fire; their bosoms heaved so gracefully when they enquired after you.

RODOLPHE. What do I care about these girls?

PETER. You are perfectly right. It is very agreeable to traverse the woods in liberty. You have no wife to trouble you, and no children to disturb you with their cries. You can go about when you please, and return the same. But, Rodolphe, in this state of liberty do you feel no privations?

RODOLPHE. My desires are few, and those which I have can be easily gratified, as my heart is always at ease when in the field, or at the tournament.

PETER. It would be well if this could continue. But the time will arrive, Rodolphe, when you will change your sentiments. A wife, and indeed all women, have their disagreeable sides. She attaches herself to her husband, like a thorn to the traveller's foot. If he is absent for a moment, she cries and faints. If he wishes to go out, she scolds; and recommences at his return. Mothers, sisters, and cousins assist at these scenes. Indeed a husband has but few real enjoyments.

RODOLPHE. Peter, I shall never marry; your experience of so many centuries confirms me in my resolution.

PETER. But love—Rodolphe—love is very pleasing; love is the balm of life, without love you can never enjoy any real pleasures; you will fade like a sterile flower which vegetates on a rock, and you will live and die without having existed.

RODOLPHE. But you treat me like a child, showing me a brilliant bauble and then hiding it again.

PETER. Seek it, Rodolphe, and endeavour to seize it

RODOLPHE. And what is it I am to obtain?

PETER. Is it absolutely necessary that you must love a wife? Must you be chained by indissoluble bonds to a thing which may soon be tired of you, and you of it. Enjoy yourself. I must be off.

RODOLPHE. Whither?

PETER. I have other affairs and must be tomorrow at Dürnstein. The flocks of the knights of Ottenwiel have, for a long time past, been devoured by wolves. All the nobles of the country have been invited to tomorrow's chase. These wolves are terrible animals; the servants have already attacked them with success. The eldest daughter of Ottenwiel is to distribute the prizes, and she is the most beautiful maiden in the country.

Peter disappeared, while Rodolphe endeavoured in vain to compose his spirits to sleep; he fancied he beheld figures beautiful as an April morn, blushing as the rose, slender as a poplar, fleeting before him. His bed seemed a bed of thorns, his chamber a cell, his castle a desert. At the first crowing of the cock he called for his arms, mounted his war-hose, and soon attained the place of destination.

At his arrival the fierce animals had already wounded three knights and killed six of the most expert huntsmen. Rodolphe fought with the vigour of a giant, and killed four wolves, the largest that had ever been seen in the woods of Germany. He was unanimously proclaimed victor by his companions, conducted in triumph to the castle, and presented by the eldest daughter of Ottenwiel with a magnificent scarf.

CHAP. II.

THIS lady was named Regina: beautiful, and in every respect calculated to inflame the heart of a young man. Her figure was elegant, her eyes black, her skin fair as the fairest lilies, and her hair floating in ringlets over her finely formed neck. The thin veil she wore betrayed the emotions of her heart, while her whole form commanded love and respect.

Many were the knights that sighed for Regina, and constantly waited her orders; but none had yet made the least impression on her heart. She often joined in their amusements and conversations, which sometimes appeared interesting and sometimes insipid to her; and she often enquired of herself what was yet wanting to complete her happiness. But the elegant and graceful Rodolphe occupied her mind. The whole of that day she saw him along. If his lips did but move she was all attention; she was deaf to the sound of the trumpet, for her ear heard only the accent of Rodolphe. "There", said she, "is the man whom my imagination has sought so long in vain among all these knights. Were my desires consulted, and the void of my mind to be filled, Rodolphe should be the partner of my joys."

Rodolphe was seated before her, immovable as a statute; intoxicated with the beauteous image of Regina; he contemplated in silence the celestial object. His very existence seemed extinct. "Oh! Love, how sweet art thou!" said he, incessantly;

and recalled to mind the words of the mysterious Dwarf. When love has once attained a certain degree it soars to infinity, suddenly manifesting itself to the object of its adoration; it fears no obstacles, and breaks the rules of good breeding; those rules which often keep the timorous lover for months, nay years, in agonizing suspense.

Rodolphe quitted Dürnstein not without the hope of having made a favourable impression on the mind of Regina, as she had deigned to cast a look of affection on him at his departure, and gently returned the pressure of his hand.

When arrived at his castle he entirely abandoned himself to his passion, and thought himself happy in having experienced the first impression of love. But he soon thought otherwise when he retired a lonely being to his apartment. He rose and sought repose in the dark shade of the woods, but returned without finding it; he rose again, and again he returned, and thus spent three successive days.

"I cannot," said he, "any longer bear this restraint, these excruciating torments. Tomorrow I will fly to her father, demand her hand, and be happy."

No sooner was this resolution taken than Little Peter was at his bedside.

RODOLPHE (*rising suddenly*). What happiness again to see you, ancient friend of my house. I am in want of your advice and assistance. I have experienced the charms of love. During three days of insupportable length, I felt, that without love, life is but an insipid repose. I have resolved to go to Dürnstein, and not to return until I have obtained the object of my wishes; then Peter, the castle shall resound with rejoicings, balls and feasts, which you can describe to my descendants for centuries to come. But you are silent! Must I be happy? Do you perceive insurmountable difficulties to that bliss my ambition leads me to hope? Speak, Peter; can Regina—will she, ought she to become my wife?

PETER. *She can.*—What father would refuse Rodolphe of Westerbourg! Who would not open his arms with joy to receive such a son-in-law? *She will*, for she is prepossessed in your favour, and impatiently waits the hour of your arrival to demand her of her father. And *she ought*, for the brave and noble Rodolphe has sworn to become the slave of a woman, to feast on her looks, and to obey her slightest caprices.

RODOLPHE. I never swore that!—

PETER. But you have sworn to marry a woman; believe me, servitude and marriage are so synonymous that it is difficult to form a correct distinction

RODOLPHE. But love is agreeable, it will soften the servitude it prepares. I assure you, Peter, that I am another man. I am the organ of Regina, and no longer myself; I obey her wishes, and nothing ought to prevent me from espousing her. A wife the worthiest, the most exquisite gift of Heaven!

Peter made various representations to Rodolphe concerning a married state, and painted a single life with the most flattering colours. But Rodolphe was deaf to all his arguments, and remained unshaken in his resolution of marrying without delay.

PETER. My duty was to endeavour to prevent this union. But as you are determined, it is now my turn to offer you every assistance in my power. Are you going tomorrow to Dürnstein?

RODOLPHE. Yes, at a very early hour.

PETER. And you will demand Regina of her father?

RODOLPHE. I will, as soon as I alight.

PETER. And you will make her your wife; the wife of the knight of Westerbourg?

RODOLPHE. Yes, eternal questioner; I will, and be happy without delay.

PETER. You will have to encounter many difficulties and great obstacles. However, I have remedies for everything. Your impatience is extreme, and you must triumph and be happy.

Little Peter then opened his wallet, and drew from thence a ball of thread, which was ornamented with numerous and different sized needles.

PETER. Here, Rodolphe, after having demanded Regina of her father, present him this ball; you will perceive a change in him, and he will immediately accord you his daughter.

RODOLPHE. Malignant spirit; how dare you mock me? Of what use can this ball and these needles be to the knight of Ottenwiel? Perhaps in your youth such a gift might be of some value; but now——

PETER. It is now that it will be of the most essential service to you. He has in vain sought this ball for twenty years past. But I will not fatigue you with my advice. Seek your happiness yourself; I have kept this trifle for many a year in my wallet, and can still keep it. Good night; in a year I will return, and enquire after your welfare.

RODOLPHE. One moment more. You gave my ancestors good counsels; I believe you would not deceive me; I will accept your present, and present it to the father of Regina. This ball must be a precious object that can decide the fate of a beautiful lady.

Little Peter disappeared.

CHAP. III.

BEFORE break of day, the knight of Westerbourg, with his ball in his pocket, was on the road to Dürnstein. His way to the castle lay through a small forest of pines, into which Regina had strolled to indulge her melancholy feelings, under the shade of the trees. Rodolphe approached her before she perceived him. A loud shriek testified her surprise; the gallant Rodolphe descended from his horse, related the purport of his visit, and ventured to imprint a kiss on the lips of his mistress, who was transported with joy, when informed of his intention; and accompanied him to the door of her father's apartment, waiting the issue of the conference in the outer hall. Rodolphe was received by Ottenwiel with politeness, and according to the custom of these ancient times, related the impression which his daughter had made on his mind, and concluded his speech by begging of him the only balm which could heal the wound. He promised an honourable and handsome provision, and should he die without heirs, the inheritance of his fortune.

"I know," added the young knight, "that you have long sought a treasure which is now in my possession. I present it to you with great pleasure, if you accord me your daughter." Filled with hope as he pronounced these words, he drew the fatal ball from his pocket, and presented it to the lord of Dürnstein.

Suddenly the brows of Ottenwiel lowered, his gracious smiles vanished, and rage was depicted in every feature. "Young man," exclaimed he, "I have long felt the most sincere remorse for the follies of my youthful days, their very remembrance oppresses my declining years; but you, you insult this repentance, you openly reproach me with a fault which I believed sufficiently concealed from the eyes of the world. God may pardon you, but I call on him to witness the oath I now take, that were you the master of the empire and treasures of the East, and were your demand as sincere as it is insulting, you should never possess my daughter!"

Rodolphe was on the point of replying, but the knight stopped him, and advised him to leave his house, if he did not wish to compel him to violate the laws of hospitality. Westerbourg in despair reached the door with tottering steps. Regina anxiously awaited his return; she called, but he fled in haste, without listening to her. The only idea which filled his mind was the determination of revenging himself on the little phantom, and tearing out his long beard hair by hair, and of preparing the most excruciating tortures for him. He did not then imagine that the spirit was laughing at his rage, and could easily avoid his best premeditated plans.

With such dispositions the knight arrived at his castle. The bell told the hour of twelve, but Peter did not appear. The furious Rodolphe vainly sought him in every corner of the house. A week of anxious expectation elapsed; at the end of which, unsatisfied vengeance, hopeless love, and continual restlessness, chained him to a bed of sufferings. A violent fever threatened his life, his faithful friends and companions in arms began to deplore his loss, when towards midnight Peter appeared at his bedside. The fever was instantaneously calmed, his senses returned; and he thus, in a feeble voice, addressed the enemy of his repose:—

"Miserable being! why thus delay your appearance? Why do you choose the moment in which my hands are too weak to revenge me? But I shall soon be removed to that world which you inhabit. There, cruel and false counsellor, my vengeance shall pursue you until it is satiated. But why, Peter, thus reduce me to misery?"

PETER. Whatever I have done, I did it for your welfare, and that of your whole family. Your impetuosity is enfeebled, and you are now more capable of discerning than you were before. Listen, and judge whether I have not acted as a friend, and preserved your honour.

RODOLPHE. May the everlasting fire of hell reward you for your trouble!

PETER. Do not interrupt me, and listen with composure to my narrative. It is about five-and-twenty years ago since the old Knight of Ottenwiel went to Palestine, to accomplish a vow which he had made to fight the infidels for three successive years. He kept his word, and many a valiant Saracen felt the effect of his sword. When the Christians assaulted the town of Joppe, he was the first who mounted the wall. The period which he fixed being expired he was only waiting for a ship to convey him to Italy. When one day walking on the sea-shore, he saw a beautiful figure, whose outward appearance announced the poverty of her station. Like you, for the first time, he felt the power of female charms. He did all in his power to gain her confidence, and to persuade her to follow him. Her father was a poor tailor working for the Christian warriors, some days scarcely gaining a sufficiency for himself and daughter; but both were as virtuous as they were poor, and constantly refused the splendid offers of the opulent knight. Although the young person was greatly attached to him, she would not even permit him to press her lily hand. This continued resistance excited the passion of the knight to such a pitch, that he married the tailor's daughter, and settled upon her the whole of his fortune. When the nuptial benediction was completed, and the knight seated at table with family of his bride, the tailor rose, demanded silence, and presented to the astonished knight on a plate a ball of thread. "Here is," he said gravely, "the inheritance and marriage portion of my daughter. It is my only treasure. It will incessantly recall to your mind the obscurity of the birth of your wife, and be a surety to you that she would rather have continued to work with these needles for the remainder of her life, than have exchanged her virtue for the most splendid riches. And you, my dear and only child." added he, "if once your husband should neglect you in a foreign land, and forget what he has sworn in the presence of the Almighty; if he should abandon you, do not forget that your hands were given you by the universal Father of all for the support of your honour and virtue; and that you can never be entirely destitute, having learnt an useful art." The first six months of this marriage passed in the most supreme felicity. The following six months were much less happy, as the knight began seriously to think of returning to his native land, and dreaded to encounter the moment when he must present himself to the proud noble of Germany with the tailor's daughter. He still tenderly loved her, but he found it hard to be exiled forever from his family on her account, to abandon the inheritance of his fathers, and never more to behold his castle. During this conflict his wife presented him with a daughter, but the hour of her birth proved the last of the mother. Ottenwiel was inconsolable. The little Regina, the very image of her mother, claimed and obtained all his attention. It seemed impossible to him to abandon the innocent pledge of a love which continued to burn, although the grave had closed over its object, and to leave with her grandfather all that he held dear on earth. He sought the means of keeping his child with him, of rendering her happy, and found them at the court of Constantine. Courtiers, ever prodigal and ever poor, procured him, for a thousand pieces of gold, a formal attestation, that he, the knight of Ottenwiel, had espoused a Greek lady of a noble and ancient family, and that by her he had a daughter named Regina. A genealogical table was drawn out and duly verified; and Ottenwiel believing himself the happiest of men, returned to Germany with his daughter, whose descent was registered on his arrival. Shortly after, he espoused a rich heiress, and became father of two other daughters; but Regina continues to be his favourite child, and he has resolved to constitute her heiress of the greatest part of his fortune.

RODOLPHE. Now I plainly see all. Now I can explain the anger of the knight, and his dreadful oath.

PETER. Are you not also convinced of the sincerity of the intentions of your friend? Not being able to curb the violence of your passions, he furnished you with the innocent means of avoiding the disgrace which menaced you. Your noble house has flourished for more than five hundred years, and ought the daughter of a tailor to contaminate the purity of its blood? Your descendants would wear a shield quartered with a ball of thread covered with needles, and would ignominiously be forced to fly all knightly amusements.

RODOLPHE. Old man! Incapable of commiserating with the sufferings of youth, it is in vain that you endeavour to excuse yourself. I abhor you forever. How could I guess this secret? What pleasure I should have enjoyed with Regina!

PETER. This adventure is not unknown at the eastern court. Malice is ever on the wing. Several German nobles are yet in Palestine: how can you be assured that one of these will not return, break your shield in the hall of the tournament, and demand of you to justify it by other than mercenary means?

RODOLPHE. Away, and let me die in peace!

PETER. Calm your spirit, Rodolphe;—be a man. I have done my duty as a father, and as a friend. I withheld you when you were plunging headlong into the precipice. If you will not open your eyes I shall find it incumbent on me to conduct and govern you until you are free from danger. Your love is violent, nature cannot resist it, and it must be satisfied. Reanimate yourself, Rodolphe, and seek your bride.

RODOLPHE. Cruel being! Will her father give her to me at present? Will he not keep the oath which my insult caused him to take?

PETER. Are there no other means but a father's consent? Are you obliged to walk in an intricate path, when you can find one which will conduct you in safety to the point?

RODOLPHE. Show me this path; were I forced to scale inaccessible rocks, or traverse the most profound abysses, I will undertake everything to obtain Regina.

PETER. Rejoice, for you shall possess her! Her passion for you is not in the least abated; the obstinate silence of her father on the subject of his refusal, has greatly diminished that confidence and affection which she evinced towards him. Indeed, she begins to feel an aversion for him who refuses to fulfil her most ardent desires, and she is now ready to throw herself into your arms. Compose yourself by sleep; then rise, mount your horse, and proceed to Dürnstein. You will find Regina, towards the evening, in the forest of pines. Explain your torments to her, expose the cruelty of her father, and never believe me again if she does not mount behind you, and fly with you to your castle. Then enjoy her charms as long as your passion continues.

RODOLPHE. No, traitor, never!

PETER. Do not interrupt me; I guess your scruples. You will have nothing to dread from the father's vengeance. He will believe himself happy, if you keep his secret; and yourself scarcely sufficiently recompensed by the charms of his daughter for your silence; and should he be fool enough to demand vengeance, rely upon my zeal. You are acquainted with my power, and know full well that I have never ceased to protect the house of Westerbourg.

RODOLPHE. I will follow the first part of your plan, but leave the second to my delicacy. I am acquainted with the laws of knighthood; I will not degrade my conscience and my honour by a criminal flight. If Regina consents, I will conduct her to my castle: the chaplain shall await our arrival, and unite us forever. The anger of the father will soon be conciliated, when the priest announces the marriage to him, and I shall have justified myself. Of what importance is it to me if the family of my wife is discovered. No one can deprive me of my fortune; and I shall be happy in her arms, although my shield should not be suspended in the hall of the knights, or I should no longer be permitted to signalize my valour in tournaments. Second my desires, Peter, unless you wish me to consider you a demon of the infernal regions, sent to seduce men from the path of virtue.

PETER (*in tears*). The Lord bless you, worthy son of illustrious ancestors! You have undergone the trial, and convinced me that virtue reigns in your heart; your love and sentiments are worthy of you, go and be happy with Regina. Honours, riches, and dignities, are not things which render an union blissful. 'Tis friendship, love, and honourable principles alone, that can form links sufficiently strong to resist the impetuous attacks of adversity. O, my son! I have assisted you in achieving a good act; and my felicity is complete for a century to come. Preserve your health, gather your strength, put your plans in execution, and expect me soon.

RODOLPHE (*astonished*). Protecting angel, accept at least the testimony of my acknowledgements, and——

But the Dwarf had disappeared.

CHAP. IV.

RODOLPHE enjoyed a profound and agreeable sleep for the first time since he had been at Dürnstein. He awoke in an ecstasy of joy. The third day he felt himself sufficiently strengthened to leave his bed and prepare for his visit to Regina. A few faithful followers were to accompany him to Dürnstein. His confessor, informed of the whole, was directed to wait in the chapel, which was ready, until midnight; for Rodolphe decided to conduct his lovely prey to the altar immediately on his arrival.

He was soon on the road with his attendants; and as the sun began to decline, Rodolphe, oppressed by sighs, crossed the little wood and sought Regina: he began to doubt his success, when he beheld her descending from the castle. He instantly met her, explained the object of his visit, answered every objection, and those which he could not remove were soon destroyed by all-powerful love. Regina suggested many difficulties, but insensibly suffered herself to be conducted to the horses of Rodolphe, one of which she irresistingly mounted, delighted at being supported by his nervous arms. Night was fast approaching, and was far advanced when they arrived at the castle of Westerbourg. They had, from a distance, discovered the illuminated chapel, and Regina soon forgot that her father was perhaps seeking her with the utmost solicitude; she suffered herself to be led into the castle by her lover, who was soon to become her husband.

They had entered the chapel, and knelt before the altar . . . when a servant of Rodolphe approached, and informed them that the ceremony could not be performed, as the chaplain had been suddenly taken ill, complained of a dreadful pain and rolled in agony on the floor. Rodolphe seized the hand of Regina, and led her to the chamber of the priest, where she herself saw the poor man who was then unable to articulate one syllable. The arguments of Rodolphe soon prevailed over the scruples of Regina, and engaged her to wait until the morrow; he tranquillized her by promising to send for a priest to a neighbouring convent, and after their union he would set off himself and carry the intelligence to the father.

They sat down to the marriage-feast; and after supper, Rodolphe conducted his bride to an apartment which had been hastily prepared for her. As they traversed a dark vaulted gallery, the rays of the moon darted through the long gothic windows Regina expressed a wish to contemplate that luminary, and was conducted by Westerbourg to a balcony. There the loving pair enjoyed the most charming aspect. It was a most clear and delightful night: not a breeze undulated the air; not a cloud obscured the brilliancy of the heavenly spheres. Nature seemed lulled into a sweet sleep; and the turret owl alone reminded the lovers that they were not the only beings who enjoyed their existence at that moment.

REGINA (*resting her head on the bosom of Rodolphe, and turning her eyes to the moon*). Do you perceive that perfect and brilliant disk? Oh! may it ever be the symbol of our love!

RODOLPHE. It will.

REGINA. May our loves ever be as pure?

RODOLPHE. They will.

REGINA. May they never decrease like that bright luminary;—may they never be hid, as it sometimes is, from mortal view.

RODOLPHE. Never! Never!—and if some cloud should

obscure them for a time, they will soon reappear with redoubled serenity.

REGINA. I wish it with all my heart.—I hope and believe it. How beautiful it is! How tranquil is all creation! Every object enjoys the most perfect repose. But whence proceeds that soft murmur?

RODOLPHE. From a grove planted by my ancestors. It is a delightful walk, which the scorching rays of the sun scarcely penetrate.

REGINA. Let us descend: sleep has forsaken my eyes. I dread being alone: my conscience reproaches me for having quitted my father; for having followed my lover, and not yet being his wife.

RODOLPHE. You shall be so tomorrow at the dawn of day.

They descended supporting each other, and soon disappeared in the shade; which inspired Rodolphe with boldness, and Regina with condescension. Ardent kisses were interchanged; and at the end of one half hour, Regina left the dark recess in the utmost disorder. Her dishevelled locks were blended with the folds of her gown; she wrung her hands; she struck her forehead; she tore her bosom, and gave herself the most odious names.

In vain the knight followed to console her; he promised never more to see her but in the presence of a priest. She saw nothing but her dishonour; she called him the ravisher of her innocence, and precipitately fled to the apartment destined for her. The intoxicated servants had luckily fallen asleep during their absence. They saw not her despair. They heard not her sighs; while Rodolphe, fearing to awake them, stole with a palpitating heart to his lonely chamber.

"Peter will be here," said he, "and will call me to account for the fault I have involuntarily committed." His fear proved groundless, Peter did not appear; and Rodolphe passed the night in seeking the means to appease Regina, to reconcile her to her father, and to commence with her a tranquil and happy life.

CHAP. V.

RODOLPHE, accompanied by a priest, was at the door of Regina's apartment by day-break. He at first tapped gently, and conjured her to open it. But a whole hour elapsed, and no answer being returned, his impatience knew no bounds, and he forced the door. Gods! what a sight for a lover.

Regina extended on the floor, bathed in her blood, grasping a reeking poignard in her hand; her steadfast, but half-closed eyes, fixed on a painting, brought from Palestine by the ancestors of Rodolphe, representing Lucretia despairing at the loss of her honour, and plunging a dagger into her breast. The countenance of Regina plainly testified that she had abandoned herself to despair like Lucretia, and perished like her.

How shall I describe the scene which followed? Rodolphe was at first overcome by a stupor, which soon changed to frenzy, and had not the priest and his servants restrained him, he would have followed Regina to the grave, and avoided the many trials which awaited him. One step out of the straight path led him by degrees from error to error, from precipice to precipice, to the borders of that abyss into which he fell.

Beware young man! Beware young woman! It is for your instruction that I have robbed the worms of this history, who had long since began to destroy it. It is easy to stray from the straight path but it is difficult to regain it.—

It was with difficulty that Rodolphe was dragged from the body of Regina, and laid upon his bed. His servants were obliged to tie his hands, and to watch him closely. The consolations of religion were offered in vain; he ground his teeth in despair.

The desolate father of Regina came to fetch the body of his daughter; but he had not the strength to demand satisfaction of the seducer of her innocence, but shed tears of forgiveness on his couch. He soon followed the child of his affection to the grave; and when Rodolphe was capable of leaving his bed and moderating his grief, the old knight was already placed alongside Regina.

CHAP. VI.

AFTER three long months' confinement Rudolph left his apartment in pursuit of his favourite amusement—the chase. He strolled in the forest, sad and depressed, and returned without game; he had not the courage to shed blood, for that of Regina continually flowed before his mind. His heart was open to all the sufferings of life, and closed to all pleasures. Little Peter made his appearance at the hour of midnight, and roused Rodolphe from the momentary sleep which closed his eyes. A long black crape fell over his shoulders, and abundant tears chased each other down his furrowed cheeks.

RODOLPHE (*trembling*). What do you wish? Whence come you?

PETER. I come from the tomb of your mistress. For these three months past, I have bathed it daily with my tears. I hoped to have seen you there, but my hopes were deceived.

RODOLPHE. Your reproach is just! It is the mildest which you could make me; but tomorrow I will visit that tomb, and pay it a last and sad duty.

PETER. Why do you avert your eye? Why can you not support my looks?

RODOLPHE. Because I am ashamed. I always dreaded the moment when I should see your return. I feared to hear your reproaches, as I had merited them.

PETER. You deserve many more. I gave you my fatherly advice; I painted your misdeed in the blackest colours, and you forgot everything. But the curtain is fallen, and if your repentance cannot obliterate the past, it may render you wiser for the future. Where is the man that never stumbled or never fell? Thousands fall an hundred times, and an hundred times rise unhurt. Your first fall was painful. This experience will teach you how to avoid such shoals in future.

RODOLPHE. Dear and good old man, every word is a balm to my wounded heart. You are right—I will forever renounce the sex, I will forever fly from women.

PETER. What precipitation, and what folly! Should he who has broken one leg never attempt to walk again? Must he remain inactive forever for fear of breaking the other?

RODOLPHE. I do not understand you.

PETER. Must you renounce love, never enjoy the delights of human destiny, because you have once been the victim of that passion? What injustice! Moderate your sorrow. Only beware not to fall, and you will again be happy.

RODOLPHE. Who? I! I could!—No, never will I forget Regina, nor lay my homage at the feet of another.

PETER. Time will render that practicable which now seems impossible. It is just to shed tears for her you love; fulfil that obligation; but then remember your sacred duties; as a man, and as a knight.

Peter disappeared, and Rodolphe was astonished that the dwarf had not reprimanded him more severely; but upon more mature considerations, he thought that he had no right to do so, as his fault proceeded from an excess of love, and as he had neglected nothing promptly to repair it. The mournful death of Regina still dwelt on his mind but he attributed her end to the over-exalted principles, to the over-pure ideas she had formed of honour.

The following day, at an early hour, he proceeded slowly, in deep mourning, to the tomb of Regina. The images of the past presented themselves to his saddened heart. "It was here," said he, "that we walked together arm in arm—here I met her; there she ran towards me—then I was happy. Love, thy enjoyments are as infinite as thy pains: thou art more bitter than wormwood; but, in return, honey is less sweet than thou."

It was one of those days in autumn, which it would be impossible to paint, and much less faithfully describe, in which Nature seems to bid adieu to its admirers, and prepare itself for its long winter sleep. Light clouds floated in the air, and veiled at intervals the declining rays of the sun, which then fell obliquely on the surrounding landscape; scarce a zephyr agitated the lofty forest trees, while a vague murmur at times interrupted the solemn scene, as the leaves incessantly detached themselves one after the other from the branches, which till then had held them firmly, and descended with a slight rustling to the mossy ground. The inhabitants of the woods no longer uttered their joyous notes, and the shrieks of their more dismal brethren were only heard at intervals. Oh, how different were these from the warblings of a father and the plaintive accents of a mother, when her young ones begin to exercise their newly acquired strength! The fields were barren, their splendour had long reposed under the labourer's cot; the eye became fatigued on beholding the desert country, and rested only with pleasure on a few verdant corn-fields, sole emblems of reviving Nature.

Let him who in such a day can walk in the fields, without recalling death to his mind at every step, hasten to make his will, for it will seize him when he least expects it.

This day made a deep impression on the mind of Rodolphe; he delighted in finding in every object an image of death; unbidden tears flowed from his eyes, and when he approached the mound that marked the spot where Regina lay—when he saw the flowers, which had been planted there, faded, and their leaves dispersed here and there, he sunk on the ground and gave vent to his anguish and sorrow.

CHAP VII

RODOLPHE, after having been repeatedly urged by his squire to return to the castle, quitted that fatal tomb with deep regret. In passing the obscure forest, he perceived through the trees lights floating in the distance, and heard the sound of horses approaching with rapidity. Six horsemen passed before him swift as lightening; one of them held a lady in his arms; she shrieked, and her cries implored assistance. The courage of Rodolphe was awakened; he drew his sword and followed the fugitives. He soon attained them, and demanded satisfactory reasons concerning this capture. The combat was engaged; the ravishers took flight and left the lady in the hands of Rodolphe, who transported her, fainting, to his horse, and conducted her to his castle.

"Noble lady," said he, when she recovered her senses, "you are in honourable hands. The knight whom you see before you is aware of his duty; he will protect an oppressed lady, and defend her to the last drop of his blood. Speak, what is your pleasure?"

STRANGER. I have long been inured to the hardships of misfortunate; they can alarm, but not vanquish me. On leaving Spires today, I thought myself the most unfortunate, the most miserable of human beings; but Providence soon convinced me that I might be still more so in the hands of robbers. I see that destiny has turned the scales in my favour, in throwing me into the arms of the most generous of knights, who offers me both assistance and protection.

RODOLPHE. I will afford you both! Speak as to a friend; what are your desires?

STRANGER. Alas! I am destitute of everything which human nature can stand in need of; all I possess are these cloths, barely sufficient to cover me. The horse which I had mounted to go to Worms is become the spoil of the robbers; but I will willingly continue my route on foot, in the hopes of not putting an end to my misery, but of receiving or procuring some relief.

RODOLPHE. I have friends at the imperial court; and if they can be of service, I will give you the strongest recommendations.

STRANGER. Oh no; the pomp of a court is not the object of my wishes: how could I appear in such a dress—I, the wife of the knight of Waldemar—I, who once enjoyed such high consideration? My views are more conformable to my present situation; I will endeavour to gain a sufficiency by embroidering veils and scarfs.

RODOLPHE. You, madam, the wife of the knight of Waldemar, and in misery? in such distress?

STRANGER. Yes; more abandoned than a child exposed in the forest by an unnatural mother; it has no idea of its situation, but I feel all its horrors.

RODOLPHE. Pardon my curiosity; deign to inform me what strange vicissitudes can thus have reduced you.

STRANGER. Five years are now elapsed since some French priests travelled through Germany, and preached the crusades by order of the Pope. My husband, animated by their exhortations, sold his castle and all his estates; raised a body of four hundred men at arms, and proceeded with them to Brundusium, where some ships were prepared to convey all the German warriors to the Holy Land. He left me a bare sufficiency for one year. "I will," said he, "send you a considerable supply by the first ship!" For he dreamt of nought but the treasures he should conquer from the voluptuous Saracens. Five years are now passed, and I have not received the least intelligence from him. But, with extreme economy, I contrived to live and to sustain myself and one servant for four years, when I sold all the jewels I possessed, and even my very clothes; and after having remained two days without any nourishment, I decided to proceed to Worms on a hired horse, to gain any subsistence by the labour of my hands, or to enter the service of some lady of quality.

RODOLPHE. Cruel Waldemar; how could you thus forget your spouse?

STRANGER. Blame him not; he far advanced me in age, but I loved him tenderly, I loved him; I loved him as a father. He undoubtedly has fallen by the hands of Saracen; or perhaps been cut off by the plague, or he would never have neglected his wife.

RODOLPHE. But your friends—your relations?

STRANGER. I am a stranger in this country; by birth an Italian, of the noble, but poor house of Orsano. Waldemar saw me during a pilgrimage at Rome, eight years ago. The little beauty which I possessed engaged his attention, and he chose me for his spouse. It is not astonishing that his family, and the nobility of Spires, should abandon an unfortunate stranger, an Italian, who perhaps has preserved too much pride during her misfortunes.

RODOLPHE. It is a most unworthy proceeding! How fortunate I am, madam, to have met you. I had long been wishing to accomplish some noble action. Consider me as your friend, as your brother. Remain in my castle till your grief is effaced, and ceases to attack the flower of your beauty. You shall not want anything which my wealth can procure you.

Agnes (which was the name of the stranger) long refused the generous offers of Rodolphe; but he continued his solicitations, and endeavoured to persuade her that she should consider the whole as a loan, which her husband would willingly repay on his return. She yielded and consented to accept, for a fortnight at most, an apartment in the castle.

The usual activity of the melancholy Rodolphe began from that moment gradually to return. He often went to town to purchase wearing apparel and diamonds for his interesting visitor.

Agnes had then attained her twenty-sixth year; the sufferings of her heart had cast a paleness over her countenance, which, however, was soon effaced by her renewing roses; her hollow eyes began to resume their former brilliancy, and harmonized with her long ebony locks. When, for the first time, she appeared before Rodolphe, her eyes moistened with tears, and her elegant frame decked with costly ornaments, he owned to himself that there were other women as beautiful as Regina.

The fifteen days soon passed, and Agnes wished to take her leave; but Rodolphe begged her to prolong her stay for eight days more: his solicitations soon prevailed. Thus her departure was deferred from week to week, and was soon no longer mentioned. Agnes loved her benefactor; she devoted her soul to him. Rodolphe tenderly returned her affection; and he would have espoused her had not indissoluble bonds linked her to another. He only perceived in distant time, the day when he could offer his hand; but it was with the less impatience that the ardent love of Agnes accorded everything to his growing passion. He lived but for Agnes alone.—Yet, sometimes, in the dark hours of night, when satiated with voluptuous pleasure in her arms, he recollected the unfortunate Regina. He also called to mind the little Dwarf, and trembled as he imagined he saw him in some corner preparing to heap reproaches upon him. But Little Peter did not appear to disturb the pleasures of Rodolphe.

CHAP. VIII.

DURING this interval, Waldemar had arrived in Palestine, and conducted all his warriors to the Christian army. He had fought five years against the Saracens, but without deriving any great advantage, and he was often unable to pay his companions. He incessantly recalled his wife to his mind with paternal solicitude; he repented his errors, and again proceeded to battle, where wounds were his only recompense.

One day, as he had retired from the sultry heat of the sun, and lay extended in his tent, he demanded of himself what Agnes might at that moment be doing, and what means she employed to subsist. "All is well with her," replied a voice, "she leads a very joyful life." The startled knight arose, and beheld at the entrance of the tent one of his friends, a compatriot of great renown in arms.

WALDEMAR. Did you just now answer me? And what has brought you hither?

THE KNIGHT. The same thirst for glory which governed you when you departed for Palestine. For this month past I have sought you in the army, to give you some intelligence of your wife. She is perfectly well off.

WALDEMAR. How that? and I left her scarcely enough to sustain in her for six months!

KNIGHT. Is gold necessary to a beautiful woman to live and be happy? My good old companion, you have very little experience.

WALDEMAR. Great God! Is it thus I must acquire it? But explain yourself clearly, raise my doubts, and put an end to my misery.

KNIGHT. Your misery! when you hear that your wife is happy? You are strange! The young Westerbourg—you know the young and beautiful Rodolphe? Thanks to your follies, your wife was quite destitute; well! he received her. Agnes had long been an inmate of his castle when I left Germany. She is sumptuously clothed, and leads a charming life, while you are in actual want under your tent. You will soon have heirs; the obliging Rodolphe, as is said, takes upon him the charge of procuring them for you at Spires. Come! you must fight valiantly, amass a fortune, in order to ensure your children a rich succession.

WALDEMAR. You lie!

KNIGHT. Reproach me when you have convicted me of falsehood. As a loyal knight, I thought myself in duty bound to inform you of your dishonour; it is now your turn to do your duty, and if you approve the conduct of your wife, I have nothing further to add.

The knight retired; Waldemar foamed with rage. "Yes," said he, "were it the demon himself, who by a false report sought to drag me from Palestine, I would return to my wife. Evil, evil be to her if I find her guilty. She ought to have suffered hunger, to have begged, sooner than barter my honour; sooner than blemish the renown which I have such trouble in acquiring here."

He embarked in the first ship that sailed for Italy, crossed Germany, and arrived one evening at Spires, overcome with fatigue.

Agnes did not think him so near her. Her birthday was celebrated in the castle of Rodolphe; numerous guests filled it with mirth. Towards midnight, Agnes retired to the voluptuous couch of Rodolphe which she had never ceased to share with him. Seven months had elapsed since she had the prospect of becoming a mother; but she had the art of concealing this circumstance from the penetrating view of other persons of her sex, and no one suspected the truth. Rodolphe, lulled into an agreeable slumber by her tender caresses, did not hear the Little Peter, who opened the curtain.

PETER. Excuse me if I disturb you, Agnes; I have something to communicate to you; your husband arrived last night at Spires. He will fetch you tomorrow; beware that he does not find you in this situation.

He disappeared instantaneously, and left the lovers involved in difficulties. Agnes doubted the truth; but Rodolphe knew that the words of Peter were never in vain. They arose, and consulted of the best means to adopt: morning caught them thus undecided. Rodolphe could not hide his Agnes; the neighbourhood knew she was at the castle. Neither could he refuse her to a husband who came to demand her. He feared the vengeance of the inhabitants of Spires; and even if he could have braved it, he would have imprinted an ineffaceable stain on Agnes. After having deliberated for some time longer, it was resolved that Rodolphe should go to Spires to sound the resolutions of Waldemar. As he was on the point of mounting his horse, Little Peter arrived. "You are in trouble," said he; "I cannot help pitying you, and although your conduct scarcely merits it, I will serve you."

RODOLPHE. O if you could, I should forever consider you as my benefactor, my friend, my father!

PETER. The knight of Waldemar knows where you are living, Agnes; he will leave Spires this morning at an early hour, accompanied by his friends, and will arrive here about twelve. He must not find you afflicted as I now perceive you; his suspicions and jealous eye would immediately uncover your secret.

RODOLPHE. Then I will bar my gates and prepare for defence.

PETER. And openly declare that the wife of another is your mistress? Imprint shame on her face and your own? Expose yourself to the ridicule and attacks of every knight? Is that what you wish, Agnes?

AGNES. Oh! No, no.

PETER. If you will confide in me, I consent to succour and save you. (*He detached his knapsack, opened it, and took out two little parcels. Rodolphe trembled, for he remembered the ball of thread.*) Here, continued he, addressing himself to Agnes, are two powders; take this first, and in one half hour you will be happily delivered; then you will take the second, which will strengthen you, and you may appear before your husband.

Rodolphe doubted the effect of the powder; he conjured Peter to save the life of his child, which would certainly be the victim of so dangerous an operation. He begged Agnes not to accept them, and left her to prepare his castle for resistance. Little Peter, taking advantage of his absence, assured Agnes that the powders would neither injure her nor her child, and that *he* would take the latter under his immediate protection.

When the trumpet of Rodolphe called his warriors together, Agnes imagined that her husband was arrived, and swallowed the first powder with all possible haste; she soon after gave birth to a daughter, beautiful as herself; and, relying on the assistance of the Dwarf, she immediately took the second powder, which had even a more rapid effect than the first; and the invigorated Agnes rose from her couch, and embraced her dear Rodolphe, who that very moment returned from his warlike preparations. With an amiable smile she presented him his little daughter, and reproached him for his want of confidence in his guardian angel. The joyous Rodolphe asked with solicitude what was to be done with the child, and how it could be concealed.

"Rely on me," said the old man; "I will be its father. And to you, Rodolphe, man of little faith, I swear on my honour that you shall one day see your little Agnes, and that she shall render you happy."

Peter took the child and disappeared.

CHAP. IX.

INSTEAD of preparing for his defence, Rodolphe gave all the orders necessary to receive a large party. Agnes retired to a distant apartment, and tremblingly awaited the arrival of her husband, thinking on the mournful time when she must exchange the loving caresses of the young and beautiful Rodolphe, for those of the aged Waldemar. At twelve, the sentry announced the arrival of the latter, accompanied by his friends. Rodolphe proceeded to the court-yard to receive them.

RODOLPHE. Who are you, noble knights, and what has procured me the honour of receiving you?

WALDEMAR. I am the knight of Waldemar; these are my friends and my companions. I was told at Spires that I should find my wife under your protection May I believe the report?

RODOLPHE. Yes, brave knight, you may.

WALDEMAR. Where shall I find her? In your lady's apartment?

RODOLPHE. I have not yet tasted the sweets of matrimony.

WALDEMAR. And you receive the wife of another under your roof? keep her for months together, and sacrifice with her the honour of her absent husband?

RODOLPHE. Who is the man that dares accuse me of such a crime? Let him appear, and I will answer him as a true knight.

I am not prepared to meet with reproaches of this nature from anyone, but much less from *you*, Waldemar. I found your wife in the hands of robbers and my arm forced them to abandon their prey. The garments of Agnes were miserable, barely sufficient to cover her frame, and I have clothed and fed her for this year past. I hospitably received her in this castle; and this faithful spouse would long since have closed the mouth of calumny, if on leaving this house she had been certain of finding an asylum elsewhere. And if your friends have abused you by false representations, let them come and confirm them in my presence; let them say why they abandoned your wife when in misery, and why they left the performance of their duty to strangers. But before you calumniate my actions, remove the stain which your neglect has imprinted on your forehead, and say why you left her during six successive years without provision!

Waldemar felt the justice of these reproaches: his eyes, the mirror of his wrathful soul, assumed a calmer expression, and for the first time they were bent towards Rodolphe.

WALDEMAR (*extending his hand*). If the reports in circulation are ill-founded we are both happy! We shall be united in the bond of friendship, and the services which you have rendered me during my absence shall never be obliterated from my mind. But where is Agnes?

RODOLPHE. In her apartment; I have not spoken to her today. She will be delighted to behold the man whose death she has so often deplored.

WALDEMAR. I will dry her tears if they proceed from a pure source.

He entered the castle, and met his wife, who presented herself to him with seeming innocence depicted on her countenance; his suspicions vanished, all reproaches ceased by the mediation of his friends, and Agnes restrained her tears. After the repast,

Waldemar clasped her in his arms, thanked Rodolphe for his attentions towards her, and proceeded to Spires, without affording her an opportunity of bidding farewell to the knight of Westerbourg.

Agnes rode mournfully by the side of her husband, entirely occupied with the image of Rodolphe; indeed her grief was so great at this separation that it was evidently manifested in her countenance, in her actions, and more particularly by her eyes, as she incessantly turned to look behind her. Waldemar saw and remarked this, his suspicions were awakened anew; and when his friends took leave of him, and left him alone with Agnes, she began to sigh and weep; he in vain demanded the cause of this grief, of these tears; a frightful certainty rushed on his mind. But, in order to be thoroughly convinced, he seemed to commiserate her sufferings, and condemned himself for having abandoned her: "As you conceived me to be dead," said he, "in justice I perhaps ought not to reproach you for having promised, or even accorded your love to another."

Agnes answered not, and soon sought a solitary couch, to mourn in silence the loss of Rodolphe and of her daughter, those beloved objects which she had been forced to quit so precipitately. Waldemar meditated plans for the discovery of the truth. At the point of day he approached the bed of Agnes who had not yet closed her eyes, and said to her, "Prepare yourself to leave Spires in an hour."

AGNES (*trembling*). And whither are you going?

WALDEMAR. To Palestine. My warriors await their leader, and I will take you with me, in order not to expose you to further difficulties.

AGNES. Impossible! Impossible!

WALDEMAR. And why impossible? You cannot remain here. I have no money to leave you; and you would not depend on the bounty of others.

AGNES. How shall I support the fatigue of such a journey? If you wish to put an end to my existence, let it rather be accomplished here, that I may avoid the sufferings which await me.

WALDEMAR. You will then not depart with me?

AGNES. I cannot.

WALDEMAR. You would rather remain behind, and depend on the bounty of some gallant knight? Is it not so, Agnes?

AGNES. I will die!

WALDEMAR. We must be off, my hours are numbered. You hesitate too long. Choose; will you follow your husband? Will you share his troubles and adversities as becometh a faithful wife? or will you retire to a monastery until I return?

AGNES. Lead me to a convent, where I may in quiet pray for you and for me.

WALDEMAR. Your will be done; the horses are saddled, prepare yourself, for I shall soon return.

Waldemar hastily left the room. Agnes slowly rose from her bed, and was scarce able to dress herself, for she continually turned her eyes to the street to see whether she could discover any of the squires of Rodolphe, or perhaps Rodolphe himself, but it was in vain. Her husband returned, requested her to follow him, helped her onto horseback and rode beside her in deep silence. They meet several horsemen, but Agnes could perceive no Rodolphe.

Towards midday they alighted at an inn. When Waldemar was ordering his men to bait the horses, and prepare a repast, Agnes stood at the door, affliction marked in her looks. Opposite to the inn was situated a small cottage, and on the threshold a fine healthy woman with a baby at her breast. This sight pierced her heart, and awakened maternal tenderness in her bosom; and a desire of clasping a child in her arms, though only the child of a peasant, engaged her to cross the street to the cottage. "Happy mother," said she, on viewing the poor shepherdess, occupied with her respectable duty; "happy mother, you have the satisfaction of seeing your child, and of feeding it! Oh, how I do envy your lot!"

SHEPHERDESS. Noble lady, it is not my child, I am only its nurse.

AGNES. And to whom does your dark-eyed foster child belong?

SHEPHERDESS. The Lord in heaven knows, for he sent it me yesterday in a miraculous manner. I was tending my sheep, and weeping the loss of my child, when an old man (I never saw one so small nor so aged) ran to me, and charged me to take care of this child, laying at the same time a purse of gold in my hand, and promising me as much more in another year.

AGNES. It is her! It is her! Thou art my dearest lost child; this is her mouth! thou art my picture, and that of Rodolphe.

"Let me also examine this resemblance," said a voice behind Anges. She turned and beheld Waldemar inflamed with anger and vengeance. A cold chill ran through her whole frame, she forgot the treasure she had in her arms, and it would have fallen to the ground had not the attentive nurse caught it on her knees. In that state Waldemar carried her to a lonely apartment of the inn, for she was unable to stand. When placed in a chair she fixed her eyes on the window, as if apprehensive of encountering those of her offended husband, who stood before her with his arms crossed.

"I insist", said he, at last, with vehemence, "I insist upon a full and simple confession of your crime. It will be the only means of saving yourself! This confession, if sincere, can alone allay my vengeance."

When Agnes was enabled to express herself, she confessed all. "Give me" added she, "the death which I merit; I have offended your honour but I will never forgive you for having left me in the most cruel distress, and being thereby the first cause of my misfortune."

Waldemar answered nothing, but proceeded to give his orders for their departure. It was with difficulty that Agnes could follow him, but there was no alterative, and ill health caused no uneasiness in the heart of an offended husband. On mounting her horse she perceived that one of the attendants carried a child enveloped in a mantle. Mortal anguish oppressed her heart, she began to weep, and found a melancholy charm in her tears, When they had ceased, she cast her looks behind her, saw the child, and her tears immediately began to flow afresh.

CHAP. X.

AGNES arrived at Worms at the end of the second day in the most deplorable state. The next morning Waldemar entered her apartment with the child in his arm. "There," said he, disdainfully, "take it and follow me."

"O, so long as I have thee with me," said Agnes, on receiving the child, "I will resign myself to my fate, were I even to be conducted to the most horrible dungeon!" Waldemar ground his teeth and passed on; Agnes followed, sobbing bitterly, with the child in her arms. They soon entered a spacious hall, where a numerous assembly of knights sat round a table.

"Judges of the Tribunal of Nobles," said Waldemar, "here is my wife, whom I have brought hither before you. While I was fighting the enemies of Christianity in Palestine, she broke her marriage vow with Rodolphe of Westerbourg. While I laboured to add to the glory of my ancestors, she disgraced me by the birth of this illegitimate child. Judge the mother and the child in the equity of your court." And casting a look of contempt on Agnes, he hastily left the hall.

"Let this unfortunate be placed in security," said the president. The guards immediately surrounded her, and conducted her to prison. The laws ordained that every female who proved unfaithful to her husband should suffer the penalty of death. Agnes was not ignorant of this, and yet she followed the guards with a firm step.

"Wherewith shall I nourish my child?" said she, sighing deeply, as soon as the prison doors were closed upon her. "Here I am alone and abandoned in this dark tower. If my tears could nourish thee, sweet child, thou shouldst not want."

She approached it to her breast, and was not a little consoled by finding that she was a mother in every respect; she waited with fortitude the moment that was to decide her fate, and when conducted before the tribunal, she confessed her crime, and presented her wretched state before she became guilty, in such pathetic terms, that many of the judges, on consulting their consciences, owned to themselves that in such a case they would have acted as she had. They unanimously desired to preserve a life, which the law condemned with the uttermost rigour. The gentle Agnes exonerated Rodolphe, by affirming that when rescued by him from the hands of the robbers, she had introduced herself to him as a widow; she added that he had repeatedly offered his hand, which she had as often refused, and that it was only on the day she heard of the arrival of Waldemar, that she declared herself to be the wife of another.

At this confession, the judges recalled the citation, which they had dispatched to summon him before their tribunal. The third day they pronounced sentence of death on Agnes, with tears in their eyes, and announced it to Waldemar; for, according to the terms of the law, the husband alone could pardon his criminal spouse, by generously forgetting her offence, and receiving her again in his house. But Waldemar was silent, and Agnes was called before the tribunal to hear the sentence.

She appeared with the child in her arms; she heard the sentence of death with fortitude, and saw the fatal wand broken over her head. "I submit," said she, "without a murmur to a death which I have merited; but if your hearts are not entirely insensible to the voice of humanity, take pity on this child. She has drank, with her mother's milk, sufficient affliction; must she also share my destiny? must she fade and die as a flower because I was criminal? Send her to Rodolphe of Westerbourg; he is her father, and he will have compassion on the little creature, although he may forget," added she with a torrent of tears, "although he may entirely forget her unfortunate mother."

The softened judges took charge of the child, confided it to a nurse, and dispatched her with it to Rodolphe. Agnes, when led back to the prison, requested to know whether anyone had enquired after her during her confinement? When she was answered in the negative, she sighed deeply, demanded the presence of a priest, and devoutly prayed with him. On the third day the guards announced to her that her hour was approaching. She threw a veil over her head, and followed them with resolution. As she placed her foot on the first step, the death bell began to toll. Agnes trembled, but soon recovered her courage. On passing through the crowd that awaited her, she raised her veil, cast a look around her, and not perceiving one of her friends, she from that moment solely occupied herself with the image of her Saviour, which her confessor had placed in her and she seemed not to perceive that her armorial bearings were broken, and the fragments cast at her feet. The executioner received her, and she steadfastly followed him.

The magistrates had ordered that Agnes should pass before the house of Waldemar; for, according to the law, he was even yet permitted to pardon his wife. He was standing on the balcony when the procession passed; the priest informed Agnes of the circumstance, she raised her supplicant hands; the people exclaimed: "Pardon! Pardon!" But Waldemar retired to his apartment, loaded with the maledictions of all the assistants. There was not one ray of hope for Agnes. The scaffold struck her with terror. Suddenly she stopped and exclaimed: "Rodolphe! Rodolphe! have you totally forgotten, totally abandoned me."

CHAP. XI.

LET us examine whether Rodolphe merited these cruel reproaches, and whether he had not attempted everything in his power to deliver Agnes.

When Waldemar tore her with such precipitation from his arms, and conducted her to Spires, he felt the separation even more poignantly than Agnes herself. In the excess of his grief, he searched in vain every apartment of his castle. It was then he felt that Agnes had been, and still continued to be all he held dear in the world. He reproached himself for not having denied her to Waldemar; for not having protected her by force of arms. "I consented to give her up", exclaimed he, "in order to save the honour of the old knight and never thought that without her I could not exist."

The idea of having become a father, and not possessing the pledge of his love, diffused a cold tremor over his frame; the agitation of his blood subsided, and was succeeded by a mournful dejection. He never had awaited the approach of midnight with such anxiety, for he expected to see Little Peter, and to concert with him the means of delivering Agnes. But the spirit never appeared. "Perhaps," thought he, "he is occupied elsewhere; perhaps even he is rescuing Agnes." With this impression he patiently awaited the morning. At the first dawn of day he mounted his horse, and pursued the road to Spires, accompanied by several attendants. On arriving, he heard that

Waldemar had left the town early in the morning with Agnes, and he immediately followed them.

In the great forest of Spires, where two roads meet at the foot of the hermitage, he interrogated the hermit, and was by him informed that several knights, with a lady, had passed in the morning, and taken the road to Italy. He took the same direction, asked the same questions, and received the same answers. At Strasbourg, he was told the knights had changed horses, and that the lady had never ceased to weep. The tears of his Agnes (whom he thought this lady must be) sunk deep in his heart. He spurred on his jaded horse, and at last arrived at an hotel in Basel. There he overtook the knights whom he had so long pursued. He had decided to demand Agnes of Waldemar, and to take her by force if he refused her. But what was his astonishment, when he heard that it was a knight of Franconia going to Palestine, whom his wife accompanied to the confines of Italy; she wept because she was going to part with a husband she tenderly loved, and whom she imagined would be exposed to great dangers.

Rodolphe returned mournfully without any fixed project; but deceived by another illusion, he lost himself in the forest of Spessart. He there heard a voice which called him by his name. This voice led him into a wild part of the wood. "You believe yourself miserable, Agnes thinks herself forsaken," said the voice from the summit of a rock; "but behold me, and judge who is most miserable, who is most neglected." Rodolphe raised his eyes, and saw his friend, the Dwarf, chained in the air, above a craggy rock.

RODOLPHE. Peter!—You here? Can I possibly deliver you?

PETER. Mount the rock and approach, that you may hear me more distinctly.

Rodolphe ascended the rock with some difficulty, and said, "What must I do now?"

PETER. You must draw the chain to the rock, that I may place my foot upon it. (*Rodolphe obeyed. Peter opened his wallet, and gave a file to Rodolphe.*) There, cut the ring which surrounds me, and deliver me from a torture which I have endured since I delivered your child into the hands of a nurse.

RODOLPHE (*filing the chain*). Does my child yet live? What does Agnes? Where shall I find her?

PETER. Deliver me first, and I will then satisfy your curiosity. (*The ring being cut, the chain falls to the foot of a rock.*) I thank you, Rodolphe. You have saved me. A superior power, a formidable enemy, had chained me above this rock, and prevented me from assisting you, and informing you of the dangers that menaced your Agnes. Oh! had you but passed sooner here! An evil spirit seems to defeat all our plans. Hasten, Rodolphe; go to Worms; tomorrow morning Agnes, convicted of infidelity, dies by the hand of the executioner.

RODOLPHE. Convicted of infidelity?

PETER. Yes. It would be too long to relate you the whole transaction. Her husband has delivered her into the hands of justice. Hasten your steps and be tomorrow at nine at the place of execution. If you arrive in time, you are certain of saving her. The populace will take your part. Haste! Haste! for on every moment of delay depends the life of your Agnes!

RODOLPHE (*descending from the rock*). And my daughter?

PETER. She is safe! She has been sent back to your castle. I will go and provide a nurse. Think only of the mother, I will take care of the child.

RODOLPHE (*mounting his horse*). Follow me, you are more active than I am, and more powerful—save my Agnes!

PETER. I would willingly do so, if it were in my power. But I am only destined to be the guardian of the descendants of the old Peter of Westerbourg. If you were in danger, I could fly three hundred miles in an hour; but to protect others I have only human strength, and could only arrive at Worms tomorrow night. But haste you, Rodolphe, or you will arrive too late.

Rodolphe set spurs to his horse, and was with difficulty followed by his attendants. In despite of all his efforts, the sun had already risen high before he attained the eminence above Worms. His squires remained behind, as their only spur was duty, and not love. Rodolphe was forced to stop a moment, his harnessed horse fell under him. He cast anxious looks towards the place of execution, which was not far distant. It was crowded with spectators. He darted like an arrow, his feet scarcely touched the ground. "Halt!" he exclaimed from afar. He flattered himself, he hoped, he mustered all his strength; the crowd rushed towards him and made way; furiously he reached the scaffold, and beheld—the inanimated corpse of Agnes on the floor, the head severed from the body; her half-closed eyes filled him with horror, and seemed to demand vengeance! At this dreadful sight he fell senseless on the ground. Agnes had ceased to live for one hour. Three times she cast her eyes around her, three times she called on Rodolphe, and left this world under the cruel impression that he had totally forgotten her; and that he could have saved her had he still loved her!

CHAP. XII.

IT was in a splendid apartment, and bound on a bed of suf-ferings, that Rodolphe, with difficulty recovering his senses, began to see and hear. Strange servants surrounded him, and a young lady, advancing with precaution, demanded, with an interesting air, whether he was better!

RODOLPHE (*extremely weak*). Where am I? Where is Agnes

The lady looked at him with tenderness, and shed tears of pity.

RODOLPHE. Where am I? Where is she whom I saw—in a dream—undoubtedly—in that horrid state!

YOUNG LADY. Calm yourself, sir knight! Men cannot resist the will of Heaven! Resign yourself to fate, or you will not even meet your Agnes in the other world.

RODOLPHE. It was then not a dream, but a reality? Horrible!—Horrible!—And I—I am the author of her death! I committed the crime! She is pure, innocent! O, wash away this blood! It burns my body, it tortures my soul! (*He closes his eyes, opens them again after a long interval, and sees the lady still standing before him.*)—Where am I?

YOUNG LADY. In the house of a friend. Count Reichard is your host; I am his only daughter, and await your commands; happy if I can relieve your sufferings, or offer any consolation to your afflicted mind.

RODOLPHE. Death is the only object of my wishes; it is fast approaching! In case it should surprise me, deprived of the use of my senses, permit me, noble and hospitable lady, to request you to thank your father, in my name, for having so generously fulfilled the duties of chivalry, in receiving me here as a parent, after having undoubtedly found me insensible on a scaffold. May I request one last favour?

YOUNG LADY. Certainly!

RODOLPHE. That my body may be laid beside that of Agnes. On mentioning her name the tears began to fall down his pale cheeks. He requested to be unbound, and when the lady had given orders to do as he wished, he with difficulty raised himself, and asked, whether any knight was dear to her heart?

YOUNG LADY (*blushing deeply*). I must speak the truth to a dying man. Yes, I love.

RODOLPHE. Make the object of your love swear—he must possess a noble soul to be worthy of your love—make that knight swear, as I know him not, never to demand your hand—never to call you his wife, before he has avenged, in my name, the blood of Agnes on the knight of Waldemar. Promise this to me; swear it, young lady!

YOUNG LADY. I promise! I swear! May God grant him strength to accomplish my vow!

The tears prevented her from continuing, and Rodolphe fell into that kind of stupor, from which the last efforts of a suffering nature seemed to have called him.

The physicians thought his recovery impossible; and the only daughter of the powerful Count Reichard, shed tears of despair on his death; alas! too certain she loved! She passionately loved him—for it was her first love.

CHAP. XIII.

RODOLPHE, fallen on the scaffold, was placed on a litter and carried away by the people, who were ignorant of the whole of his melancholy tale. They passed before the palace of Reichard. Clara, his daughter, then only sixteen years of age, was at the window. She saw the pale knight on the litter; she saw the wind sporting among his long locks, that sometimes covered his discoloured face, and at others left it exposed to view. Alarmed at this terrible and affecting sight, she called her father, and the count ordered him to be carried into his palace. His whole history was soon known, and the soul of Clara filled with esteem, admiration, and pity. "His heart must be noble," whispered she to herself, "if he loves so tenderly," and she added, "may I one day meet with a knight that will love me as he loved; who, if I was to die, would fall insensible beside my inanimate corpse!"

She frequently visited Rodolphe. When the fever inflamed his cheeks, and he fixed his looks on her, she said: "How beautiful he is, even at the gates of death! How expressive are his eyes!"

It would be useless to describe all the symptoms of the love, which by degrees subdued the soul of Clara with irresistible force. Pity and love are so nearly allied, that it is difficult clearly to distinguish them; sometimes we render homage to pity, when love is in reality the only object of our adoration.

Notwithstanding the decision of the physicians, and notwithstanding the reasons with which seconded this decision, Rodolphe did not die. Nature triumphed over the obstinacy of his fever. At the expiration of two months, he was enabled to leave his couch; and the third, saw him completely restored to health. The affectionate attentions of Clara greatly contributed to allay his suffering, and to hasten his reestablishment. Rodolphe was ignorant that she loved him; her father suspected it still less, and both attributed her kindness to the tender and compassionate heart of the young lady. One beautiful morning, Clara had seated herself near the window, and cast her eyes on the fields, covered with brilliant dew-drops. She delighted in thinking of the inexpressible happiness she should experience in traversing those fields with her lover, as her looks traversed them at that moment; and what bliss she should feel in embracing him, in the purity of her love, when suddenly Rodolphe entered the apartment in complete armour. His countenance was on fire, and tears furrowed his cheeks.

RODOLPHE. Lovely Clara, I have just been taking leave of your respectable father, who will be ever dear to me. I confess it, I cried tears like a child. May God permit me once to thank him more worthily than with tears! Generous countess, it is with the same intentions that I come hither. How can I acquit myself towards you? (*falling on his knees.*) Clara, you have had for me the attentions of a sister, of a mother! Agnes herself could not have surpassed you in tenderness. Adieu! May you ever be happy.

CLARA (*alarmed*). What, Rodolphe! you are going? you— you going to leave us?

RODOLPHE. Yes, noble lady; I must depart to accomplish a vow, and fulfil a duty. I must have satisfaction of Waldemar; I must appease the soul of my Agnes. You, madam, are freed from the oath and the promise you made to me when I thought myself on my deathbed; it was that which first restored me to tranquillity. I thank you a thousand times. May Heaven ordain that your hand be disposed of to some virtuous man; may your pleasure never be mingled with sufferings; may your heart never experience one thousandth part of the pain which love has heaped on me.

CLARA. Depart?—Depart?—You cannot do it! you are too weak! wait another month!

RODOLPHE. Pardon me, if after all your kindnesses I must refuse your first request; I must go.

CLARA. Oh! remain at least a week!—You will not?—but a day! half a day!

RODOLPHE. I would willingly do so if in my power. Yourself must approve the reasons of my departure, when I inform you that last night the spirit of Agnes appeared in a dream, and demanded vengeance.

CLARA. Then go! But return! oh! return soon!

RODOLPHE. Alas! I cannot even satisfy you on that point. If the justice of my cause gives me victory over Waldemar, I will proceed to the Holy Land, to seek a glorious death; it is also one of the vows I have made. My heart is dead to love; I will no longer sacrifice to it. I have felt all its pleasures, but they have been so surpassed by the sufferings which it inflicts, that they shall tempt me no more.

CLARA (*pale and trembling*). You will then not return? You will not return—(*her tears prevent her from continuing*).

RODOLPHE. You are much affected! I do not merit these tears, they are too precious! May Heaven shower its benedictions on you! Adieu forever!

CLARA. And you go without leaving me a token which may recall—but what am I saying? Depart, revenge yourself and die! I have but too great a cause to remember you, never to forget you.

She precipitately retired to her apartment, and carefully closed the door. Rodolphe addressed her yet a few words but his heart soon breathed vengeance and glory. After having liberally rewarded the servants of Reichard, he mounted his horse.

On the road his active mind retraced anew the beautiful Clara bathed in tears; he reflected on her conduct, and was astonished at having remaining so long without perceiving that love had perhaps subdued the heart of the young lady; and that love was perhaps the instigator of the attentions shown him by her during his illness and of her sorrow and tears at his departure. But as he was yet free, or as more properly speaking his heart was yet devoted to Agnes, he reproached himself for this idea of vanity, and spurred his courser towards the castle of Westerbourg. His dependents received, with transports of joy, a master whom they thought already laid in his tomb. All was merriment and joy; Rodolphe alone was melancholy. He occupied himself incessantly for several months with preparations for his departure. He arranged his affairs, and named an administrator of his estates in case he should not return.

Rodolphe, having settled everything, was to depart on the morrow. At midnight Peter approached his couch.

RODOLPHE. Welcome, Peter! Your assistance is useless! my Agnes is dead; and with her all the enjoyments of my life.

PETER. Alas! I know all!

RODOLPHE. Tomorrow I depart to revenge her death on the cruel Waldemar. Good and faithful Peter, ancient protector of my family, strengthen my arm, that my vengeance may be complete. After that leave me, abandon me to my fate, and reserve your assistance for a happier being! You could with all your power not give me one moment of joy. Peter! Love is as odious to me as food to a sick person. I will go to Palestine and seek an honourable death. Hasten its steps.

PETER. Despair not, Rodolphe! time insensibly heals every wound however poignant; it disappears by degrees, and in the end leaves no trace of its existence.

RODOLPHE. I defy that cruel benefactor; I will daily rebuild what he has destroyed; I will preserve my melancholy and continually renew it. But where is the unfortunate offspring of Rodolphe and Agnes?

PETER. She breathes.

RODOLPHE. I constitute her heir of all my estates; I will give them her. Watch over her life; if anyone offer to deprive her of this inheritance, it is your duty to chastise him.

PETER. I promise and will keep my word. But you say you have determined to revenge yourself on Waldemar?

RODOLPHE. I have.

PETER. And you expect to find him at Spires?

RODOLPHE. I do.

PETER. Six months have elapsed since he left the country for Palestine; five since he embarked at Brundusium; and his ship has long since reached the shore of the Infidels.

RODOLPHE. Then I will follow him: he cannot escape from this world, and I will seek him until I find him.

PETER. Your intention is just and laudable, and you would incur eternal shame in not revenging the death of Agnes; and whatever dangers you may encounter on the road, never quit the steps of Waldemar, and you will undoubtedly attain your end.

RODOLPHE. If I was as certain of raising Agnes from the dead, as I am of accomplishing my vow, there would yet be some ray of hope reserved for me in this world. Peter! Peter! perhaps you could have saved her?

PETER. Have I not already informed you, that it is for you alone I possess supernatural strength? And did you not find me, when returning from your researches, in the most disastrous situation, even in the impossibility of informing you of what was going forward?

RODOLPHE. I remember it well; but what power was thus capable of enslaving you?

PETER. This must yet be a profound mystery to you. But one day you shall know the causes of things which now seem as miracles to you. Wait patiently, and do not reason on things you are incapable of comprehending: no one can oppose the immutable decrees of fate. If you proceed with a steady determination you will attain your end; but the greatest evils await you if you waver.

And Peter disappeared.

CHAP. XIV.

THE echoes of Westerbourg had scare repeated the early sounds of the watchful cock, when Rodolphe left it never more to return. He was accompanied by thirty warriors, who had sworn on the altar to share the good and evil fortune of their leader. He took the road to Italy, and intended sailing from Ravenna to Palestine. They scarcely left Strasbourg, when they saw, seated on the road-side, a young man covered with dust and rags—"Generous knight," said he, addressing himself to Rodolphe, "if you are acquainted with the miseries of human life, if you have a compassionate heart, take pity on a poor orphan; permit me to follow you. I will tend your horses, I will serve your servants, if you only deign to accept of my services."

The prayer of the unfortunate youth deeply affected the heart of Rodolphe. He ordered his attendants to give him a horse; and, on arriving at the first town, he had him decently clothed. Rodolphe was soon repaid for his generosity, by the gratitude of the young man. He carefully observed every movement of his eyes; he attentively read his will in every gesture, even the most insignificant; and when the fatigued warriors forgot their master in the inn, and slept beside their bottle, he was constantly beside him, and awaited his orders. One day, Rodolphe being pleased with his attentions, said to him: "I will call you Clarus in remembrance of a noble lady who during a long illness tended me with the same kindness." The grateful squire kissed his hand, and bedewed it with his tears. "I perceive," added Rodolphe, "that you have good and noble sentiments; continue to fill your duties with the same fidelity, and I will prove to you a father."

"Be so," replied the young man, "and naught will be wanting to complete my happiness."

They continued their journey, and had already crossed the greatest part of the high mountains of Switzerland, when one of those frequent storms after a sultry summer's day was announced to them, by the distant rumble of thunder. They hastened the steps of their horses, to arrive at the place of their destination; the tempest and night soon overtook them. Enveloped in total darkness, they strayed from the beaten track, and lost themselves in the forest. The lightning at times discovered to them the dreadful abysses ready to swallow them up; they receded in terror, and lost themselves more and more. At last the storm ceased, and their courage returned; but they sought in vain to regain their road.

As midnight was fast approaching, they beheld a glimmering light in the distance; they endeavoured to approach it. This light proceeded from an illuminated castle rising on a rock from the centre of the forest. They followed the narrow and winding path which led to it, and soon arrived at the gate, which, however, was closed. Rodolphe called the sentry, but received no answer. He ordered one of his men to knock; the gates suddenly opened, and the knight entered with his followers into a spacious court. There he stopped, expecting someone would demand his name, but a mournful and uninterrupted silence reigned through the whole building. The horsemen began to speak of spectres and goblins; some even determined to retreat, when to their great astonishment they found the gates closed behind them, and so securely that all their efforts to open them were fruitless. Suddenly the tinkling of a little bell was heard in the distance; the sound increased gradually,

as larger bells began to toll, till at last the ears of Rodolphe
and his companions were deafened by their continued din; the
horses' manes stood on end, and their trembling riders could
scarce withhold their fury.

When, suddenly, from the spacious steps leading to the
castle-hall, descended a funeral procession illuminated by
thousands of torches, accompanied by several hundred men.
The trumpets sounded, and the bells ceased; they marched on
before the astounded Rodolphe: the procession was closed by a
magnificent coffin, which was conveyed to the chapel, when all
resumed its former silence. An old servant descended the steps
with a torch in his hand, and thus accosted Rodolphe:—"My
lady presents her regards to you, and begs to inform you that
although she saw you arrive from the castle window, you will
pardon her negligence for having detained you so long, as
the regret she feels at the loss of her daughter, whose funeral
you saw, had totally occupied her mind. Descend from your
courser, and accept of such hospitality as can be offered you by
a widow; your horses shall be well fed, and your servants shall
want for nothing." Rodolphe was cheered up by this obliging
invitation, and boldly followed his conductor. Clarus did not
leave him, and the horses were conducted to the stables.

The guide conducted Rodolphe through a great number
of smaller and larger apartments, all beautifully furnished and
illuminated; at last they arrived at a closed door:—"Wait here,"
said he, "while I announce you." The old man entered, and
soon returned to introduce Rodolphe. The eyes of the knight
were at first dazzled by the riches of the chambers; but, casting his looks around, he perceived that it was surrounded by
guards richly dressed, and before him stood a Little Woman,
not above two feet high; white hairs fell on furrowed countenance. Like Little Peter, she held in one hand a knotty stick,
and in the other the straps of a leathern knapsack hanging
from her shoulders.

"Welcome, Sir Rodolphe of Westerbourg," said she, "I have expected you for near five hundred years. I did not believe that you would honour me with a visit today, much less that you would come of your own accord; therefore, you are doubly welcome! You change my sorrow into joy. I lost a beloved daughter, and I hope to find a son in you. But you are tired from the length of your day's journey; you are in want of repose, and are now not able to understand the subject on which I wish to converse with you. Rest yourself; tomorrow we will talk at our leisure."

The tears of the Little Woman began to flow afresh at the mention of her beloved daughter, and she retired. Rodolphe was conducted to his apartments by several servants. Clarus followed him, and laid down beside his master's bed. All that passed seemed so astonishing, so supernatural to the squire, that he remained all the night in a deadly tremor, and was quite surprised to see Rodolphe sleep in such security. But the knight was accustomed to adventures of this nature; he doubted not but the woman was either the wife of his friend the Dwarf, or at least one of his relations, and firmly relied on the assistance of Peter, having been accustomed from his infancy to regard him as his protector; he, therefore, rested in peace, and sought to recover the strength necessary for the continuation of his journey.

CHAP. XV.

JUST as Clarus, somewhat cheered by the approach of day, endeavoured to compose himself to sleep, a gentle rap was heard at Rodolphe's door. He ordered Clarus to open it; and the Little Woman, the mistress of the castle, entered in deep mourning.

LITTLE WOMAN. How have you slept, Rodolphe?

RODOLPHE. Perfectly well, as I was certain I reposed under the roof of a friend of my family. Excuse me for receiving you in bed.

LITTLE WOMAN. It is my fault; but my age removes all temptations on your part, and screens us from the tongue of calumny. I am impatient to know your sentiments. But I wish to speak alone to you.

Rodolphe ordered Clarus to leave the room, and the Little Woman continued.—"I told you yesterday that I expected you for many centuries. I knew not when you would come, and I was forced to be ever ready to receive you. At every birth of a son in your family, I imagined it must be you—you who had been promised me; but I expected in vain. Little Peter, whom you know, is my husband. For five centuries we have lived in continual dissensions. An inevitable fatality forces him to work against my deliverance and his own; or, that is, whatever I do, he undoes. At the moment he is consumed with rage and vexation at knowing that you are with me, and under my protection. Several months ago, I succeeded in chaining this obstinate spirit to the summit of a rock in a desert, but you yourself delivered him. Why am I not allowed to inform you of everything?—But your resolution must be unrestrained, and your actions ruled by your own conviction. It depends on *you* to be our friend or our enemy—to save or to lose us—to render us happy or unhappy, as *my* power is circumscribed."

RODOLPHE. What must I do?

LITTLE WOMAN. You can be the author of my repose, and that of Little Peter. By the same means you can render yourself master of innumerable treasures; you can be initiated into a number of the secrets of Nature: and you can (mind the only counsel which I can give you)—you can assure to yourself above eternal happiness.

RODOLPHE. And how can I do this? What must I do to attain it?

LITTLE WOMAN. Nothing easier. You are a bachelor; marry my last daughter tomorrow, and all is accomplished. I have brought up a hundred daughters on your account, as I was forced to be ever ready to receive you. I cultivated their beauty; I formed them in the mould of virtue; but they all died successively: they withered and perished in the vain hope of seeing you arrive. Yesterday I had two; I was robbed of one of them, undoubtedly, by a stratagem of Little Peter. One, only one remains to me; she is less beautiful than anyone of those whose loss I have lamented, and yet she surpasses in beauty all the young ladies that you have ever seen. Receive her from my hands; marry her before me, Rodolphe, and you will make her, yourself and me happy.

RODOLPHE. Venerable lady! I believe your words, and I will, perhaps, one day enter into your views; but it is impossible now. An irrevocable vow forces me to embark for Palestine. I will pass at your castle on my return.

LITTLE WOMAN. You must not go to Palestine! Your misery and ours would be inevitable. You must decide today, this very day, or the interest which I have in your welfare will compel me to take others resolutions.

RODOLPHE. Then take them, for my answer is clear and constant—no. You force your guest to say things he would have spared you. Whatever be your intentions, they cannot be pure. You endeavour to excite my suspicions against Little Peter, the ancient protector of my family. You call him your husband, and you behave toward him with the greatest treachery. You wish to give me a wife, who, being educated by you, would treat me in the same manner. You pretend to inspire me with confidence, and own to me that it was you who chained the Dwarf to the summit of the rock, to prevent him from saving the unhappy Agnes. Woman, that action renders you forever odious in my sight; never will I subscribe to your wishes.

LITTLE WOMAN. Blind man! Was your union with Agnes not horrible? Your union with Regina, was it less so? And do you not perceive that you are wandering from the path of virtue in pursuing an outraged husband, who acted according to justice and the laws, and who revenged himself only when he was justified in so doing?

RODOLPHE. What a stupid excuse! But you yourself said that my will was free. Well, that will decides my departure.

LITTLE WOMAN. And you will not even see my daughter?

RODOLPHE. Neither see nor speak to her. She must be a prodigy of beauty if she resembles your beautiful self!

LITTLE WOMAN. Reflect! she is beautiful. She saw you yesterday without showing herself: she loves you tenderly.

Dear Rodolphe, you are prepared! Do not plunge yourself into misfortune. You can see my daughter, and speak to her.

RODOLPHE. I depart this moment.

LITTLE WOMAN. Then depart if you can. I must be your physician whether or no.Night, as 'tis said, inspires wise counsels; perhaps you will become prudent for the first time in your life; for the present you must remain here.

The Little Woman retired, and the irritated Rodolphe sprang from his couch. He called the faithful Clarus, and ordered him to tell the horsemen to saddle their horses as soon as possible; but before Clarus left the apartment, the Little Woman entered with her guards. "Conduct that knight to the tower," said she. "It is for you alone, Rodolphe, that tower was built long since. Its door will close on you, and the hand of my daughter alone can open it. I shall take care you remain faithful to her. Once a year I shall demand of you whether you have changed your resolution. The necessaries of life shall be regularly supplied you, and you shall not be in want of time to reflect. Away! your resistance is useless."

Rodolphe had not the strength to draw his sword, he was forced along by the conductors, and could only grind his teeth. Clarus, the faithful Clarus, followed his steps, and entered the tower with him, unperceived by the guards. In the centre of the prison was a lamp, that shed but faint rays of light; no opening was perceptible: the door through which he had passed was so artistly hidden, that he did not observe the smallest trace of it, and it seemed as if he had been walled in.

Rodolphe had not perceived Clarus enter the tower. He admired the attachment of that young man, who for his master imprisoned himself for life. "I hoped one day to have rewarded your fidelity," said he; "but that is no longer possible. If I can speak to the hag, or one of her servants, I will beg her to spare innocence, and to set you at liberty."

"Oh! no, no!" said the young man, with tears in his eyes; "permit me to remain, to live, to die with you! I was already devoted to you, but now your firm resolution, your noble resistance, make me your slave. It will be my greatest pleasure to serve you! Let me, therefore, enjoy it."

"Well," replied Rodolphe, "remain as long as you will find charm in sharing my misfortune. If I recover my liberty, I give you my knightly word you shall never leave me!"

"I will recall this promise to you mind," said Clarus, with a smile.

CHAP. XVI.

A TABLE, covered with luxuries, rose in the midst of the tower at the accustomed hour of dinner; but neither Rodolphe, nor his page, approached it. Plunged in a deep reverie, they did not even perceive the inviting odours they exhaled. The table stayed one hour, and then disappeared through the floor, when a voice exclaimed—"If you think, Rodolphe, that you can end your days by starvation, you are mistaken; for in future the air shall nourish you and the vapour rising from the earth shall quench your thirst."

Rodolphe answered not. In the evening he again refused the feast prepared for him, and a little while after he threw himself on his bed, and Clarus lay down in a corner, without uttering a word. The continued tears of the young man, the heavy weight of grief which overloaded his eyelids, soon procured him a profound sleep. Rodolphe, on the contrary, rolled about on his couch, and already reproached himself for not having consented to see the daughter of the old woman. Filled with this idea, he heard someone tapping gently against the wall. "Are you asleep, Rodolphe?" said a voice. "Do you not hear?"

RODOLPHE. I hear! Who calls?

PETER (*outside*). It is the voice of your faithful friend, Little Peter, who, not being able to give you any assistance, is come at least to console and inspire you with courage to resist the temptations prepared for you.

RODOLPHE. Can you not enter? Can you not tell me what I ought to do?

PETER. The walls are impenetrable for me. I cannot even see, and scarcely make myself understood, by a small opening barely visible.

RODOLPHE. O, Peter! Why did you not inform me of this? Why do you always come too late to my assistance?

PETER. I could not oppose the decrees of fate, nor prevent you from falling into the snare with which you are menaced. The future is not entirely disclosed to me; if it were, I should not have taken such measures when I saw this tower building. But it would have been possible to have saved you, had you recompensed fidelity according to its merits. Where is the faithful Clarus?

RODOLPHE. Clarus is sleeping in the corner; he followed me into this horrid prison unperceived by myself or the guards.

PETER. Clarus is with you! Happy Rodolphe, you are saved. Awake him, and tell him to take out of the wall the stone on which you hear me tapping.

RODOLPHE. Why can I not do that sooner than that poor boy?

PETER. Your endeavours would be useless; his hand alone can do it.

Rodolphe awoke Clarus, ordered him to take out the stone, and what the knight could not have done with all his might, the young man did with one hand. The stone was square, and the space left was just sufficient to admit Little Peter.

Clarus, on seeing the Dwarf, recoiled with terror; but Rodolphe convinced him of his error, he calling the old man his father, his saviour.

PETER. When my wife built this tower, I could not discover her intentions; for we have the faculty of mutually concealing from each other our projects: I thought she was constructing it to keep the little daughter of your dearest Agnes. It was with this idea, that one day while the workmen were reposing, I threw this stone among the others, after having endowed it with the virtue of being able to be removed by the hand of any woman. By this lucky stratagem, I contrived to ensure myself an entrance into the tower. When building the foundations, I was prohibited from altering anything whatever: but happily the masons used this stone, and thus enabled me to come to you.

RODOLPHE. I do not understand you. You say that the hand of a woman alone can remove this stone? And yet that young man has succeeded in that attempt.

PETER. The time approaches in which truth will be evident. Tremble not, Clarus, Rodolphe's heart is grateful; he knows his deliverance depends on you alone. You will be astonished, Rodolphe! Have you no idea who this young person is? It is Clara, it is the daughter of Count Reichard, who took such care of you during your illness; who followed you when you abandoned her; who disguised herself to await you on the road from Strasbourg; who has served you for love; who for love determined to share your prison; who for love made a vow to die with you.

RODOLPHE. Is it possible? Ah! I confess the resemblance often recalled to my mind the remembrance of Clara, and has occupied me for hours together, and strengthened my resolution of demanding her hand on my return from Palestine. Speak, noble lady; is it true? Speak; one word from your lips would render me your slave forever.

CLARA (*blushing*). Yes, I am Clara. Pardon a giddy creature, who could not exist without you. Pardon my folly, for having left my father's house contrary to the rules of propriety, and followed you. But I was resolved never to discover myself to you. I had determined to remain with you until you had recollected the unhappy Clara, or until your heart was subdued by another.

RODOLPHE. You alone shall govern it—you alone shall possess it; if you design to accept a gift so unworthy of you.

CLARA (*falling into his arms*). O, Rodolphe, how happy am I!

PETER. Then be grateful: render him happy, by dragging him from this prison.

CLARA. And how can I do this? Speak, I will this instant do everything in my power.

PETER. This tower completed, I assisted at its inauguration, unperceived by my wife; I then discovered her object in building it. "When Rodolphe inhabits this tower," said she, "as it shall be impossible for him to be untrue to one of my daughters, so also no spirits, or human hand, except that of one of my daughters, shall be enabled to open this door." Long since Rodolphe, I trembled in foreseeing the fatal period, when I should not be permitted to warn of the danger which I myself could not avert. I did not expect that issue would prove so favourable. Clara, it depends on you alone to fulfil the conditions imposed by my wife. The hour in which you resign your charms to the knight, and accord him all that is most dear to a woman, will be the hour of his deliverance. Act now as may seem most proper to you; it is not in my power to constrain you, and I will not undertake to persuade you. But that no one may discover you in this place, and thus destroy the means of escape which are yet possible, take this belt, (*he draws one from his knapsack*) as long as you fulfil the condition prescribed, you will discover the door, and be able to boldly open it.

Peter passed through the opening, and Clara replaced the stone with her trembling hands.

CHAP. XVII.

FEW would reproach Rodolphe for preparing his deliverance that very night?—Few would reproach Clara for granting his requests, as he solemnly promised to conduct her to her father, to unite himself to her, and then to proceed with her to Palestine?

As soon as the lovers awoke, the eyes of Clara were directed to the door; she distinctly perceived its locks and bars. After having taken off the belt which rendered her invisible, she hastened to take the hand of Rodolphe to deliver him and herself. Locks and bars gave way to her hand, as the Dwarf had predicted; the door opened, and Rodolphe saw his followers in the yard preparing for their departure. "Whither are ye going?" exclaimed he, darting down the steps. Suddenly the door closed, and Clara, who had not yet left the prison, could not open it again.

Rodolphe's men expressed the most sincere joy at beholding their master so unexpectedly. They had seen him conducted to prison, without being able to offer any assistance; and they were on the point of leaving the castle by order of its mistress, and of returning home to deplore his loss. "Bring me my horse," said Rodolphe, "and saddle one for my faithful Clarus, whom I——"

He turned and perceived that Clara was not with him; he saw that the door of the prison was closed; he ascended the steps as swiftly as he had descended them, and called Clara.

She feebly answered: "The locks and bars have disappeared! Perhaps I must expiate here a crime which I committed for you alone. I am happy in the certainty of your liberty, and my sufferings will be nought if you can find the happiness you merit."

"I cannot be blessed without you!" exclaimed Rodolphe. "Advance," said he to his guards, "and assist me in forcing the door." They all ascended and endeavoured in vain to open it.

Then a voice from the castle exclaimed, "You are giving yourself useless trouble; no human power can henceforth open that gate. Rodolphe, my mistress wishes to speak to you before your departure."

Rodolphe, at that moment, remembered that one of the daughters of the old witch could open the prison door; he immediately accepted the invitation, and hastily mounted the stairs, to beg her to deliver his dear Clara. The old woman met him in the anti-chamber. "Unfortunate!" said she to him, "I can no longer oppose your wishes; and if you persist in your resolution you are irrevocably lost. This morning I was suddenly informed of the horrible secret, which I did not so much as suspect, and which was concealed from me with such cunning. Miserable sinner! it depends on you to save yourself while you are yet in this castle, and to repair all the crimes which you have committed."

RODOLPHE. If your inflexible heart retains one grain of pity allow me what I refused yesterday; allow me to speak to your daughter.

LITTLE WOMAN. Willingly! Enter that room, you will see her, and be able to judge what a treasure you have renounced.

Rodolphe, without replying, darted into the room, and stopped at the door, fixed as a statute. Instead of a deformed dwarf, a sort of monster, which he expected to see, he found in an arm-chair a beautiful and charming young lady. She was dressed in black, and that dress enhanced the dazzling whiteness of her complexion; her silky hair negligently floated over her graceful shoulders, and was descended to her feet. At that moment she was wiping away a tear that had escaped her large blue eyes, and she rose quite alarmed from her seat, when she perceived the knight at the door.

"Are you come to take leave of me?" said she, in a sweet accent, "or are you come to insult my tears? They flow less for you than for the miserable Clara." At the name of Clara, the knight recovered from the astonishment which seemed to have petrified him.

RODOLPHE. It is to beseech, to implore your pity for that unfortunate lady, that I present myself before you. I know that you have alone the power of opening the door of the tower. Return me my liberator, my dearest Clara, who abandoned her father to follow me, who consented to sacrifice her honour to save me.

EUPHROSINA. If it were possible, I would not shed here useless tears. The tower could only be opened twice; the first, at the order of my mother, to receive you; the second, by my hand, or by the effect of your infidelity, to deliver you. Both cases have taken place; and from henceforth the door is closed forever; if you do not change your resolutions.

RODOLPHE. Forever? Closed forever? And what will become of Clara?

EUPHROSINA. I cannot inform you. I cannot read the book of futurity. All that I know, and which my mother told me is, that you can save her if you repent, if you undergo a rigorous abstinence. Go to Palestine and mortify yourself. During that time, you must not even touch the lips of a female, not even look upon one with desire, nor return any advances made to you. When that time has expired, and you have strictly observed the rules prescribed, Clara will be at liberty, and you will be enabled to render her completely happy.

RODOPLHE. I will then save her by these means as there are no others. But if you deceive me——

EUPHROSINA. If I deceive you, may my name ever be branded with shame in the eyes of the world; and may the flower of my virginity become the prey of the meanest of your servants.

RODOLPHE. I will then begin my pilgrimage, fast and mortify my flesh; and may I be forever accursed, if I do not accomplish my vow.

EUPHROSINA. You have taken a terrible oath, tremble to break it.

RODOLPHE. Grant me, I beg you, a second request before my departure. That is, once more to speak to Clara, to console her.

EUPHROSINA. That is impossible, for your penitence is already began.

RODOLPHE. Permit me then to ask one last question. Are you then really the daughter of the little old woman?

EUPHROSINA. I am her adopted daughter. Fate permitted her to adopt and educate one hundred young ladies; I am the hundredth and last; it is on your penitence that depends— But perhaps I have already said too much.

LITTLE WOMAN (*entering*). Yes, my daughter, you have said too much. Rodolphe, your resolution is noble. Go, let nought deter you. O, if I could guide you! If only I could warn you! Pay attention to these words, and learn them by heart: "*Three times the sinner as fallen, three times he has been raised again; six times the Lord has forgiven, and the seventh time he has pronounced a dreadful judgement.*" Remember, that for every service that was rendered you, you answered by a sin! Remember this incessantly, and go in peace.

Rodolphe was in the most cruel anxiety. The instructions of the old woman tore his soul; those of her charming daughter, had penetrated his heart, that heart that only beat for Clara, which was devoted to that unfortunate lady. He, however, secretly repented for having so rudely refused the offer of the old woman. "Then," said he, to himself, "I was innocent; then my heart was not engaged, was not enchained, I could then have made my choice."

These thoughts, by degrees, awakened in him a mistrust in Little Peter. After some reflections, he felt undecided, whether he should court his protection, or that of his wife. But the deliverance of Clara being nevertheless a sacred duty for him, he promised himself to accomplish it, by a penitence of three years, as that was the only way of saving her. He renewed his promise to the old woman, and wished to depart. She then opened her little knapsack, and drew out a straw hat rolled up, which she presented to him.

LITTLE WOMAN. Take this hat; as long as it covers your head, no one can give you pernicious counsels, or corrupt your heart. If you take it off, innumerable seductions will overwhelm you anew. Endeavour but to govern your passions, and you can yet aspire to happiness in this world.

Rodolphe took the hat and thanked her.

LITTLE WOMAN. One word more. A truly penitent mind forgives its enemies; therefore, if you should ever meet Waldemar, you must forgive him. Rely on the justice of Heaven; and if you are in tribulations, bear it patiently; if you are overcome by misfortunes, repent; if dangers menace you, hope; and never despair, even should the sword be suspended over your head.

EUPHROSINA. When you return, after three years of severe penitence, be certain that Clara and myself will be at the balcony; and that we will meet you, with trumpets of joy, if we perceive the hat still on your head.

LITTLE WOMAN. Depart! I have done all that is in my power. It now depends on you alone to accomplish your vow.

Rodolphe left the room with precipitation, descended into the court, threw off his sword, his buckler, and his armour, and ordered his followers to return to his castle, and expect him at the expiration of three years. He put on a coat of coarse brown cloth, bound it with a cord, took a staff in his hand, put the straw hat on his head, and left the castle; turned towards the gate with a sigh, and then raised his eyes to the window were Euphrosina was sitting. As soon as he was on the main road, he began singing the hymns which he had learned in his youth; his heart felt movements of contrition; he plainly discovered that he had sinned, that the blood of Regina and Agnes, that the miseries of Clara fell upon him. "The old woman cannot deceive me," said he, "all that she orders is good and meritorious. Little Peter only inflamed my passions; she endeavours to extinguish them. Yes, I will follow her instructions alone."

CHAP. XVIII.

RODOLPHE continued his journey for seven days, strengthening himself more and more in his resolution. He already beheld the frontiers of Italy, when a sudden blast of wind loosened his hat and blew it off. He instantly perceived Little Peter at his side, who beckoned and endeavoured to speak to him. But Rodolphe ran after his hat, and replaced it on his head. Little Peter disappeared.

The same accident happened several times while crossing Italy, but he remained firm in his resolution; and Little Peter never was able to converse with him. Arrived at the sea-coast, he embarked on a ship for Palestine. He had the precaution to tie his hat on his head with a riband, that the wind might not carry it off. The penitent soon discovered from afar the whitening coasts of Syria; and already delighted in the prospect of ending his voyage, when two Saracen galleys appeared bearing down upon them. Their ship being ill-equipped, and having only pilgrims on board, endeavoured in vain to escape by flight. The Infidels boarded, massacred those who resisted and took the others prisoners. Among the latter was Rodolphe. At the commencement of the engagement, forgetting his new state, he threw away his staff, seized a sword and valorously defended himself. The Saracens snatched his sword from him, but pitying his youth and beauty spared his life. He was chained in the hold, received scarce sufficient bread to nourish him, and was disembarked with the other captives. "Suffer without a murmur," said he to himself, when laden with heavier chains to conduct him to the town.

There the prisoners were arranged according to their age, and the fate of each was decided. The pirates sold to peasant sthose who promised the least; and several merchants bought the others by degrees. Six of the most beautiful, amongst whom was Rodolphe, were destined for the sultan, as that prince published an edict in every sea-port town, that he expected from the pirates a present of two hundred of the most beautiful Christian slaves.

"Penitence must be opposed to misfortune," said Rodolphe again; when he was conducted to the capital with his companions. He constantly wore his pilgrim's coat and his straw hat. The poor captives had much to suffer during this long voyage; but they were well fed, for fear their beauty might fade and thus the tribute lose its value. They arrived at their destination, and were soon after presented to an officer of the sultan.

"The requisite number," said he, "has long been made up; but the master of the seraglio is in want of some intelligent eunuchs; conduct these slaves to him, and your present will be equally acceptable to my master." One of the slaves, who understood the language of the country, announced to his companions the fate which awaited them. The unfortunate victims were horror-struck, but their pitiless conductors were deaf to their entreaties, and they were unmercifully dragged to the superintendent of the eunuchs, who approved of them, and ordered them to prison.

"If thou wert menaced with the most horrible outrage— hope," said Rodolphe. But the last ray of hope vanished, when early in the morning several blacks entered the prison, armed with sharp knives. They bound his companions one after the other, dragged them out and executed the cruel operation. Rodolphe had hid himself in a corner, and when the last sufferer was led out, despair mastered his resolution. "Is this the reward of my penitence? is this the end of my suffering? Am I to return to my native country covered with infamy" exclaimed he, tearing the hat from his head. "Why did I not follow the advice of my friend? And now he will abandon me."

PETER. He will not abandon you; he pities your blindness, and hastens to save you. Do you now see whose advice you are to follow? Can you conceive who can lead you to happiness? But you are more in want of succour than reproaches. (*He opened his knapsack and took out a red parrot.*) Take this bird; it has for three days left the apartment of the favourite sultana, who is inconsolable for its loss. The sultan has sworn by the beard of Mahomet, and proclaimed, that he who shall bring this parrot may make a demand, which, if in his power, shall be immediately fulfilled. Take it then, and request your liberty; it will be immediately accorded you. I shall soon see you again. Tell the first man that enters, that you caught it at the bars of the prison, and that you would wish to see the sultan.

Peter disappeared.

Rodolphe obeyed tremblingly; he imagined he beheld the bloody knives ready to execute the sentence on him. But as soon as he heard the cries and rejoicings of the negroes, who threw away their barbarous instruments, and saw him treated with the greatest respect, hope again began to reanimate his drooping spirits, he determined never to follow the advices of the old woman in future.

CHAP. XIX.

A S soon as the sultan was informed that a slave waited with the favoured bird, he gave order for his immediate admission; he even went to meet him, and sent to fetch the sultana, before he heard the demand of the miserable slave. She flew, and arrived, raising her veil, to kiss her dear fugitive; and the astonished Rodolphe recognised in her the beautiful Euphrosina, the daughter of the little old woman. Scarcely believing his own eyes, he remained immovable as a statue, when Euphrosina, turning towards him, said to him in German, "Is it you, Rodolphe, who have found my bird?"

SULTAN (*to Euphrosina*). Do you know that slave?

EUPHROSINA. If I mistake not, he is a German knight of my acquaintance. He is so astonished to find me here, that he cannot express his ideas. By his dress, he was going on a pilgrimage to Jerusalem, when he was taken prisoner.

SULTAN. Ask him what he desires, I will accord it him. I will keep my oath.

RODOLPHE. Is it you, Euphrosina? You in this place? You the mistress of the Sultan of Egypt?

EUPHROSINA. My lord, he demands his life and liberty.

SULTAN. I accord him both; and moreover, a permission to travel over all Judea without obstacles.

EUPHROSINA (*to Rodolphe*). Go, you are free. Where is your hat?

RODOLPHE. I wish I had never placed it on my head. As a reward for my obedience, I was near suffering a horrible mutilation! and doomed to find you in the arms of the sultan!

EUPHROSINA. Did I promise to be faithful to you? Have you persevered to the end? Have you seen danger menace you without despairing? The hat will remain three days in the prison. After expiration of that term, return with or without it, and you will have your firman. A blind and constant faith is generally rewarded. Trust not to your eyes and ears, and you will be happy.

RODOLPHE. May the thunder crush me, if——

EUPHROSINA. Swear not. You have three days to reflect, and your penitence will last three days longer. You cannot return to Germany before three years and three days; and in that time, if you have followed my advice, Clara and myself will await you on the balcony of our castle.

Euphrosina kissed her parrot, and left the apartment of the sultan. The despot followed her, after having given orders to suffer Rodolphe to depart. The knight retired, without being able to recover from his surprise. Everything he had seen and heard seemed incomprehensible to him; he knew not what to believe, he knew not what to think. He decided, at last, to demand of Little Peter the explanation of these strange occurrences, and strolled about the town to seek him. Night approached, and he found but a common inn to rest in. After having satisfied his huger with a piece of bread, he laid down on the straw, and endeavoured in vain to close his eyes in sleep. Suddenly, he perceived beside him—not the ardently desired Little Peter, but his little wife. "What do you wish of me?" said the astonished Rodolphe.

LITTLE WOMAN. I come to strengthen you in a project half-forgotten; I come to regenerate your sentiments, and to free your mind from temptations which it is apt to fall into.

RODOLPHE. I need no preceptors! I am not in want of such a guide as you are, who mocks me, conducts me to the border of a precipice, and indulges me by vain promises, only to precipitate me with the greater facility! But you have a charming daughter?

LITTLE WOMAN. As virtuous as she is beautiful.

RODOLPHE. Virtuous! Poor old woman; you are a very indifferent enchantress, or I should not be in want of many persuasions to prove that you have lied. I saw your virtuous daughter this morning

LITTLE WOMAN. I know it.

RODOLPHE. I saw her in the arms of the sultan.

LITTLE WOMAN. I know it.

RODOLPHE. You know that and talk of her virtue? Out of my sight; I perceive you are too old to blush. If you have made your other ninety-nine daughters mistresses of emperors and kings, you are but an indifferent moralist. Whoever preaches virtue, ought to set the example, or shame will be his just reward.

LITTLE WOMAN. Rodolphe! Rodolphe! you know me but little! You will repent too late. A blind confidence alone can save you. You think that the road to happiness is easy, and that you will find no thorns in the path of real glory. I am permitted to warn you three times. Beware Rodolphe, only three times. You have already followed once——

RODOLPHE. And that once was sufficient to acquaint me with your sentiments. I beg you not to trouble yourself for a second or third time; it would be in vain, you cannot add to the horror I feel for you; abandon me to my destiny, whether good or evil.

LITTLE WOMAN. My son, be not precipitate; reflect, consider, and determine accordingly. Think of the unfortunate Clara! She has deplored your fatal perverseness.

RODOLPHE. Less fatal than a captivity which she has not merited. What has that innocent maiden done to you that should thus imprison her? What have I done myself to become your laughing stock, that you should offer me a daughter for a wife, whom I afterwards find the arms of the sultan?

LITTLE WOMAN. Every crime exacts a punishment, every sin a sincere repentance. Examine your own conduct, you will see that it is useful; it is indispensably necessary you should impose on yourself a voluntary punishment. Blood, innocent blood, demands expiation of you! Crime blackens your conscience, and it must be purified.

RODOLPHE. What then must I do?

LITTLE WOMAN. Remain firm in every temptation and trial; support difficulties with the assurance of having merited them, and despair not in the greatest of dangers, even when you are apparently without resource.—Where is your hat?

RODOLPHE. In prison, where you would have devoted me to the most cruel and infamous treatment.

LITTLE WOMAN. If you know the full value of a good counsel, fetch it. Recommence your pilgrimage, be patient and you will be happy.

RODOLPHE. I will neither trust to your promises, or to your counsels! I——

LITTLE WOMAN. Fool that you are!—three-days' reflection are given to you; and during that time the hat will remain in the prison, as my daughter informed you.

RODOLPHE. Well, I consent once more to follow your advice; but explain me one thing.

LITTLE WOMAN. I exact unbounded confidence.

RODOLPHE. I promise, if you will inform me by what chance that Euphrosina, whom I left in the wild mountains of Switzerland, has been raised to the rank of a sultana; if you swear to me by all that is sacred that she——

LITTLE WOMAN. Stop there! Curiosity must not enter into the motives of your penitence.—You must obey. But why are you uneasy concerning my daughter, when Clara—that Clara whom you seduced and sacrificed, expects satisfaction from you? The sole object of your pilgrimage must be her deliverance and your own. My daughter now follows another destiny; and I must continually repeat to her, to you, and to myself:—Trust not either to your eyes or your ears.

RODOLPHE. But you cannot persuade me, that a girl can be virtuous in the arms of a sultan——

LITTLE WOMAN. Trust not to your eyes or your ears!

RODOLPHE. That she ever——

LITTLE WOMAN. Trust not to your eyes or your ears! Nor let the time of reflection pass without profiting by it.

RODOLPHE. One single question. Can I see your daughter? Can I speak to her during my pilgrimage?

LITTLE WOMAN. Yes; and she can answer you when you demand news of Clara. But beware, Rodolphe, that impure thoughts enter not into your mind during your penance; otherwise you are inevitably ruined.

She vanished, leaving Rodolphe in the utmost irresolution. Sometimes consulting his conscience he determined to follow the wholesome advice of the old woman, and persist in his trials; sometimes he reflected on the dangers to which he had thereby been exposed, and renounced the enterprise, discouraged by the difficulty. "Little Peter," said he, at last, "will explain the whole to me; he will inform me how the beautiful Euphrosina came to this spot, and whether I can ever attain that happiness which the sultan seems to enjoy with so much exultation."

His fickle heart burnt for Euphrosina with the same ardent fire as he felt before he left the castle in which he found her in Switzerland; with that love which he had often owned to himself during his pilgrimage, and which was revived with greater force at the sight of the beloved object. Clara had made but a slight impression on his mind. He had been pleased by her extreme attachment to him when the tower; but the facility of the enjoyment greatly contributed to diminish his affection. It was not for Clara that he did penance; it was in the interested hope of one day finding Euphrosina with her.—It was not for love of virtue that he loaded the old woman with reproaches concerning the union of her daughter with the sultan, but jealousy: this was the only reason why he did not refuse her advice with disdain, and why he pretended to follow it; he desired to find an occasion of often seeing the young beauty, and to disclose to her a passion which gained incessantly upon his mind.

CHAP. XX.

RODOLPHE quitted his sad couch, after having vainly expected his friend Peter, and left the inn without any fixed intention. He often approached the walls of the seraglio; but he could nowhere satisfy his curiosity. The second night passed, and Peter did not appear; the second day vanished, and his love was doubled, without one single ray of hope. The third night was passed in vainly expecting the arrival of his good friend Peter, but he did not appear: Rodolphe imaged that his wicked wife had chained him a second time. The third day he resolved to approach the throne of the sultan, to demand his firman, to fetch the hat in the prison, and patiently to await the decrees of his destiny.

Rodolphe presented himself at the palace. He was conducted to an interpreter, and thence to the principal governor. The aga give him a firman, with four purses of gold, wished him a prosperous journey, and begged him to pray for the health of Euphrosina. "Is she ill?" said Rodolphe to the interpreter.

"The favourite sultana is very ill," replied he, "all enchanters and physicians who have attended her despair of her recovery; the whole palace is in tears. Numberless couriers are searching the empire for relief; and the sultan has promised the Christians to return them to the territory of Ptolemais, if they consent to send their best physician!

Rodolphe trembled at this information. He would have given all his castles in Germany to procure the smallest relief, to save her whom he loved every instant more and more, or even only to speak with her. The interpreter left the apartment; and Rodolphe, in crossing the last court, perceived that the door to the prison was open. "I will fetch the hat," said he; "I will conform myself to the wish of the aga; I will continue my pilgrimage, and pray for the health of Euphrosina. Both the mother and daughter have promised that I shall see them again; would they have promised it if they did not read the decrees of fate?"

He entered the prison, sought the hat, found it in a dark corner, put it on his head, and tied the riband. As he was on the point of leaving the prison, he was struck with the clanking of chains; he recoiled from the door. The noise approached; and he perceived some Christians approaching, conducted by a strong guard. The slaves were pushed in, and before he could look round him, the door was already closed.

Profound obscurity, and a death-like silence, interrupted only occasionally by the sobbing of the miserable captives, seemed sole rulers of that dreary place. Rodolphe retired to a corner, harassed by the most frightful ideas. He thought it most expedient not to await the end of his misfortune, and, therefore, took off his hat.

But not withstanding his ardent wishes, the Dwarf did not appear. Rodolphe feared that he had been imprisoned with the slaves; and, at the expiration of one hour, this fear changed to a certainty. During this time his torments were redoubled for he soon perceived he should never be enabled to leave it without the assistance of his good friend, Peter; and the possession of the hat announced many other evils. But then he considered again, that as the hat alone could extricate him from his situation, and inform him of the fate of Euphrosina, he replaced it with confidence on his head. He knew not as yet who the prisoners were with whom he was confined, but was not long ignorant of their destiny, as they began to converse.

A VOICE. I wish to God this night were eternal.

A SECOND VOICE. I wish it would pass with greater rapidity than all the others, that it might put an end to this insupportable life! A longer existence would be for me a most cruel torture.

A THIRD VOICE. You wish to see the end of your torments! But you will yet suffer for days, if tomorrow, according to the sentence of the cruel aga, we are thrown on the fangs.

SECOND VOICE. However dreadful these torments may prove, they will yet have an end—an end which I have sought in vain until his hour!

Silence again resumed its empire; and Rodolphe was thrilled with horror in reflecting on the miserable death these Christians were to endure. Desirous to inform himself how they had incurred such a dreadful punishment, he wished to speak to them, and infuse some consolation into their minds, when he heard a deep moaning beside him.

A DOLEFUL VOICE. Oh, Agnes! I have merited this!

RODOLPHE (*astonished*). An Agnes then also affrights your conscience.

THE SAME VOICE. Who uttered these words? If the horrors of death do not deceive me, and if I were in Germany, methinks I should know that voice.

RODOLPHE. I certainly know yours! Are you not the knight of Waldemar?

WALDEMAR. I am. And you, are you not—? I dare not pronounce the name of her seducer—of him whose head I loved to see in my dreams exposed on the place of execution. Did you not fly your judges? And does not justice overtake you in this prison, where, yourself excepted, none but innocents are confined?

RODOLPHE. Yes, I am Rodolphe of Westerbourg. I have fled no judges, but I have undertaken a long journey to revenge on you the murder of the innocent Agnes.

WALDERMAR. Then revenge it tomorrow during our execution. I know not for what crimes you are confined here: but if the same torture awaits us both I shall yet enjoy some pleasure in this world. What delight for me to see you suspended besides me! You will reproach me for the death of Agnes, and I will reproach you for her seduction. This idea comforts me! Rodolphe! Rodolphe! Her death shall fall upon you. You seduced her, and forced me to take the barbarous step with which she reproaches me continually in my dreams. May your conscience bear all the terrors which have assailed my mind since my departure from Germany. The blood which was shed shall burn on your heart. You will die like me in despair; and the supreme Judge will pronounce a terrible sentence against you.

RODOLPHE. I will endeavour to obtain his mercy, by forgiving you. I will not revenge the death of the innocent; I will not demand satisfaction of you for innumerable torments which you have caused me to endure. Listen; I am not so miserable as you think; I am not confined to this prison for any crime. It was by chance that the gaolers closed the door before I could leave. But it is, perhaps, in my power to procure you, by my intercession, if not your liberty, at least some alleviation to your pains.

WALDEMAR. I will not lay myself under any obligation to you; and if it depended on you to give me life or death, I would choose the latter. This second crime would also fall on you, and the certainty of your damnation would be a healing balm to my wounded heart. Cease to fatigue me with useless addresses: I will listen no longer to you.

He raised himself with difficulty, and moved to another part of the prison; but the companions of Waldemar, who had entered his service in Italy, immediately crowded round

Rodolphe. They had heard of the possibility of obtaining the deliverance of their master; and dreading death more than Waldemar, they conjured Rodolphe to do for them all that depended on him. He related to them how he had fallen into the hands of the Saracens; how much he had suffered in that same prison; by what accident he obtained his liberty, and the firman of the sultan; and how, at last, in seeking his hat, he had been locked in with them. "Tomorrow morning," added he, "as soon as the gates of the prison are opened, I will hasten to the aga, who gave me this firman, and intercede in your favour."

The soldiers relied on his promises, and informed him, that after a prosperous and speedy voyage across the bosom of the Mediterranean, and almost in sight of the shores of Syria, a tempest had driven them back to sea. The storm lasted three days and three nights, and the pilot knew not whither to direct their course in a vessel which was become a total wreck. When the sky resumed its serenity, they discovered land, but before they reached it, they were boarded and taken prisoners by an Egyptian galley. They suffered the greatest hardships; and were at last placed, with Waldemar at their head, as labourers in the gardens of the sultan: there they profited by the small particle of liberty they enjoyed to form a conjecture by which they hoped to regain their entire freedom. Waldemar conducted the whole; a renegado, in which he had confided, betrayed them. They had the night before been seized, conducted to the aga, and sentenced to be thrown on the fangs.

CHAP. XXI.

NIGHT insensibly passed during these mutual relations. Rodolphe had often but vainly attempted to enter into conversation with Waldemar. He persisted in not answering him, and cherished in his heart the blackest of projects.

At the point of day, the prisoners heard the jarring of locks; the doors opened, and the guards entered. The miserable victims were thrilled with horror; but Waldemar advanced boldly, while Rodolphe retired to the remotest corner, with the intention of leaving the prison to the last, to implore the sultan's mercy for those unfortunates.

The guards had already surrounded all the captives, and were conducting them out, when Waldemar stopped, and addressed himself to the chief in the Arabian language, which he had learnt during his long residence in Palestine. "You are not strictly fulfilling your duty," said he: "one of our accomplices has hid himself. Yesterday you forgot to chain him, and he hoped to escape: but being equally criminal with us, he must suffer with us."

The officer turned round immediately, searched the prison, and discovered Rodolphe. He ordered him to be bound. The knight attempted in vain to resist, in vain he endeavoured to protest his innocence, and call on the other prisoners to bear witness: the guards paid no attention, as they did not understand the language; and as they were ordered to throw on the fangs all that were in the prison, they rejoiced that none had escaped their vigilance.

The march began, Waldemar applauded himself inwardly for the success of his vengeance: his companions deplored their lost hope; and Rodolphe cursed the hat, which his chained hands could not tear from his head. The most profound silence pervaded the streets through which they passed. Rodolphe met no one whose assistance he might implore. The guards hastened their pace; for, according to the custom of those times, the criminals were all to be executed before sunrise.

They arrived at the place of execution. One after the other was thrown on the fangs. Already the cries of the unfortunate sufferers resounded in the ears of those who awaited the same destiny. Waldemar, seized by the executioner, threw on Rodolphe a look of insult and triumph. "I will not bid you adieu," exclaimed he, "for I hope too to see you again." He had scarce completed the sentence, when he was precipitated, and it was Rodolphe's turn. In that terrible moment, he exerted his utmost efforts to strike the hat on one of the soldier's pikes, to tear it from his head, and try for the last time whether Little Peter had totally forgotten him. He succeeded in his attempt! the riband was untied, the hat fell to the ground, and Little Peter stood beside him. He hastily loosened the cords which bound the hands of Rodolphe, and said, with the same precipitation, "Show your firman, and you are saved. I shall be at the inn," and he vanished.

Rodolphe, between life and death, seized the favourable opportunity to present his firman to the officer of the guard. They were all astonished, respectfully kissed the seal, unchained Rodolphe, and conducted him before their aga, who ordered him to be set at liberty.

Before he followed them, he seized his cursed hat, and threw it on the fangs: "Hang on that iron," said he; "and if thou art endowed with any feeling, expiate the tortures which thou hast twice made me endure; but thou shalt no longer deceive me or any other mortal."

Chance, (if it be true that chance does exist in this world,) chance directed a light breeze to sustain the hat in the air a while, and suffered it to fall slowly on the head of Waldemar. One fang had caught the knight's right leg, and he seemed destined to suffer longer than his companions. Rodolphe did not think of looking into the precipice; but, in departing, he heard the imprecations of Waldemar, and the last agonizing sighs of his followers. He hastened to the inn he had lately occupied, and impatiently awaited the arrival of Little Peter, who made his appearance towards midnight.

RODOLPHE. Why do you make me wait so long?

PETER. Do you not merit it? Ought I not in justice to have abandoned you to your fate? For you repay my friendship with nought but ingratitude.

RODOLPHE. Oh! pardon me my dear and only friend, pardon my giddiness: your long absence and my increasing passion induced me to obey the wicked old hag. Believing my-self quite abandoned by you, I flattered myself that she would fulfil my desires.

PETER. If you were in search of death, you would soon have encountered it.

RODOLPHE. But why did you wait so long? Why did you not hear me? Why did you make me believe that your old wife had chained you a second time?

PETER. Because I wished to convince you, with evidence, that my wife only seeks your ruin, and your ultimate death. If you are not the wiser for it, accuse yourself in future; for then I will entirely forget you, even in the most imminent dangers.

RODOLPHE. I banish forever all distrust; I will confide in you as my only support; I will follow you as my only guide. But, my friend, I expect the same faithfulness on your part: you must not refuse me your advice and assistance when I am most in need of them.

PETER. And why?

RODOLPHE. O Peter! I love.

PETER. Is it possible.

RODOLPHE. I Love——I scarce dared own it to you. I love the adopted daughter of your wicked wife.

PETER. I suspected it.

RODOLPHE. You only suspected it?

PETER. Guessed it if you like; if some motive of that kind had not influenced you, you would never have followed her advice, nor again placed the hat on your head.

RODOLPHE. Now that you know my passion be not offended, but tell me rather how I may satisfy it.

PETER. With difficulty.I have no power over Euphrosina. I dare not, I cannot even approach her.

RODOLPHE. But can I not do that?

PETER. Certainly you can; but the most ardent love is without power, artifice alone can conclude the work which passion has commenced.

RODOLPHE. I heard yesterday that Euphrosina was very ill.

PETER. That illness will at least procure you an opportunity of seeing her with the consent of the sultan.

RODOLPHE. What bliss! Oh! if I could only see her: I hope to triumph over every other obstacle. But my friend, tell me first how Euphrosina came to this place—how she passed into the arms of the sultan: tell me without prevarication is he, or is she not the mistress of the sultan?

PETER. You are become jealous Rodolphe, I never perceived that weakness in you before. I will first satisfy your curiosity, and then you can act as you may think proper. I will relate to you what I am allowed to discover. Euphrosina loved you the first moment she saw you.

RODOLPHE. Oh! that thought alone makes me happy!

PETER. Yes; she loves, perhaps more ardently than you love her: it is the first time she loves. Her mother has herself cherished that inclination which she now endeavours in vain to root out. She intended employing Euphrosina to captivate you, and drag you into the abyss; but seeing that you have escaped her artifices, she is preparing other snares for you. According to the decree of destiny, your death alone can liberate her. But those are incomprehensible things for you. I will return to Euphrosina. She fainted on hearing of your infidelity to her with Clara, and shed abundance of tears at your departure. She wished to leave her mother, and follow the beloved of her heart to Palestine. As my wife kept you in her dependence by the magical virtue of the hat, and delighted in beholding your future miseries, she soon accorded the desire of her daughter; and some days after your departure, they followed. My wife was well aware that Euphrosina loved you passionately; she hoped by her means to prevent you from recurring to me. You were already in full sail when they embarked. Her enchantments had secured every part of the ship against storms. She had more particularly fortified the sails against my power; but she neglected to conjure the wind, and did not think that it could burst them by its violence. A tempest threw the vessel, without injuring it, on the coast of Egypt. Notwithstanding the power of the old woman, Euphrosina was made a slave, and conducted to the sultan as a present worthy of him.

RODOLPHE. And the sultan?

PETER. Was inflamed by the most ardent desire for that beauty.

RODOLPHE. Unfortunate, I——

PETER. He watches, he anticipates all her wishes, and thinks only of the means of making himself agreeable.

RODOLPHE. I shudder.

PETER. But all these evident proofs of a lively passion are returned with cold disdain. She thinks of her Rodolphe only, and promises to be faithful to him to her last breath. Moreover, a belt wove by the old lady protects her from all the violence which the sultan may meditate. Awed by the talisman, he can only languish and pray; but he cannot command.

RODOLPHE. I feel new life.

PETER. Too soon, my poor friend; too soon. This belt will protect her against your efforts, as well as against those of other men. No power on earth can deprive her of it. The protection of my wife will extend over her as long as she continues to wear it. She must quit it without constraint; and she has sworn to the old woman—she has sworn on the altar never to abandon it.

RODOLPHE. Oh! assist me, advise me! What must I do to surmount this obstacle?

PETER. Here ends my power, and you must act alone. If love, all-powerful love, is of no avail, you must leave this place without having gratified your desires. Prudence and artifice can alone obtain the victory.

RODOLPHE. Furnish me only with the means of seeing her, of talking to her.

PETER. I will do all that depends on me. I have already taken my precautions; it is in your power to see her for hours together tomorrow. She is ill, very ill; I am the cause of her illness. I threw into one of her favourite dishes a powder, which incessantly consumes her entrails, and which will infallibly cause her death in two days, if a remedy is not speedily supplied.

RODOLPHE. Oh, horrible monster!

PETER. Hear me out, and judge afterwards. My wife, who approaches Euphrosina as I do you, soon discovered the cause of her illness. In seeking an antidote, she was informed that the illness could only be cured by a plant growing on the Upper Alps of Switzerland, which must be culled at midnight during the full moon. She flew thither, relying on the virtue of the belt during her absence. Yesterday the moon began to decrease, and she is thereby forced to wait four weeks until the return of the full moon. During that long interval, you may, without being opposed by her, try all the eloquence of love.

RODOLPHE. But if the illness gains ground upon her, and the poison destroys her vitals——

PETER. And if your impatience prevents me from continuing, your perplexities will augment, and we shall lose a most precious time. Whosoever prepares poisons must be provided with antidotes. Here, (*he opened his knapsack, and took out three papers*), take these powders, announce yourself as a physician: swear on your head, that the sick sultana will recover if she takes your medicine, and you are at liberty freely to approach her. Give her every morning one of these powders, and the third day her health will be completely restored.

RODOLPHE. I thank you a thousand times, my worthy friend! But if the old lady be tired with waiting so long on the mountains, and come and find me with her daughter?

PETER. Always mistrustful! Know then, that to protect our friends, we have both the power of traversing space in an instant; but we cannot return without having found what we sought. Desirous of procuring the plant, she never thought of the decrease of the moon. She may sigh and moan, but she must remain in Switzerland until the return of the full moon. During that interval, you will have no other obstacle but the belt. Remove that, and you will be happy.

RODOLPHE. One word more.

PETER. Again suspicious.

RODOLPHE. One but only one question. It is so long since I have seen you, that I am in want of some information. When I lately returned the parrot to the sultan, I saw Euphrosina, and spoke to her. Well! not a word, nor a look discovered that love which you paint in such glowing colours.

PETER. Because she scrupulously follows the advice of her mother; because, her part was planned before she entered the seraglio; because, deceived by my wife she imagines that three years' penitence can alone render you worthy of becoming her husband. She thinks that Clara will determine on taking the veil, and thereby resign her lover to her.

RODOLPHE. You named Clara! What has become of that unfortunate girl?

PETER. She is yet in the tower, and laments your death.

RODOLPHE. She believes me dead?

PETER. Yes; yesterday when visiting her I gave her that false report.

RODOLPHE. Barbarous! and why?

PETER. Because you are indeed dead to her; and because being informed of that, she will resolve on taking the veil, the only means of leaving the prison.

RODOLPHE. And how?

PETER. If she ardently wishes it, the door will open instantly, and she will be permitted to enter a monastery. No witchcraft can oppose the effect of such a path.

RODOLPHE. She was a very good, a very amiable girl!

PETER. But too gentle, too languishing for the ardent Rodolphe. The charming, the lively Euphrosina will please you more, and captivate you longer.

RODOLPHE. You talk as if I already possessed, as if I could call her my Euphronsina.

Peter strengthened his feeble hope by some assurances, and disappeared to enquire, as he pretended, after the state of Euphronsina.

CHAP. XXII.

RODOLPHE presented himself early in the morning at the gates of the palace, announced himself as a physician, and was immediately introduced to the desolate sultan. "Invincible monarch of Asia and Africa," said he, "I was the person who lately had the pleasure of finding the parrot of the favourite sultana. I just heard that she was ill. Skilled in the knowledge of medicine, and possessor of several secrets of great importance, I flatter myself with the hope of being able in three days to return her to your embraces perfectly recovered, if I am permitted to see and approach her without obstacles."

"If that were in his power," said the sultan to the renegado who served as an interpreter, "half my treasures would scarcely be a sufficient recompense: but several persons have already ineffectually attempted it, and only increased her torments. Yesterday evening she desired me forbear bringing any more doctors, and to let her youth and nature combined, operate her recovery; I promised it her, and I will keep my word."

"He warrants on his head the efficacy of his medicine," said the renegado; and the sultan, who seized every opportunity, preceded him to announce his arrival to Euphrosina. An eunuch soon fetched Rodolphe, and conducted him to the apartment of the seraglio.

"What do you bring me, brave knight?" said Euphrosina, in a feeble voice. "I am informed that you expose your life to see me; I am charmed by this proof of your esteem: the dying Euphrosina thanks you; but it is not in your power to save me."

RODOLPHE. If I do not save you, I shall esteem myself happy in dying with you. I heard of your sufferings; I suspended my pilgrimages; I implored the assistance of Heaven. Take now one of these powders, and it will relive you much.

EUPHROSINA. I will accept death itself from your hands.

RODOLPHE. The Lord preserve me from giving it you!

Euphrosina took the powder in some lemon-juice: soon felt her pain abate, and seemed disposed to slumber. Rodolphe wished the sultan to retire; but he could not make him understand as no interpreter was present. He at last had recourse to intimating that Euphrosina was in want of repose. The sultan understood him, and left the apartment, after having begged Rodolphe also by signs to stay and watch her.

EUPHROSINA (*after the departure of the sultan*). I do not sleep, I only closed my eyes; but your powder has calmed my sufferings.

RODOLPHE. How happy I should be if I could save you!

EUPHROSINA (*opening the curtains of her bed*). Where is your hat?

RODOLPHE. I carry it under my coat, for it could not place it on my head in the presence of the sultan.

EUPHROSINA. Do not lose it! This hat is the only means, as my mother informed me, of protecting you in future against every seduction; it can alone—I ought not to tell you, but illness makes us poor miserable creatures much weaker—it can alone bring you back to me, by its virtue, when three years of your penance are expired.

RODOLPHE. And can I, may I, then hope that I am not indifferent to you?

EUPHROSINA. Yes, you can Rodolphe; I am enchanted with the warmth of your questions; it proves to me that a reciprocal passion glows within you. Yes, Rodolphe, I love you.

Be strong in temptation, and close your heart against every seduction, that you may one day be worthy of Euphrosina. When I was taken ill my mother was with me; she informed me that you had recommenced your pilgrimage, and that she hoped you would support yourself in every danger. The care of my health forced her to leave me; and since that moment I have in vain expected her.—Perhaps she sent you to cure me, and to endear you more to my heart.

Euphrosina afterwards related to Rodolphe all that Little Peter had previously informed him of and concluded, by saying that she hoped, with the aid of her mother, to escape from the sultan. "I hate him," added she, "if it is possible for me to hate, and I shall be the happiest of mortals if, when delivered of his importunities, I can accompany you in your pilgrimage as my mother promised me."

Already Rodolphe had declared his ardent love to Euphrosina; he had already imprinted a kiss on her hand, and she returned it with a gentle pressure, when the impatient despot entered the room with an interpreter. Euphrosina immediately closed her eyes. "She sleeps," said Rodolphe.

"She sleeps," whispered the interpreter.

The sultan, struck by such a sudden change, conceived a great esteem for Rodolphe, nourished him with delicacies from his table, and lodged him in an apartment in the seraglio, that he might be near the patient in case of danger. That same day Rodolphe conversed several times with Euphrosina whose health ameliorated speedily. The only subject of their conversation was their love,—that love which they confessed without reserve, and which they swore to keep inviolate to the end of their lives.

CHAP. XXIII.

LITTLE PETER presented himself at night before the couch of Rodolphe. "How do you sleep on Persian carpets?" said he. "You have played exceedingly well the part of a physician with the sultan, and of a hypocrite with Euphrosina. Continue, and you will do more than I had imagined; be bolder tomorrow in giving the powder,—a kiss will not be refused, but that is all that you can obtain while she wears the belt her mother gave her."

Peter disappeared, and Rodolphe sunk into a refreshing sleep, delighted with the prospect before him. Before the sultan had quitted his bed of down, Rodolphe was with Euphrosina; she thanked him for the repose his powders had procured her during the night, and added: "I dreamt of you Rodolphe, you imprinted a kiss on my lips."

"I must realise that dream," said Rodolphe, in a transport of joy; and embraced his Euphrosina. A feeble patient can scarcely resist the nervous arms of an ardent lover: she returned his embrace, and begged him to desist, as they might be surprised by some slave, or by the sultan himself. Adam, before his fall, never received more innocent kisses from his Eve.

Rodolphe administered the second powder. "When," said he, "I clasped you in my arms I felt a large belt that must encumber you during your illness; you ought to take it off, that nothing may disturb your repose."

"I dare not—I cannot," replied Euphrosina hastily; "it is the gift of my mother; and I may not quit it before you have sworn eternal fidelity to me at the altar; it is, moreover, so thin, that it does not cause the least inconvenience."

They were continuing, when the sultan entered. He was so exceedingly delighted with the prosperous state of the health of Euphrosina, that he extended his hand for the physician to kiss, and promised to accord him everything if re-established her completely.

The sultan sat the whole day beside the bed of his favourite. Rodolphe was permitted to be present, but it was of little avail to him; what do I say? he was forced to see, without uttering a sentence, the sultan caress the hand and cheek of Euphrosina; and to hear him talk of his approaching felicity. The lover, who has been in the same situation, can alone form an idea of the torments of Rodolphe—more horrible than the torments of hell; and if Mahomet is damned for the evil which his false doctrine has spread over the face of the earth, his greatest punishment must consist of seeing the demons embrace his beautiful houries in his presence.

Husbands! beware that ye do not convert this into a place of suffering for sensible spouses, by taking their presence to great freedoms with other females. Women, beware! and become not the demons of your husbands, in abandoning him who has devoted his soul to you, and by according to others what belongs to him alone.

In order to be able to speak from time to time to Euphrosina, Rodolphe owned to the sultan, that he perfectly well understood the Italian language. The interpreter was dismissed, and Euphrosina soon profited by his absence.

"I wish," said she, "I was delivered from this constraint. My mother promised me I should, and now she abandons me!'

"I wish it also with all my heart," replied Rodolphe, "but do not despair."

"Perhaps she sent you to my assistance, and has destined you for my deliverer."

'Oh! If you could but achieve so glorious an action."

"If you should see her before me, I conjure you to speak to her concerning it."

"I promise it to you!"

Such were the discourses which the lovers ventured from time to time, and which the sultan took for isolated exclamations or questions relative old acquaintances in their native country. Thus passed the second and third day.

CHAP. XXIV

LITTLE PETER visited his friend on the third night

PETER. You are asleep, Rodolphe? I must awake you. The new moon will soon rise above the horizon, and you have only stolen a few kisses. In this manner we shall not advance much more in a year; we have but a few weeks before us.

RODOLPHE. I ventured to speak about the belt yesterday; but——

PETER. Do you think Euphrosina is capable of breaking with facility an oath so solemnly taken, or of parting with a treasure she has so long enjoyed? It must be the work of all-powerful love; it is in the excess of that passion alone that you can expect her to make such a sacrifice; but you must excite that excess. Act, and I will fail in nothing that can second your flight. Remember that we cannot leave this place without having unbound the belt, as by its virtue Euphrosina continues to be the power of my wife, although absent. If that talisman were on the vessel, she could direct it whither she chose; and you may easily conceive that it would not arrive in a safe harbour.

RODOLPHE. Do not doubt my activity and zeal. Am I not the most interested? But, although ardently desirous of succeeding, I cannot discover the possibility. The sultan never leaves Euphrosina; he comes at the break of day, and remains until past midnight.

PETER. You are the physician, and can easily desire him to leave the apartment. I see I must instruct you; for time flies and with it a most precious occasion. Approach early tomorrow morning the bed of Euphrosina. Tell her that her mother, who is now become your own, appeared to you; that she yielded to your importunities, and chose you as the instrument of her flight. The simple and loving Euphrosina will easily credit your assertion. Then demand of the sultan, as a reward for her recovery, a ship completely equipped; and, moreover, one hundred Christian slaves, whom you must say you intend to conduct to their country, where you will arrive under the auspices addressed to Heaven for their liberator. He will accord you everything being far below his promise. Lastly, return Euphrosina to the enchanted despot.

RODOLPHE. What? Return her? And see her——

PETER. Do not interrupt me; return her to the sultan, and say that she is in the bloom and flower of health, but that you cannot answer for a relapse; that you even foresee an approaching one, if she does not observe a diet calculated to restore her strength, which consists in bathing and taking plenty of exercise. In undertaking the cure, you will pretend to yield to the prayers of the sultan, and put off your departure for a fortnight or three weeks. Fix on the garden of Damiette for the walks of your patient; they are closest to the sea-shore and may favour your flight. In order to be always within call, you will be lodged in one of the neighbouring houses. Tomorrow, I will bring you the herbs which Euphrosina must bathe in, they have great secret virtues which act on every fibre. The chaste Euphrosina will scarce dare expose her charms to her own eyes, and will, before she enters the bath, dispense with all the slaves, and lock the door herself; but here is a key which opens every lock. As soon as you believe Euphrosina is in the bath, boldly open the door. She will attempt to fly, but follow her; and if in her security she has taken off the belt, your victory is complete. But if she has preserved it even in the bath, beseech and implore; and if you do not succeed, you may seek your fortune elsewhere, and continue your pilgrimage, for I can be of no further service to you. But, at all events, have your ship in readiness, and slaves on board. Make them swear that, until their return unto their native country, they will serve you faithfully; and will even, if required, shed their last drop of blood for you. If you triumph over Euphrosina, hasten your departure.

RODOLPHE. But how—by what means?

PETER. You can also open the garden-gates with the key I gave you: you will arrive on the sea-shore; there a skiff will await you, and conduct you to the ship, ready to sail at a moment's notice.

RODOLPHE. But the guards that protect the harbour, and observe every skiff?

PETER. I will keep them otherwise employed.

RODOLPHE. And the sultan?

PETER. Will take a soporific draft, which will keep him in bed the greatest part of the day; and when he awakes, he may seek at leisure what he will never find.

RODOLPHE. Peter!—you make me the happiest of mortals.

PETER. Stop awhile! The belt is as yet safely knotted; everything depends on that. Tomorrow I shall be with you.

Rodolphe, faithful to the advice of his friend, presented himself early before the door of Euphrosina. He surprised her at the window, in a light morning gown. She received him with transports of joy and gratitude. She gave and took acknowledgments of their love. But in vain the alabaster whiteness of the most beautiful neck seduced his eyes; the cruel belt forbade any bolder enterprise; and only permitted him to renew his kisses on the lips of Euphronsina.

But not to lose a time so precious, he informed her of the will of her mother, as Peter had commanded him. Euphrosina believed everything, and easily consented. She was charmed that Rodolphe so far enjoyed the good graces of her mother; but was rather astonished that the latter had not appeared to her. "A hostile star deprives you of that happiness," replied Rodolphe; "and she is desirous of accustoming you to forget her by degrees: for she foresees, as she solemnly assured me, the approach of the day of our union and her deliverance."

"I will never forget my mother," said Euphrosina, with a sigh.

"Not even in my arms?" replied Rodolphe; and he fondly embraced her.

A slight noise announced the approach of the sultan. Before his entrance, Rodolphe had become a physician, and Euphrosina a feeble convalescent. All that Peter had predicted took place; the ship and the slaves were accorded, and the new system joyfully adopted,

Before the close of the day, the flotilla of the sultan proudly cleft the waves of the Nile, and directed its course to Damiette. During the whole of the voyage, the jealous Mussulman sat beside Euphrosina. Rodolphe, the physician, was, it is, true, admitted in her presence; but he could not find one moment to speak to her alone. On arriving at Damiette, Rodolphe perceived with joy that the sultan retired to his palace, placed Euphrosina in a distant pavilion, and assigned him a lonely gardener's lodge not far from it.

CHAP. XXV.

THAT same night Peter visited his pupil, and excited in his heart all the desires of approaching happiness. He gave him the herbs, and encouraged him to attempt the attack.

Rodolphe awoke in one of the finest and most delightful summer mornings; he rose from his couch, walked into the garden, and seated himself beneath an orange grove. The zephyrs, in floating voluptuously over their branches, covered him with flowers, and cooled his burning face. Near the arbor was the pavilion of Euphrosina. An avenue, formed by the all-delighting hand of Nature, discovered to the knight the window of her chamber; and it was not long before a most beautiful hand opened the blinds; Euphrosina, desirous of inhaling the air of a fine a day, placed herself on the ledge. Not conceiving it possible that she was observed, she paid no attention to the gentle wind which agitated the transparent veil that covered her bosom, and which was insensibly detached. The eyes of Rodolphe were riveted on the charms of Euphrosina. "I must," said he, "this day embrace that angel; I must imprint a kiss on those coral lips; or I will present myself to the kislar aga, and desire him to deprive me of my life."

He left the grove impressed with these ideas. Euphrosina retired with a blush, replaced her veil, and opened the door. She received him as innocence receives its seducer. The sultan soon after appeared. It was arranged in his presence, that

Euphrosina should enter the bath towards the setting of the sun. The longest day of Rodolphe's life was drawing to a conclusion; the herbs were prepared; the slaves had arranged the bath; the sultan had retired; and the knight, enraptured at the approach of his happiness, was busily employed in the necessary preparations.

Everything took place as Peter had foreseen. Euphrosina carefully dismissed all the eunuchs and slaves: "You may return in two hours," said she, closing the door. It was natural that the physician should remain in the proximity to call the slaves, and give assistance in case of any accident. Seated in the anti-chamber, the minutes seemed centuries to him. An hundred times his ardent passion prompted him to employ the key, and as often cold reasoning persuaded him not to lose all by too great precipitation. At the expiration of a few minutes he locked the anti-chamber, suddenly opened the door of Euphrosina's apartment, and advanced into it. The beauty had already entered the bath, and on perceiving the knight, endeavoured in vain to retire. Her garments were scattered around; in vain she attempted to seize the nearest; Rodolphe rushed forward and clasped her in his arms.

RODOLPHE. I thought I heard you call; pardon my tender earnestness; pardon the invincible power of love, if I am lost in the beauty of your charms; if I forget—if I——

And he kissed the most beautiful bosom which ever adorned a human being; for she, in her security, had taken off the belt.

EUPHROSINA. Noble and generous Rodolphe! if your sentiments are pure, I conjure you—yield to my prayer, and leave me.

RODOLPHE. Celestial beauty! what cold heart would consent if it saw what I see? Who could——?

Euphrosina disengaged herself from the arms of Rodolphe, darted to her couch, and endeavoured to hide her charms in the cover, which she had left in the greatest disorder. Rodolphe followed her; he implored, he sighed, he became more enterprising, and was on the point of triumphing, when that chaste Euphrosina perceived her belt beside the bed.

At this sight, the recollection of the order and instructions of her mother, rushed upon her bewildered mind; she redoubled her resistance, and endeavoured to seize the belt. Rodolphe observed every movement; he saw the talisman, grasped and hid it in his bosom. The instant before he was decided to pursue the half-gained victory, the instant after he determined not to make an ill use of his triumph, but to listen to the prayers of innocence, and to spare unveiled chastity. His intoxicated passion immediately subsided, and was succeeded by a pure and virtuous love. Rodolphe blushed at his temerity, sunk on his knees before the bed of Euphrosina, implored her pardon, solemnly swore never to be guilty of the like offence, shed tears of repentance, and was easily forgiven by the sensible Euphrosina, who was much affected; embraced the knight with her lily arms, and covered his lips with kisses. She resisted no longer, and would have yielded had Rodolphe continued his solicitations; but the calm lover returned within the bounds of reason, began to converse of virtue, marriage, and domestic happiness.

"I will inflict a punishment on myself," said he; "I will deprive myself during three days of your divine looks; I will not demand one kiss until the priest has united us forever. You are perfectly recovered, and need not bathe any longer." At these words, he left the most beautiful of women, without having solicited one more favour.

He did not think of retiring to bed before midnight, and had till then walked in the garden, unconscious that his beauty was considering him from the window. Other thoughts occupied his mind. He was ashamed of his past life, and resolved firmly to return to his castle and to live happy. He threw himself on his couch, more discontented than the traveller, who, having wandered during the whole of the day, perceives in the evening the inn which he left in the morning. He anxiously expected his friend, Peter, in order to impart his resolution to him, and demand his advice. Peter did not arrive, and Rodolphe, who felt himself inconvenienced by his clothes, undressed, and in so doing, the belt which he had placed in his bosom, fell to the ground unperceived by him. "What a fool I was," said he, suddenly, "not to profit of that which was so feebly refused."

Peter instantly appeared on the opposite side, and answered, "Yes, a fool indeed."

RODOLPHE. Oh, there you are, my good friend! Why did you not come sooner?

PETER. Imprudent man! You were near never seeing me again. Before all, pick up that belt and throw it into the fire; but beware not to touch it with your hands; its influence is fatal, it deprives of strength, and makes a child of a hero.

Rodolphe executed the order of the Little Peter, and the flames consumed that wonderful texture.

RODOLPHE. You are right; since I destroyed it, I feel more fire, more activity, more boldness within me.

PETER. Happy are you so soon to have got rid of that fatal poison! As long as you wore it you were in the power of my wife. She already had planned new schemes to destroy you.

RODOLPHE. Fool that I was, I perceive all. It was this belt which prevented me from enjoying the best of opportunities——

PETER. Certainly: it acted upon you, and hemmed your desires within the bounds of modesty; and it prevented the languishing Euphrosina, notwithstanding the ardour of her desires, from allowing you more than kisses.

RODOLPHE. What must I term myself? What punishment ought I not to inflict on myself! Never will I recover such an opportunity, and yet I feel I am lost if I do not possess her.

PETER. Remember how she remained at the window, watching you for hours together; how she sought you with her eyes; how many useless signs she made, being scarce able to support the fire which you have awakened in her veins. Remember all that, and remember also, that being deprived of her belt, she is exposed to every seduction; remember that the sultan will profit by those favourable moments, and that he will perhaps rob you of that happiness which you so foolishly neglected.

RODOLPHE. Unfortunate! Unfortunate! I am lost! Is it possible——

PETER. Be not alarmed; your friend has provided against every danger, and hopes to see you at the height of felicity. I have mixed some poppy juice with the beverage of the sultan; he is plunged in the most profound sleep. The fatigued slaves are slumbering also; sleep forsakes Euphrosina alone. She is now walking in the orange grove, and seeks to cool the glowing fire that consumes her; I need say no more.

Rodolphe left the apartment at the same time with Peter. At the expiration of an hour, he returned overwhelmed with favours, and transported with joy; but Euphrosina reached her couch, sad and melancholy.

I will here remark, for the consolation of every chaste female, and to warn all women of frivolous and light minds, that she deeply felt the loss of her innocence; that she would willingly have sacrificed half, nay the whole of her life for that hour, that single hour, which, in the voluptuousness of pleasure appeared so delightful; but the hour had passed never to return again. The counsels, the lessons of her mother again rushed more forcibly on her mind; she dreaded her approach, instead of, as in her days of innocence, awaiting her arrival with the most lively impatience. Punishment follows vice step for step; of this the murderer, the seducer, the robber, the miser, and the prodigal are ever convinced:

A pure conscience is the greatest treasure upon earth, but the haunted conscience of the criminal is a more excruciating and more terrible punishment than death itself.

CHAP. XXVI.

THE only consolation afforded to Euphrosina, was her excessive love for Rodolphe. "I have given him all I possessed," said she, with a deep sigh; "he will recompense me by an unbounded attachment." The hope of flying in his arms from the persecutions of the sultan; of soon becoming, by the benediction of the priest, the partner of his joys and troubles, occupied her mind incessantly. Thus she endeavoured to soothe a conscience which it was not in her power to calm.

On retiring to sleep, she perceived the loss of her belt, and sought it in vain in every corner. "It has disappeared with my innocence," said she. "Oh, if it could but return with my innocence, I would never quit it!" The loss a treasure enhances its value. The consciousness of this truth banished sleep from her eyes for some time. She slumbered in sadness, and awoke in melancholy. She received her lover with shame in her eyes, and beheld him with tenderness only after he had renewed his oath of being faithful, and of abstaining from her presence till the approaching celebration of their marriage.

The sultan, who had risen rather late, appeared next, and informed himself with solicitude of the effects of the bath. Euphrosina assured him that she was singularly fortified, and the despot became more enterprising. The absence of the talisman had deprived Euphrosina of the power of commanding that reserve on his part which she had done hitherto.

Rodolphe was forced to see him imprint ardent kisses on her lips, notwithstanding her resistance. But love and artifice soon triumphed. "Sublime monarch," said Rodolphe, "I implore as a slave, and advise you as the physician of Euphrosina, to spare her for twenty-one days. If you do not attend to this advice, and accord this prayer, you will never arrive at the height of felicity; the illness will return with redoubled violence, and then neither myself nor any physician can cure her. Accord her that delay for your mutual happiness. Shun her looks, that the irresistible power of love may not undermine your resolution, and I will answer with my head, that you will afterwards triumph without danger or difficulty."

The sultan believed Rodolphe, and promised a rigorous abstinence during that period, if Euphrosina promised on her part after that time to accord him everything. Rodolphe made a sign of approbation to Euphrosina, who accepted the conditions; the sultan, elated with hoped, instantly retired.

The day following, Rodolphe presented himself before the throne of the monarch. "An inexpressible desire of returning to my country," said he, "has brought me hither. The use of the bath will have re-established the health of Euphrosina in the time prescribed. Fulfil now your promise; order the ship to be delivered to me; order the slaves to be liberated, and grant me a sufficiency of provision to reach my native country. You will be amply recompensed in the voluptuous embraces of Euphrosina; and the enjoyment of supreme felicity will, perhaps, sometimes recall to your mind the physician who contributed to it; and who, in the most distant regions will not cease to implore the benedictions of Heaven for you."

The sultan faithfully fulfilled his promise. The ship, which was already fitted out, was that the same day placed in the possession of Rodolphe, and the next day it was filled with provisions and magnificent presents. According to his firman, Rodolphe could set sail at any hour of the night or day which was most agreeable to him; and, according to that same firman, every vessel which he might meet was to suffer him to pass without obstacles, and even render him assistance in case of necessity. Rodolphe had also the permission himself to deliver one hundred Christian slaves. His soul was affected on seeing these liberated captives, among whom were several German knights, at his feet, on hearing them pronounce their thanks, and voluntarily taking the oath of serving him unto their death.

Thus several days passed quietly on. Rodolphe, in despite of his oath, passed the evenings, and perhaps even whole nights in the arms of Euphrosina. He often conversed with his friend, Peter, who approved of his designs, advised him to hasten his flight, and assured him of his assistance.

The time when the moon would complete her course was approaching with rapidity; already nineteen days had been spent in preparations for the voyage. Towards midnight, Rodolphe glided into the orange grove to fetch Euphrosina, and conduct her to the ship, under the powerful protection of Little Peter. "All is ready," said he, "the sultan sleeps profoundly, the soporiferous beverage presented by my hands, will make his sleep of long continuance. The guards profit by my generosities, and are rejoicing in the interior court. A favourable wind fills the sails of the vessel which has already left the harbour. The slaves whom I have delivered, await with impatience their lady; come and receive with me their homage and their oaths of fealty." She tremblingly and silently followed. Rodolphe opened the garden gates with his key; entered the boat with his lovely prey, and three of the liberated Christians rowed them to the ship. The anchor was weighed, and when the sun arose above the silvery surface of the sea, the fugitives were far away from the coast of Egypt, which, towards midday, to their inexpressible delight, had vanished from the distant horizon.

CHAP. XXVII.

THE lovers returned thanks to Heaven for their deliverance, and the slaves already expressed their joy at the hope of soon embracing their wives and children. Several of them had some knowledge of nautical affairs; the trembling Euphrosina incessantly interrogated them, and was assured by them, that the most expert pilot could not attain them, even with a favourable wind. In the evening, the loving couple contemplated the movement of the waves, and the fish that were bounding on their surface; the pilot fell asleep on the rudder, and the rest of the crew drank to the health of their liberator. "Who is swimming there, near the ship?" said Euphrosina, quite alarmed to her lover, who was beholding the heavens. "Is it you, my faithful friend, Peter?" said the knight, looking below him and recognising the Dwarf; "What news do you bring? and why do you not approach?"

PETER (*swimming near the vessel*). Unfortunate! you think yourself in security, when you are in the most imminent danger. Save yourself and save your friend, while it is yet time.

RODOLPHE. What has then happened? what is the matter?

PETER. Your ship is in the possession of my wicked wife; the moon has attained her destination; the old woman is returned; and, in opposition to all my endeavours, she has forced the ship to form a circle. Tomorrow, your astonished eyes will see the coast of Egypt; and, in the evening, a strong current will force you into the harbour. Then evil to Rodolphe! evil to Euphrosina! evil to all those who accompany you! The sultan will exercise a terrible vengeance on you; and if I can save you, who can save Euphrosina?

EUPHROSINA. Great God! what voice! what menaces! What means all this?

RODOLPHE. Approach, my only friend!

PETER. It is not possible; my wife retains me by a secret power.

RODOLPHE. Then help—advise me!

PETER. You must help and advise yourself; all I can do is to warn you. One of the slaves that accompanies you, has that hat in his possession which you threw away, and which twice led you to the brink of destruction. Its influence, which my wife exerts to the highest degree, the vessel, and the whole crew. You are in her power. Haste, therefore; assemble all the slaves; endeavour to persuade the possessor of the hat to give it up, and throw it into the sea. But beware, no human power can deprive him of it by force; he must deliver—he must resign of his own will freely, or you are all inevitably lost. If you succeed, you will soon see me on the vessel; if you succeed not, I will do my utmost to save you, but I fear it will be in vain.

Peter disappeared. Euphrosina demanded some explanations of Rodolphe, but he was in a hurry; he promised to satisfy her another time, and immediately assembled his hundred slaves. Not one had the hat which Rodolphe knew so well; none would own having seen it, nor preserved it among their clothes. "I will seek every corner of the ship," said he, "and if I find it—if I discover the perfidious traitor who could break his oath for a miserable hat, his punishment shall be terrible."

A German gentleman advanced from the midst of the slaves. "Noble and generous deliverer," said he, in a tone of humility; "be not irritated against us; I can, perhaps, throw some light on your search. Listen, and do not judge with too much severity. You entrusted the commandment of the ship to me when it was yet in the harbour. As I was leaving Damiette, for the last time, and hastening towards the sea-shore; I met two disguised templars. These monks, whilst we were languishing in chains, had often visited us in secret, to distribute alms and to keep up our spirits by their pious exhortations. 'You can,' said they, 'reward us an hundred fold for what we have done for you, by taking on board your ship a brave old German knight, who miraculously saved, and who has secretly resided with us.—The Lord will bless you if you this good action.' I had not forgotten the strict order given by you not to receive anyone on board, but gratitude to ancient benefactors triumphed over my duty; I yielded to their importunities, and thought that yourself might one day thank me for this act of humanity. They brought the knight, and I received him on board; I concealed him amongst the casks in the hold; I have not yet had time to speak to him, and scarce found a moment to convey some food to him; but I perfectly well recollect that this pilgrim had a hat such as you seek and describe."

RODOLPHE. Where is this old man?—Where is he?

GENTLEMAN. I will bring him hither. But hearken unto the voice of mercy; pardon my fault—spare the old man.

RODOLPHE. Ungrateful man! you know not what dreadful calamities your disobedience has prepared for me. Conduct the man to my cabin, I will speak to him.

They separated, and the Gentleman soon entered the room with the German knight.

RODOLPHE (*horror struck*). Heavens! I see what I should never have imagined? Waldemar! here?

WALEDEMAR (*clad as a pilgrim, with the straw hat on his head*). Yes, 'tis I; and you are my deliverer; my saviour! I would rather perish in the most obscure prison—I would rather be suspended to the fangs, than owe my liberty to the destroyer of my repose and my happiness, and the author of my ignominy.

RODOLPHE (*perceiving the hat*). Cease your maledictions, old man; place your resentment within bounds; forget as I have forgotten. If I thought as you did, I would return on you the sufferings which you have caused me—I would revenge the atrocious conduct by which you endeavoured to have me thrown on the fangs: but I repeat it, I forgive all and forget all. Tell me how it is possible that you saved your life, when I saw you precipitated—when my ears heard your doleful cries: relate that miraculous adventure, and then accord me one favour.

WALDEMAR. I will relate nothing to you, nor satisfy your curiosity. Men like me never deign to commune with such miserable wretches as you; but if you have a favour to ask be quick, that I may once more enjoy some pleasure in this life by refusing you.

RODOLPHE. Inflexible man! Have I merited this treatment? Do you not perceive that a hundred hands are prepared to sacrifice you at my command?

WALDEMAR. Kill me if you can!

RODOLPHE. Will you not yield?

WALDERMAR. Never! never!

RODOLPHE. You will remain irreconcilable?

WALDERMAR. Until death!

RODOLPHE (*to the Gentleman*). You have transgressed my orders—you concealed this old man in my vessel—you must expiate your crime. If in one quarter of an hour you do not bring me his hat, I will have you thrown into the sea: repair the evil you have caused; I await you on the deck; bring me a decisive answer.

Rodolphe retired, and Waldemar followed him, exclaiming with derision: "That is what you wished to ask me; you are then also acquainted with the virtues of this hat?" And turning to the Gentleman, he continued: "Fear nothing; the hat is broad enough to protect us both; I defy anyone to deprive me of it by force; who will have the temerity to touch me? Be assured that you are under my protection, and that no harm can result to you."

The poor gentleman implored Waldemar to have pity on him. "I have," said he, "made an ungrateful return to my liberator; his anger and demand are both just: be grateful for the service I willingly rendered you; accord him the hat which can be of no possible service to you, and may injure him."

WALDERMAR. Of no use to me? Then listen to my tale, which I have related to no mortal man, and then judge whether it were possible for me to give up this hat even to my best friend, which you desire me to give to my most cruel enemy. I bore, like you, the chains of slavery, and worked in the gardens of the sultan. I endeavoured to recover my liberty but I was betrayed, and condemned, with all my accomplices, to be thrown on the fangs. The next morning, the cruel sentence was executed; I was precipitated; and I remained suspended on an iron pike, which pierced my thigh. Imagine my horrible situation; I experienced the most excruciating torments; and, as the pike had not mortally wounded me, I foresaw that my sufferings would be prolonged. I endeavoured to raise myself with my hands, and saw some of my companions in the same agonizing tortures; while others, more happy, had already resigned their breath. I implored Divine Mercy, when this hat lightly settled on my head. My suffering abated instantly; the fang on which I hung bent like wax, and I glided gently to the earth. Some dogs, who were licking our blood, showed me a path leading to the fields; I was soon on the great road: I hid myself until midnight, and repaired, unperceived, to some priests, whose secret place of abode was known to me. They took care of me, healed my wound, and conducted me to you.

GENTLEMAN. And you attribute your miraculous deliverance to this hat?

WALDEMAR. Certainly.

GENTLEMAN. And by what reason?

WALDEMAR. You may easily imagine that the hat was precious unto me from thenceforth, but it has become much more precious within a few hours. Overcome by misfortune and grief, I fell asleep on my bed in the hold; but was soon awakened by a slight rustling; I looked round, and perceived beside me a Little Woman, scarce two feet high. "Rejoice," said she to me; "Heaven is appeased, you have gained the palm of resignation. God and your wife are reconciled. You know as yet not what a treasure you possess in that hat; learn to appreciate its value. I own it leads the penitent into an infinity of tribulations, but if he, in whose possession it is, suffers with patience, its powerful aid will always be assured to him; it protects him when even in the jaws of death; it sustains the swimmer on the waters, and looses the fangs of the sufferer. An ungrateful youth, who has lost himself, once possessed it—he imprudently threw it away, and it fell to your share. Keep it, and transmit it to your heirs: but swear to me to fulfil one condition and scrupulously to observe it." I took the oath. "In a little while," continued she, "you will be requested to deliver up the hat; you will be threatened with death if you refuse it: but let nothing affright you; your hat protects you against every danger and every power. Untie not the riband which fastens it to your head. Let no threats or prayers induce you to quit this ship; it is in my power, by means of the hat; I conduct it where I choose. On this ship are two sinful souls, whom I endeavour incessantly to reclaim: if one is irrevocably lost, I will, at least, do my utmost to save the other. The vessel belongs to Rodolphe of Westerbourg. He has seduced my only, my virtuous daughter. Persevere, and believe firmly that the hardened ruffian can neither injure you, nor any of your companions." The Little Woman disappeared; you fetched me, and her prediction is accomplished, but I will strictly follow her directions.

GENTLEMAN. Poor old man, your misfortunes have deranged your brain but I am resigned. No crime can escape punishment, and penitence cannot expiate blood. I am a murderer, whose remorseful conscience conducted him to the tomb of the Saviour of the world; I thought myself sufficiently punished by ten years slavery; by fasting, praying, and endeavouring to perform every good action in my power. But far from me that deceiving hope! A miserable hat renews my sufferings. I will present myself before my judge, who will keep his oath, and order me to be thrown in to the sea. But I have merited it: if I were in his stead, I should sacrifice him who had transgressed the orders of his liberator as I have.

WALDEMAR. I will follow, and see who dares to touch you. Learn from me, that an austere penitence reconciles the criminal to Heaven.

GENTLEMAN. The only means by which I can be saved, is to do as I was desired; act as you please; I am resigned.—Do you know our captain?

WALDEMAR. Know him? Ah, but too well! He is—he has—But I will not inflict a deeper wound; it would be more painful than all the sufferings I have hitherto endured.

CHAP. XXVIII.

THE gentleman presented himself, accompanied by Waldemar, before Rodolphe, near whom stood Euphrosina, who had interrogated him, and in the agitation of his mind, he confessed the whole of his treachery, and related to her how he had deceived her, and given her false news concerning her mother; how his friend had had the art of keeping away the old woman, and how she had returned to revenge herself by means of the wonderful hat. Euphrosina, thunderstruck with these unexpected confessions, began to perceive the whole extent of her misfortune, and felt all the horror of her crime. She trembled at the idea that Rodolphe had renewed his connexion with Little Peter. Her mother had, during her youth, related to her the artifices and the malice of that perverse spirit, warned her to beware of his snares, and now she was suddenly caught in them. Rodolphe was endeavouring to appease her, when Waldemar entered with the gentleman.

RODOLPHE (*to Waldemar*). Well! have you decided? Will you save your deliverer? Or do you wish to see him precipitated into the sea?

WALDEMAR. I am resolved not to give you the hat, and to protect a friend by its power and virtue.

RODOLPHE. Consider your danger. Force me not to violate the respect I owe to your age; stifle not that pity which pleads for you in my heart; force me not to lose, when I wish to save you.

WALDEMAR. Hear me, Rodolphe: when I found my unfaithful spouse in your arms; when I witnessed the proofs of affection which she bestowed on the fruit of her iniquity, I swore eternal hatred to her and to you. In those blasphemous moments I considered everlasting damnation as the highest pitch of my ardent desires. I revenged myself on my wife in a terrible manner. Her death drove me from my native country, and led me to Palestine, where I was followed by remorse and regret. My heart was filled with a desire of double revenge. I beheld in you the cause of her infidelity, and the author of her death. I should have enjoyed the most excruciating torture to have seen you partake of it. I should have been at the height of felicity, if I had seen you in the depth of misery. A chance (no it is not a chance), but special Providence, delivers you this day into my hands; and yet, behold, I reject all desire of vengeance—I pity you; I——

RODOLPHE (*transported with joy*). Is it possible? You will——

WALDEMAR. Let me continue; I am no longer your enemy; I am but the instrument of a superior power. An austere penitence has reconciled me with Heaven; I am forgiven, why should I not forgive you?

RODOLPHE. You will then return the hat?——

WALDEMAR. I will not return the hat; I have sworn it, and will keep my oath. This hat through my means, shall replace you on the road to virtue; it gives me unbounded power over you, but I will not abuse this power; I will obey only the decrees of Providence, which deigns to offer you the means of escaping damnation by penitence.

RODOLPHE. But old man, if——

WALDEMAR. Cease your prayers and threats; they are useless. I am as immovable as a rock. Be assured, that I know and appreciate the power entrusted to me by means of this hat. If I ordered your slaves to bind, to flog, or to torture you, they would be forced to do so, although against their own inclination. But far from me such vengeance! I leave your punishment to Him who scrutinizes the human heart, and judges it in his justice. But will keep my oath; I will not resign my hat, and will let the vessel sail whither the winds may drive it.

RODOLPHE (*drawing his sword*). They shall not hinder me from piercing the heart of a——

WALDEMAR. Ah! will thou kill me?—Well, Rodolphe! well——

RODOLPHE (*dropping his sword*). Unfortunate that I am, my strength abandons me! I am lost!

EUPHROSINA (*in tears at the feet of Waldemar*). If your heart is yet open to the divine impulse of pity; if you are not a stranger to the compassion which the repentance of an unfortunate ought to inspire; save me, save my Rodolphe. He has deceived me, he has seduced me, he has excited against me the anger of my mother; but if, under the guidance of her power, we are re-conducted to Damiette, a more terrific chastisement awaits him and me. When I am delivered up to the sultan, he will perhaps make him endure before me the most excruciating torments. Oh, Waldemar! if you have ever loved, if you have ever felt all that love can do, you must feel how misfortune—even when merited—endears the loved object to your hearts, you must know, that in such moments, pity, pardon; mercy, anguish, fear and hope, are all confounded in that one word, Love; in that all-powerful word whose magic chains us to the very murderer. He was an hypocrite; he had perfidiously seduced me: I ought to hate, to abhor him; but I behold him unfortunate, unassisted, and my resentment vanishes. I see the sword of vengeance raised over him, and I throw myself into his arms; I stretch forth my suppliant hands to receive the mortal blow which menaces him. All my hatred turns on the authoress of my misfortunate, on my mother, who abandoned me, and left me unguarded against his seductions, allowed me copiously to drink of the poison of love, and now desires that I should conceal its effects.

WALDEMAR. Do as you please, poor deluded wretch! I do my duty. If you take an interest in protecting a seducer, in not correcting a criminal by trials, in not warning him from the precipice by chastisement, you can do it unopposed. But if you will listen to the voice of age and experience, leave the monster who derides the most sacred laws. His conscience is loaded with the reproaches of all the women whom he has dishonoured; his mind defiled with blood.

EUPHROSINA. Oh, I will wash away that blood with my tears! I will bear the punishment which awaits him! He has sinned for love, and will expiate his fault. I swear to you, I swear to my implacable mother, never to quit him; I will be his faithful companion, I will serve him as a rampart.

WALDEMAR. I repeat it, and repeat it again! Do as you please!

The gentleman who accompanied Waldemar added his entreaties to those of Euphrosina; but the knight remained inflexible. He assured them several times that he was not the enemy of Rodolphe; that he sought not to revenge himself, but only to keep his oath. "I conduct myself," said he, "like a physician, who forces his patients to take those medicines which must save them."—He then left Rodolphe a prey to the greatest despair. In vain Euphrosina sought to console him by the most tender and affectionate effusions of her love; he heard her not, and his conscience was oppressed by the blackest remorse. Waldemar ordered the pilot to tack, and was reluctantly obeyed by the slaves, who seemed incapable of resistance. The wind filled the sails; and at the rising of the sun, they beheld the shores of Egypt in the distance. The ship resounded with lamentable cries; every one sighed, prayed, and trembled for his life. But Waldemar was deaf to their entreaties, and continued to steer towards the cost.

The inconsolable Euphrosina was continually on the deck, and had completely exhausted her eyes with tears. She who once thrilled with horror at the very name of Peter, who beheld in him the most cruel of demons, now expected him with the most anxious solicitude. She hoped to obtain from him the means of salvation, or at least, a good advice; but her impatience was deceived: the presentiment which plunged Rodolphe into a melancholy despair was but too soon realised; Peter did not appear again, and Euphrosina persuaded herself that her barbarous mother had again chained him to exercise a more cruel vengeance on Rodolphe. "I will remain with you," said she to him; "I will intercept the blows with which you are menaced. Nothing, no nothing but death shall ever separate me from you."

All eyes were fixed towards Egypt: the confused masses became more and more distinct; the towers were soon discernible; the domes were next perceived, and lastly, the houses. One of the slaves turned once more with tears in his eyes towards his country, to bid it a last adieu. When addressing this pious homage, he discovered a ship at no great distance, which followed them in full sail. At this news, all the crew turned to that side, with hope in their looks; but this soon vanished, for, on the approach of the ship, its colours declared it to be Egyptian, and announced to the miserable Christians a more prompt slavery than they expected. Waldemar ordered the ship to be brought to: he was obeyed with tears. What a lamentable scene to behold the whole crew prostrate themselves, and to hear them recommend their souls to Heaven in broken and plaintive tones!

The ship soon after attained them. On the deck were several Mahometans in arms, and in the centre, the sultan himself. The flight of Euphrosina had been announced to him, and he would have followed Rodolphe in vain had not Waldemar ordered the ship back, and expressed his astonishment on perceiving astern of him, that ship which he thought was far before him. "Surrender," said the interpreter; "deliver up the ravisher and his prey; the generous sovereign of the world will have pity on the others, and permit you to return to your country."

Waldemar answered, "We yesterday took the firm resolution to return them to the hands of our benefactor, and not pay his generosity by black ingratitude. Prince, you see the proof, as we were returning to the coast of Egypt: receive those whom you seek, and deign to accord our prayer."

INTERPRETER. Bind them, and bring them to the feet of the sultan.

EUPHROSINA (*advancing precipitately*). You need not use any violence. We voluntarily submit to the decrees of destiny, and spare you the horrible perfidy of dragging your liberator into those chains from which he disengaged you. Come, my Rodolphe, come! We go to death; we will die together.

Rodolphe, who until then had remained dumb, rejected the consolation of Euphrosina, and abandoned himself to despair, now advanced.

RODOLPHE. Here I am! bind me if you can.

His unfortunate companions were incapable of performing the act; they shed tears, and several offered to encounter death for their deliverer. "If our arms," said they, "were not reduced to the greatest state of debility we would defend you, and force such as endeavoured to approach you, first to trample our bodies."

INTERPRETER. Bind them, if you wish to avert the punishment which awaits you.

RODOLPHE (*to his companions, seizing the hands of Euphrosina*). Adieu! I accuse you not of perjury, I absolve you of your oath, and wish you a happy return to your country. And you, Waldemar, I forgive you *my* death. But if the Almighty hears the prayers of a sinner, may the blood of Euphrosina burn on your conscience, and torment you beyond the grave.

He then prepared to step on board the sultan's vessel, who was making every preparation to have them soon in his power and already menaced Rodolphe with his sword, and spoke of the tortures prepared for him.

EUPHORSINA (*to Rodolphe*). Brave his threats, seize the opportunity, and follow me.

At these words, she precipitated herself into the sea; Rodolphe obeyed her example, and immediately followed her. The two ships instantly launched their boats, and endeavoured to seize them. The waves sometimes raised them up, and sometimes dragged them into the abyss, until Euphrosina disappeared entirely. The strength of Rodolphe had resisted the force of the waves, and he was seized by the Mussulmen who followed him. They placed him in the boat, bound him with cords, conveyed him to the ship, and threw him into the hold. The sultan, furious at the loss of Euphrosina, resolved to dispatch him by slow tortures. The soul of Rodolphe was prey to the most profound despair. He had swallowed so much salt water, that he soon became incapable of feeling the horror of his situation; he lost all ideas of the past, and not one of the sultan's ship's crew had the humanity to afford the assistance necessary to sustain exhausted nature.

CHAP. XXIX.

WHEN Rodolphe had recovered his senses, he found himself in the most profound obscurity and the most appalling silence. On stretching forth his hands he felt some straw under him, and beside him a cold wall. This last circumstance induced him to believe that he was no more in the hold of the ship, but in a prison. He felt no pain, only hunger and a burning thirst: while seeking something to satisfy it, he seized a hand.

PETER. Be not afraid, it is the hand of your old friend Peter.

RODOLPHE. Peter! Peter! You here? Then I am not entirely lost. Is Euphrosina saved?

PETER. Yes.

RODOLPHE. Where is she? Where is she? Has your wife dragged her out of the waves? Is she fallen into the hands of that implacable soul?

PETER. No; I caused the waves to swallow her up; and carried her under the waters out of sight of the sultan, and placed her on the shore of the fishermen's isle to return to your aid; but, unfortunately, I arrived too late: the barbarians had already dragged you from the sea, and bound you with a cord which my wife had enchanted. I could, therefore, no longer assist you, as she held you under her power. I returned to Euphrosina, who had been conveyed to a hut by an old fisherman. I have secured the hut against all surprise, and was some time before I could reach you.

RODOLPHE. Come, my faithful friend, conduct me to my dearest, that I may return her lively attachment, her undaunted love; that I may swear eternal constancy——

PETER. Stop, Rodolphe, you lose yourself! Do you know where you are?

RODOLPHE. Apparently in a prison,

PETER. The deepest and safest in Damiette.

RODOLPHE. From which you can deliver me?

PETER. You are mistaken, if you think me powerful enough to overcome so many obstacles. I cannot force iron gates; I cannot render you invisible, nor change you into aerial substance, which would be necessary to drag you from this cell.

RODOLPHE. What will become of me?

PETER. Horrible torments are reserved for you: the enraged sultan has fixed this day for your death. It is in his presence that you are, not to be put to death immediately, but slowly tortured until your end: he is preparing boiling oil to bathe you in; you are then to be healed with balm of Mecca, and then to be plunged into hot melted lead.

RODOLPHE. Great God!—Great God! And you cannot save me?

PETER. All my endeavours prove fruitless; and until this moment I have discovered no means whatever. I shall probably be forced to see the last shoot of a long race of heroes, whom I have protected for so many centuries past, destroyed.

RODOLPHE. Oh! Peter, you have not for me that friendship of which you boast. Why did you not let me die on the fangs? Why did you only save Euphrosina?

PETER. Because I believed her to be your most precious treasure—because I thought I was rendering myself worthy of your affection. I thought that the most cruel death would be more acceptable to you, than to see Euphrosina in the hands of the sultan: and that you would say, "The barbarian shall not enjoy what he has sought with so much ardour;" and that idea would contribute to soften your sufferings.

RODOLPHE. Sad and frivolous consolation! Will not his piercing eyes discover the place of her retreat? Can you swear to me, upon your word and honour, that he will not find her, and that his passion will never be satisfied?

PETER. I cannot; and I wish you were convinced of the impossibility of my saving you! That certitude would induce you to follow the only means of delivering you, and prudently sacrificing a treasure which you would be as likely to lose after the most horrid of deaths.

RODOLPHE. I do not understand you, explain yourself more clearly.

PETER. You will soon understand me, if you listen to me. The sultan still passionately loves Euphrosina: the idea of having lost her, is unto his love like pouring oil upon a furnace; and the hope of vengeance cannot moderate his regret. He will accord your life and liberty, if you will reveal to him the retreat of Euphrosina, and if you return to him what you can never possess.

RODOLPHE. Who?—I?—impossible! That would be too shameful——

PETER. It would be barbarous if you did it without an inducement; but two evils menace you at the same time If Euphrosina is discovered, you will not escape your punishment: if you die first, I cannot long conceal the authoress of your death; and, therefore, between two such evils, it would be unpardonable in you not to choose the least—not to evade a death by sacrificing an object which you can easily replace.

RODOLPHE. I should thus betray her who has braved the waves for me; I should repay all her kindnesses with such ingratitude; I should deliver her into the hands of the man whom she abhors! Never.

PETER. Leave such reasoning to men who inhabit gilded palaces; it is not for inhabitants of such dark prisons. There is certainly nothing laudable in betraying a beloved benefactress: there can be nothing more cowardly, more barbarous, than to deliver her to the man she detests; but if you are desirous of prolonging your days, there are no other means. I have nothing more to say to you: If you wish not to be a martyr to constancy, and to assure yourself a longer existence, you must renounce all these high sounding virtues. Do as you please; but this I advise you: when the guards fetch you, request them to conduct you before the sultan; repent of your crime, and promise to return him Euphrosina, if he accords your life and liberty. He will immediately consent: too happy in having her restored, whom he believed dead. Tell the guard that accompanies you to direct the boat to the nearest island. When you are disembarked, you will find on the shore several fishermen's huts: you will see suspended on one of them the veil of Euphrosina; conduct the guards thither, and deliver her up.

CHAP. XXX.

THE PRISONER soon felt his hunger and thirst redoubled; that circumstance greatly contributed to abate his love towards Euphrosina. His imagination exaggerated all the horrors of his approaching death; and, before the guards appeared, he had resolved to exchange his mistress for life and liberty.

When the guards arrived, he demanded to be conducted to the sultan, before he saw the terrible preparations, and without awaiting the fatal moment. After having offered to discover the retreat of Euphrosina, he requested mercy. The delighted sultan promised him everything as soon as Euphrosina should be delivered into his hands. A boat conducted the perjured Rodolphe to the island; he soon arrived at the hut which concealed the tender Euphrosina. He found her partaking of a frugal repast, seasoned with her tears, during the absence of her lover. At the sight of the guards, she rose astonished; but when Rodolphe advanced from amongst them, she embraced him in a transport of joy, and exclaimed, "Oh! Rodolphe, all my pains, all my sufferings are at an end: even if you fetched me to death, I would undergo it with pleasure, if I could find it in your arms." (Rodolphe turns from her). "You avert your eyes! Are then the news which you bring me worse than death?"

RODOLPHE. They are!—Seize her; deliver me of my torments.

The guards surrounded her: in vain she questioned, prayed, sighed—she could not learn the cause of this barbarous treatment; they dragged her away. But, oh! how was her heart rent when she beheld Rodolphe remaining behind: when she began to suspect that he perhaps had revealed the place of her retreat.

Rodolphe was free: for the order of the sultan was to let him go wherever he pleased as soon as he had delivered Euphrosina to the guards. His eyes refused to behold her dragged into the boat; her lamentable shrieks augmented his torments. He entered the hut, and partook of the meal prepared for Euphrosina—of that meal which she had seasoned with her tears. He has no sooner appeased his hunger and thirst than he regretted his barbarous treachery; but reflection, and cold reasoning, persuaded him that what was done could not be undone; and soon triumphed over the last scruples, over the last emotions of his conscience. He remained in the hut until the evening, expecting soon to see and hear his friend, Peter. He had already fallen into a sound sleep on the bed of straw, which Euphrosina had moistened with her tears, when Peter awoke him, and ordered him to follow.

RODOLPHE. Whither are you going to lead me?

PETER. You must leave this place. Tomorrow, a caravan leaves Damiette for Arabia, and a ship sails for France. You may proceed to Jerusalem, or return to your country—choose.

RODOLPHE. What do you advise?

PETER. Nothing;—I have hitherto conducted you as a child in lead-strings, and I have always assisted you with my counsels. The hour is come in which I must abandon you to yourself. You are acquainted with your enemies; you can distinguish good from evil, and know the causes of pleasure or pain. Go whithersoever you please, I can give you no further advice.

RODOLPHE. I desire to return to my native country.

PETER. Very well; this is the last time that I am permitted to see and converse with you without being called.

RODOLPHE. What! you would abandon me?

PETER. Murmur not against the decrees of destiny; they are capricious. The thing is, and cannot be otherwise. But in order to part as good and ancient friends, here take my only treasure—take all I possess—take my knapsack: you will find money to defray the expenses of your journey; a knife, a rope-ladder, a book, and a ring. Do not consider these last articles as objects of indifference; and although they seem of little value at present, they will become precious in future. If you open this book on the left side, I shall appear before you; if on the right then my wife will obey the summons.

RODOLPHE. I will never see her again.

PETER. Be immovable in this resolution; it heartily delights me. Adieu, Rodolphe! Remember that life is but short—that youth vanishes with rapidity—that old age walks on crutches, and that it is followed by innumerable miseries. Enjoy the first—think not of the latter. Banish all anxiety and unpleasant thoughts: enter the house of pleasure, and fly the house of mourning. It now depends on you to seek happiness and gaiety, or to wander in the dark paths of misfortune and melancholy. You are then going to Franconia?—You are returning to your native country?

RODOLPHE. Is that your advice?

PETER. I have nothing more to say. You must obey the dictates of your own heart;—you must act alone, and be responsible for your actions. You can call me or my wife at pleasure. If you open the book to the left, I shall appear, as I told you before, but not as your friend, or your counsellor, but as your servant; as a slave ready to obey all your commands, however trifling or insignificant.

RODOLPHE. Oh continue to be always what you were! You have extricated me from so many dangers and difficulties. If you do not direct me, if you leave me to myself, I shall soon fall.

PETER. Be not insatiable. Among the many millions of human beings inhabiting this earth, there are few that have found, like you, a support in the hours of misfortune and tribulation: yet they live, and do not fall. Adieu!—Are you going to Jerusalem or Franconia?

RODOLPHE. To Franconia: I wish to revisit my native country. I was always happiest in my castle, in my woods.

PETER. If you take the right on leaving this hut, you will find in the harbour a ship laden with the merchandise of a great caravan proceeding to Jerusalem: if you take to the left, you will find in the bay a ship that will set sail early tomorrow morning for the west, and on which you will be received with the greatest pleasure.

RODOLPHE. Be for once, this once more, what you have been so long to me, my friend, my adviser. What road am I to take? Which is the best to conduct me to happiness in this and the world to come?

PETER. Your mother brought you into this world thirty years ago. The hour of your birth is passed; I can no longer advise you. I have been your friend for six years, and shall be your slave during twelve. Adieu!

RODOLPHE. Stay!—one word more. What does Euphrosina? Where is she?

PETER. I can give you no answer, while you thus interrogate me. When the book calls, I come, I talk, and obey. Adieu!—take the right or the left, as you please.

And the Dwarf disappeared.

END OF BOOK ONE.

BOOK TWO

CHAP. I.

RODOLPHE remained immovable on his bed of straw. All that Peter related, struck him with astonishment. He resolved to depart as soon as the day should break; but he had not decided which road to take. "To the right, or to the left," said he, to himself. "The choice is important. What shall I do in Palestine? I shall not find happiness there. There, war, famine and the plague, preside by turns. The road to the right leads thither: it is to the right I must open the book when I wish to see the wife of Little Peter; there is nothing but misery and sufferings on the right; I will go to the left, and enjoy this life while I can: it is the last advice which my friend, Peter, gave me."

He therefore, determined to follow this resolution. But his mind was troubled. "What is Euphrosina doing at this present moment? What is become of her?" He opened the knapsack. "To the right or the left?" said he, the book opened to the left. He immediately heard the hut shake. He raised his astonished eyes, and beheld before him a gigantic figure, whose head threatened to break the roof: it was eight feet high; dressed like Little Peter, in brown cloth. Its beard descended, like the beard of Little Peter, to its knees; but instead of a knotty stick, it grasped a large club.

RODOLPHE (*trembling*). What do you wish with me? I did not summon *you*!

GIANT. No! Did you not open the book to the left?

RODOLPHE. It was not to speak to you, but to my good friend, Peter.

GIANT. Different services require different degrees of strength, and in consequence a different form. You see in me the Little Peter, who will serve you as well in the form of Great Peter. What did you wish?

RODOLPHE. You the Little Peter?

PETER. Yes; what signifies my outward form, if I execute your wishes? Speak, and see whether I shall not blindly obey you.

RODOLPHE. I can scarce believe you; I shall not be able to accustom myself to your horrible appearance. Be rather what you were.

PETER. That is impossible. You called me; what am I to do?

RODOLPHE. I desire to know what Euphrosina is doing this moment.

PETER. I will fly to Damiette, and bring you word immediately.

Peter disappeared; and Rodolphe rubbed his eyes, to ascertain whether what he had heard was a dream or a reality. He knew not what to think, before the Giant again stood near him.

PETER. Euphrosina is very ill. A violent fever has attacked her, and the sultan is in imminent danger of losing her.

RODOLPHE. Poor Euphrosina!

PETER. The sultan has given the strictest orders to seek and seize you, wherever you may be, and to drag you before him.

RODOLPHE. And why?

PETER. Because he imagines hat you had poisoned her, before you returned her to him.

RODOLPHE. What must I doWhere shall I hide myself?

PETER. Order, and I will obey.

RODOLPHE. Must I fly? Shall I remain here?

PETER. Order, and I will obey.

RODOLPHE. Insupportable obstinacy! I will know your advice.

PETER. I am your slave,—you are my master; when you command, I will obey.

RODOLPHE. Poor Euphrosina! I cannot save you then. Your death is the object of my desires; it will relieve you from your sufferings. (*He leaves the hut; Peter follows.*) The day begins to break. What shall I do? Oh, Peter! Peter! it is not generous in you thus to abandon me, when your advice is more necessary than ever.

PETER. Master, you have both reason and spirit; you have a head and a heart like other men; you know how to reflect, to act, and desire. What can you possibly complain of?

RODOLPHE. Of being deprived of your counsels.

PETER. Order, and I will obey.

RODOLPHE. Will you incessantly repeat these same words to me?

PETER. Continually, until you understand them perfectly.

RODOLPHE. You said the sultan had ordered me to be brought before him?

PETER. I did.

RODOLPHE. Will his guards find me if I go to the right?

PETER. I do not know.

RODOLPHE. And if I take to the left?

PETER. I cannot tell: I consider neither the past nor the future; I can but obey your commands.

RODOLPHE. I am horribly deceived! I am as a child exposed by an unmerciful mother, which is not enabled to sustain its own existence.

PETER. Happy is the child exposed for a good reason by its mother, if she at the same time gives it a faithful servant, who seeks it sustenance when it hungers, and brings it drink when it thirsts!

RODOLPHE. But who does not warn it of the approaching danger; who does not point out to it the precipice, to the brink of which it has been led by its imprudence?

PETER. But who protects it when he hears its voice? Who comes to its assistance when it beckons? Man must act freely, must choose unrestrained; but he is also responsible for his choice and his actions.

RODOLPHE. Well then! I shall return to my country. These perpetual efforts in search of bliss exhaust me; I desire to enjoy peace; I will no longer be exposed to the extremes of poverty and affluence. Can I rely on your assistance, if the soldiers of the sultan should discover me?

PETER. Order, and I shall obey.

RODOLPHE. Where shall I find the ship that sails for France?

PETER. The path down to the left leads to the bay where the ship put up last night, in consequence of contrary winds. The sails are already unfurled. Make haste, if you wish not to be too late.

RODOLPHE. I am going. (*Takes the knapsack, and runs along the path.*)

PETER. Am I to follow you?

RODOLPHE. I will call you when I am in want of your services.

Rodolphe soon arrived at the bay, after crossing to the main land in a boat: saw the ship ready to sail; addressed himself to the captain, whom he found on the shore, and begged him to receive him on board. "I am," said he, "a German knight, who, after having borne the chains of slavery, had retired to yonder island, and who ardently desires to see his country once more. Receive me on board, and I will generously compensate you for your trouble."

"You are welcome," replied the captain, "you are welcome; I will be a brother unto you. We also have endured the hardships of slavery; but we now return to our dear native country, having been ransomed by our generous monarch. Ascend the ship, the wind is favourable, and I am as impatient as you to arrive in Europe."

CHAP. II.

THE passage was favourable: at the expiration of one month, the released slaves beheld the land of Liberty; they soon discovered the towers of the famous Marseilles, and came to an anchor in its port. As, during the whole of the journey, Rodolphe he had not been in want of the services of his new attendant, he never called him; but he regretted that he was no longer his friend and counsellor, and that he only waited upon him in the capacity of a servant. He paid his passage, thanked the captain, took leave of him, and lodged in one of the best hotels at Marseilles.

Marseilles was then very populous, and its commerce flourished. A great number of French noblemen resided within its walls. Rodolphe often met their suites, and remarked some beautiful ladies in the train. His heart, which had long been insensible to exterior objects, opened at their sight. He resolved more closely to examine the female sex of that country, and to fill the void of his soul.

There remained a considerable sum of money in the knapsack which Peter had given him. Rodolphe bought arms, clothes, and horses, which were not all paid for, though the bag was empty.

The governor of Marseilles had some time before publicly announced that a tournament was to be held in the town of Sens, where the marriage of the rich heiress of Provence, the

Countess Beatrix, was to be celebrated. The day of her union with Charles, the prince of the blood-royal of France, was to be that of this superb *joute*.

Rodolphe beheld with a jealous eye the knights that arrived from the further extremities of the continent, and they were making splendid preparations to prove their valour before the royal family of France. A desire of displaying before the French knights the strength and courage of the German nobility, awakened in him a sense of honour; but every time he put his hand into the little knapsack, he found only the knife, the rope-ladder, the ring, and the book. "Of what use are all these objects to me," said he, after each fruitless search. "If Peter continued to be my friend, I could consult him on this emergency. But Peter, my servant, cannot second my intuitions."—"But there is no harm in trying," added he, opening the book to the left; when the giant instantly appeared before him.

RODOLPHE. I wish to engage in the tournament to be given in the honour of Beatrix; but I am in want of money to equip myself splendidly. Can you procure me some?

PETER. Order, and I will obey.

RODOLPHE. Bring me three thousand pieces of gold.

PETER. Am I to borrow them? Am I to steal them? Am I—?

RODOLPHE. Oh, fie! you must borrow them, and I shall return the sum in two years hence.

PETER. What security will you give?

RODOLPHE. My word of honour as a knight.

PETER. When am I to bring the money?

RODOLPHE. As soon as possible.

Peter left him, and immediately returned, with the sum required.

PETER. Here it is. I have given as a security your word of honour; it depends on you alone to keep it.

RODOLPHE. I will pay the debt when I return to Germany.—Peter, I am delighted with your zeal.

PETER. I am always happy in proving agreeable to my employer.

Rodolphe immediately ordered everything in the most magnificent style; he hired a number of servants and squires, and left Marseilles for Sens. The knights, on their arrival, proceeded to the judge of the tournament to prove their knighthood. Rodolphe presented himself, justified his nobility, and placed his coat of arms and his shield beside the other illustrious concurrents; but he returned to his hotel with sadness in his heart: for although none surpassed him in magnificence, many were far superior to him in strength of body and heroic appearance. There was assembled the flower of the French knighthood; and among them pre-eminently distinguished the famous William of Dampière, the valorous Count of St. Paul, and Raoul de Couci, victor in every tournament, who already boasted of the laurels they hoped to gain. The other competitors were silent, for their valour was known to them, and they had more than once experienced the vigour of their arms.

Rodolphe heard these proud pretensions, and anger flamed in his countenance. "I cannot then aspire to victory," said he; "I may distinguish myself, and attract the attention of the ladies by the splendour of my armour; but I cannot hinder them from averting it with contempt, when the redoubtable Dampière, or the proud Couci, bear me off my palfrey. Had I not done better in returning to my castle, and not presenting myself at the tournament?"—Lost in these reflections, he lay down to rest, and rose again in the same melancholy mode.

He ordered his horse to be saddled, and took an airing early in the morning, on the banks of the Yonne, to re-animate his courage. Returning, he met a numerous and brilliant cavalcade. It was the Countess Beatrix, with her royal spouse, who came to enjoy the refreshing breezes of the grove that shaded the river. Many knights and ladies were in their train; and amongst the number, the beautiful Jane, youngest daughter of the rich Count of Ponthieu. On their approach, Rodolphe respectfully turned his horse aside, and saluted the ladies as they passed with grace and elegance.

The charming Beatrix saw him stop, returned his bow with an affable air, and politely asked his name and country.

RODOLPHE. I am a German knight! My name, Rodolphe of Westerbourg. I have just returned from Palestine, where I hoped to gain laurels—but where I wore the chains of slavery. At last, freed from captivity, I intend returning to my native country.

PRINCE CHARLES. You are welcome in France, brave knight. Will you not remain with us?

RODOLPHE. The tournament, to be held in honour of your royal marriage brought me hither from Marseilles. I have exposed my shield and arms, and I hope I shall be judged worthy of the honour of entering the lists.

BEATRIX. Oh! it is undoubtedly your shield which so much pleased the Countess of Ponthieu; the herald informed us it belonged to a German knight. (*Turning to Jane.*) Here, my dear Jane, is the knight whose shield attracted your attention yesterday.

JANE (*to Rodolphe, with a blush*). It is worthy of your taste.

PRINCE CHARLES. You are not yet married?

RODOLPHE. No; prince. A knight who has worn the bond of slavery, thinks not of the silken chains of love.

PRINCE CHARLES. You are at liberty at present: the ladies of your country will soon teach you to bear those charming bonds. Follow my example.

RODOLPHE. I wish to Heaven I might choose as well as your highness.

BEATRIX. Knight, your discourses announce not a slave: you are gallant.

RODOLPHE. I am sincere.

PRINCE CHARLES. Will you choose a lady for your mistress on the day of the tournament?

BEATRIX. Choose among those composing my suite.

PRINCE CHARLES. You could not find a better opportunity: return to town with us, and come to court as often as you please. All the French nobles will render every possible honour to so brave a man: our ladies will be happy to become acquainted with so graceful a knight.

RODOLPHE. Prince, your bounties overwhelm me.

The march continued: Rodolphe mingled in the train, conversed with some, and rode beside the amiable Jane.

RODOLPHE. Beautiful countess, you heard the command of the princess?

JANE. What command?

RODOLPHE. "You must," said she, with goodness, "choose a mistress amongst the persons of my suite." Dare I—may I wear your colours on the day of the tournament?

JANE. It is an honour which I cannot refuse, but which I do not merit.

RODOLPHE. Does the divinity merit no altars?

JANE. You flatter.

PRINCE CHARLES. Oh! I see the German knight has already chosen. You give a proof of your good taste; but beware, sir knight; there are many other pretenders that wear the colours of that lady: you will have to encounter many a bold champion.

RODOLPHE. I was certain of that: the countess may justly be compared to the light of day, to whom we all pay due homage.

BEATRIX (*smiling*). Then do not approach too near, for fear of being scorched.

They returned to Sens. Rodolphe took leave of them before the castle, and retired to his hotel. All his senses were wrapt in the idea of the beautiful countess; he declared he had never seen her equal in beauty: he compared to her all those whom he had loved, without even excepting Euphrosina, and decided, without hesitation, that she surpassed them all.

CHAP. III.

THAT same evening, Rodolphe proceeded, richly attired, to the palace.

He attracted the attention of the whole court, but found many subjects of discontentment. The Countess Jane seemed, indeed, to distinguish him; but she was besieged by so many knights, that he could only address a few words to her. The Count St. Paul. and Raoul de Couci, who fatigued Rodolphe with their boastings, drove him to the last extremity. They openly declared themselves the admirers of Lady Jane; and often ridiculed the poor German, who dared to declare himself their rival, by wearing the colours of the object of *their* adoration. Raoul de Couci robbed Jane of a rose, which he triumphantly placed in his bosom. Rodolphe could contain himself no longer; he left the hall, and swore to reconquer that rose at the tournament, or die in the attempt. When he arrived at his hotel, his blood began to calm; he recollected his oath; but felt not the courage to keep it. It is true, that during the life of his father he had obtained great renown in tournaments but since that time he had never been within the lists. How could he then flatter himself to vanquish the most celebrated champions of the day?

He threw himself on his bed, reflected again on his perilous situation, and seized the book, opened it to the left, and the giant appeared before him.

PETER. Master, what are your commands?

RODOLPHE. I am, in a few days hence, to fight at the tournament. What must I do to vanquish all the champions?—You are silent?

PETER. I can but obey, and not give advice.

RODOLPHE. Can you not procure me arms which no man can resist?

PETER. I can.

RODOLPHE. Then bring them hither.

Peter disappeared, and returned with the arms.

PETER. Here is what you wish: these lances would unhorse Goliath himself. Here is a sword, a club, and a dagger, that are irresistible.

RODOLPHE. I return you many thanks; and will return you, many more, when they have covered me with glory.

PETER. You are certain of gaining the prize with them.

RODOLPHE. Do you know the Lady Jane?

PETER. I do.

RODOLPHE. Have you ever beheld such a beauty?

PETER. Nothing is more arbitrary than beauty: a universal, incontestable beauty does not exist on this globe; therefore, I cannot answer your question.

RODOLPHE. I love the countess—I love her more than ever I loved before.

PETER. I wish you success:—the countess esteems courageous people,

RODOLPHE. By means of your arms, I shall appear the most valiant knight.

PETER. Are you any longer in want of my services?

RODOLPHE. I must have an armour proof against all attacks, which must, at the same time, be more brilliant and magnificent than any I have hitherto seen.

PETER. Am I to bring it hither?

RODOLPHE. I await your return.

PETER (*returning with a resplendent armour*). Here is the armour.

RODOLPHE. It is very beautiful! It is a pity that I cannot use it; for I this moment recollect, that all champions must swear, on entering the lists, before God, and upon their honour, not to use, either for attack or defence, any enchanted arms, which these, as I suppose, undoubtedly are.

PETER. You are right.

RODOLPHE. Then they are of no use to me.

PETER. Am I to return them?

RODOLPHE. But then—then I shall not obtain the prize: the ladies will behold me with contempt: I shall not be enabled to reconquer the rose, which Raoul so triumphantly placed in his bosom.

PETER. You must certainly expect that mortification. Valiant and experienced knights will appear in the lists; and to be the most experienced the most applauded——

RODOLPHE. Appears difficult, nay, impossible. And yet the Lady Jane only admires persons of distinguished valour!— You said so yourself.

PETER. I said only what all the court, what the whole of France has said before me.

RODOLPHE. But perjury, dishonours—perjury is a horrible sin! It may entail not only the punishments of this world, but also eternal damnation in the next. (*Peter takes up the arms.*) Stop awhile.—Perjury!—Perjury! The word is terrible!—But leave the arms; I will consult with my conscience; I will examine whether I can triumph over this passion.—I will call you when I am in want of you.

Peter retired. The voice of conscience rose in arms against the dreadful scene; but the voice of love contended in favour of his passion for the beautiful Jane. He thought of the means of distinguishing himself before her, of being honoured by her; but he discovered none so efficacious as those of bearing down all before him at the tournament, and gaining the palm of victory over all the other concurrents. He repeated the word "perjury" so often, that in the end it appeared much less terrible, and the thoughts of Jane made it sound even agreeable to his ear. On the day fixed, he buckled on the armour, seized the arms which Peter had brought, presented himself at the barrier, and took the oath without the slightest emotion whatever.

CHAP. IV.

THE lists were opened; but I have neither the leisure, nor the intention of describing this pompous display of valour: it was one of the most brilliant which graced that century. The whole court of France was present; attended by the flower of the Spanish, English, and Italian nobility. Five hundred knights successively entered the barriers: many tried their fortune with Rodolphe; but he invariably defeated all his antagonists, of whom twenty-seven were unhorsed.

Dampière, St. Paul, Courci, had fallen before him; and none dared afterwards oppose so formidable a champion. A general acclamation rose in favour of Rodolphe: many of the ladies detached their ornaments and jewels, which they threw into the lists, as a token of their approbation.

From among these testimonies of the favour of the ladies, he carefully gathered up every flower, every riband, every thread which the beautiful Jane, delighted with his exploits, showered on him, and fastened them to his breastplate.

Before the tournament was ended, the unanimous voice of the ladies, the people, and the judges themselves, proclaimed Rodolphe victor. It was not necessary to assemble and deliberate, as on other similar occasions: the valour and superiority of Rodolphe were too evident—the vanquished knights themselves termed him "Invincible." The Countess Beatrix ordered the prize to be awarded him; it was a rose of precious stones, to serve as an ornament for his hat: Jane and another lady carried it to him on a velvet cushion. According to the custom of those times, Beatrix and Jane embraced the brave knight. When he received the kiss of Jane, the whole assembly exclaimed, in a transport of joy, "What a beautiful couple!" But the old Count of Ponthieu frowned, and felt the most poignant grief at the idea of his daughter marrying a simple knight, while he intended to bestow her, like her two eldest sisters, on sovereign princes.

When the table was prepared, the count called Jane aside. "It was with pleasure that I saw you," said he to her, "render that justice which is due to valour; but I desire you to desist from such conduct in future, as you might thereby encourage his pretensions. Close your ears to the folly of the people. The courage of Rodolphe certainly merits to be recompensed; but the recompense would be too great, if he obtained the daughter of the Count of Ponthieu. She is issued from blood-royal, has two kings for brothers-in-law, and cannot become the wife of a simple German knight."

During this paternal exhortation, Jane fixed her eyes on the floor, and promised to conform herself to her father's desires; but her heart was no longer at liberty: the valiant knight had triumphed over it and she would have preferred his hand to the most brilliant crown. But, aware of the sentiments of her father, she rigorously obeyed his commands.

Rodolphe sat at the table, beside the royal bride. Several merry old barons wished to place Jane on his left. Prince Charles even sought her with that intention; but she prudently concealed herself in the crowd, and seated herself at the lower end of the table. Rodolphe certainly thought himself honoured by the place which had been assigned him; but he would willingly have exchanged it with Raoul of Couci, who accidently sat beside Jane—the beauty for whom he had voluntarily perjured himself, and whose admiration and love he coveted above all things. Rodolphe sought her with anxious looks, and soon perceived her engaged in a close conversation with his odious rival. Jealousy mastered his mind and devoured his senses. He relished neither the meats, nor the exquisite wines. He thought himself forgotten—despised by Jane. The king and all the nobility of France drank his health, and of all the ladies. Jane was the only one that did not throw him her nosegay. During that customary ceremony, she was occupied with her dress, and negligently dropped her flowers on the table. Rodolphe was deeply hurt by this indifference: his heart was oppressed; the tears trickled down his cheek. When he left the table, he refused to dance, or to take any liquors: he excused himself on account of great weakness; and returned to his hotel, accompanied by the acclamations of the whole populace.

Before he retired, he sought Jane, to ask her to permit him to wear, as an eternal remembrance, the gifts she had showered on him during the tournament; but Jane had guessed his intention, and studiously endeavoured to avoid him.

Rodolphe retired to his chamber, a prey to the most desponding melancholy, and the most poignant jealousy. "It is for you that I have perjured," exclaimed he, "that I have dishonoured myself, and it is thus you repay me! Woman I must obtain your love; I must possess you, or die. I have never experienced such torments! My heart has never been consumed by such burning desires!"

After numberless resolutions, which were abandoned as soon as formed, he seized his book, and opened it to the left. Peter entered.

RODOLPHE. O Peter! I am most miserable.

PETER. Master, I pity you.

RODOLPHE. Your arms were of the most essential service to me; I vanquished all my rivals; but Jane (it is not your fault)—but the beautiful Jane, whom my heart adores, returns my affection with the most cruel contempt. What can I do to obtain her love?

PETER. My duty is to obey you;—it is the only one which I can perform. I am grieved to stun you so often with a repetition of the same words; but it appears absolutely necessary, for you do not yet seem to understand them properly.

RODOLPHE. Barbarian! Get you gone, if you cannot be of any service to me; I will not see your face any longer. But, no! stop; listen to my immutable resolution. If Jane refuses me, if she disdains the offer which I shall make her of my heart and my hand, I will ravish by force what she so unjustly refuses; I will drag her from the arms of her father, and loudly claim the reward of my valour. Can you assist me in this undertaking?

PETER. I can.

RODOLPHE. And how?

PETER. Order and I will obey.

RODOLPHE. Can you procure me at Marseilles a vessel completely rigged, ready to sail at a moment's warning? Can you conduct me safely to Italy with my beloved Jane?

PETER. I can, if you give me permission to steal the vessel, how, and where I may think proper.

RODOLPHE. I care not, so long as I have the vessel in my possession.

PETER. But it is of importance to you; for I must have an illumined warrant from you to commit such a theft.

RODOLPHE. Then do whatever you please; only let the ship be ready when I am in want of it.

PETER. You may rely on my punctuality.

RODOLPHE. Can you also procure some horses that can transport me with my prey, unrestrained, and (mark this) unobserved, by anyone.

PETER. I can, if you permit me to kill the proprietor of the horses.

RODOLPHE. Kill! Have you changed your nature as well as your form? I cannot give my consent to a murder.

PETER. In that case I cannot procure the horses, which will be absolutely necessary to accomplish your design.

RODOLPHE. Away! Leave me! I will no longer converse with you.

PETER. I obey.

RODOLPHE. Will you return if I call you again?

PETER. I am ever ready to receive and execute your orders.

RODOLPHE. A murder is a hundred times worse than a false oath. No—no murder shall be laid to my charge. Leave me, or make more reasonable conditions.

PETER. As I cannot fulfil your last wish, I will execute the first.

Peter disappeared.

Rodolphe passed a lonely and sleepless night, while the inmates of the castle danced and enjoyed the splendid scene. Before he quitted the banquet, he had sought Jane without being able to find her; and she now sought him with equal anxiety. The old Count of Ponthieu was drinking with other companions at the round table; Jane was dancing in the hall; she endeavoured in vain to discover the brave knight to dance with him the dance of honour, and to compensate for the restraint she had been placed under by her father. Oh! If Rodolphe had only suspected it, if he could have known it, he would have flown from his solitary couch, and would not have ceded, for all the treasures of Babylon, the favour of once feeling the gentle pressure of his mistress's hands.

The next day, the king himself inquired after the health of Rodolphe; and being informed that it was completely restored, he invited him to the banquet. As soon as he presented himself, the beautiful Jane smiled on him with unrestrained benignity. Her father had become rather intoxicated; and, overcome by excess, remained in his chamber; but he had permitted his daughter to return to the banquet, as he was quite delighted with her conduct during the supper. The two lovers soon found an opportunity of conversing together unobserved. Rodolphe, when declaring his love to Jane, lavished upon her the most passionate encomiums. She answered him in very near the same tone: that the attachment of such a valorous knight must ever prove agreeable to her; but that the pride of her father was so excessive, that he would never accord to a simple gentleman a hand, which reigning princes had demanded in vain. Rodolphe took the flattering side of this speech, like the bee that culls honey from the bitterest flowers. Of what importance was the consentment of a father to him, if he was certain of the love of the daughter? He pressed her to declare her sentiments on the subject; and learnt with evident satisfaction that Jane was far from being indifferent to the proofs of valour which he had displayed in the tournament. He desired nothing more to convince him of the reality of her love for him.

CHAP. V.

THE celebration of the marriage lasted during two days. Rodolphe saw Jane several times, and became every time more and more enchanted with her charms. But the count having recovered his health, returned to the banquet, and interrupted, by his presence, their tender intercourse. The third day, Jane approached a lady sitting beside Rodolphe, and informed her, that her heart was oppressed with all this tumultuous joy, and that the next day she would take an airing on horseback. "For," said she, sighing, "I must soon leave this town with my father, and I do not think I shall ever meet with such delightful company." The languishing tone with which she pronounced this sentence, the stress which she laid on the last words, everything strengthened Rodolphe in his resolution. He retired as soon as etiquette would permit him to his hotel, and opened his book.

RODOLPHE. Peter, I am in want of your assistance; let the horses and the ship be ready: tomorrow morning I shall fly from this place with Jane. If she follows me willingly, nothing will be wanting to complete my happiness; if she refuses, I shall drag her from the very arms of her father.

PETER. The ship is already stolen; it will be quite ready; the horses will soon be saddled, if you authorize me to kill the proprietor.

RODOLPHE (*coldly*). You must accompany us during the journey under a visible form, to be at hand if necessary.

PETER. I will obey your command.

RODOLPHE. Go, then, and execute my orders.

PETER. I do not perfectly understand you; explain yourself more clearly; am I to have the horses ready, and kill the proprietor?

RODOLPHE. I demand the execution of my orders—the conditions do not concern me. Do whatever you think proper, so as to ensure success to my undertaking. Why is my consent so materially necessary?

PETER. It is indispensable to me; I am but the instrument of your orders: I am your hand, which you can use for good or evil. As you alone are responsible for all the actions I commit, so you alone can authorize me.

RODOLPHE. A murder is horrible; and ten times worse when the victim is innocent. Make better conditions.

PETER. You order me to sow tares, and you would wish to reap corn. Remember, once for all, that in order to accomplish a criminal design, criminal means alone can be employed. I must use black paint to blacken a white wall, as neither red nor blue can serve my purpose.

RODOLPHE. Then blacken that which cannot remain white; let nothing oppose my passage: prepare the horses, and let them conduct me to Marseilles, as I informed you.

PETER. Have you any further orders for me?

RODOLPHE. None whatever.

PETER. Everything shall be ready in a few moments.

RODOLPHE. Do you promise me success?

PETER. I promise that you shall arrive at Marseilles unobserved; and that the ship will conduct you to the shores you wish to behold.

Peter had no sooner left the apartment, than Rodolphe began to doubt of the success of his enterprise, although so well planned. "Carry off the beautiful Jane!" said he, to himself. "Yes, I can do it; but how will she view this violence? Will she abandon her charms, accord the tenderest return to him that tears her from the midst of her family, and of a splendid court, to make her his mistress? That is a question which I cannot answer."—"My valour," continued he, "has made a great impression on her simple heart; her eyes betray its tender emotions: she esteems, she loves me; but her love, although so ardent, is as pure as her heart. She will not willingly resign herself to me; and an enjoyment exacted by force cannot satisfy a passionate lover, any more than the odour of exquisite dishes appeases the famished person who cannot reach and enjoy them."

After these reflections, he determined not to carry off Jane himself, but to commission Peter to do the act. His intention was, when she was in a distant country, when she believed herself hopeless and defenceless in the midst of a horde of barbarians, to prove his fidelity by tearing her from their hands. "Then," exclaimed he, triumphantly, "gratitude will accord what force could not have obtained!—then, she will deliver herself with transport into the arms of her liberator; and she will accord everything to him who endangered his life for her." He immediately opened the book as usual, and Peter entered.

PETER (*with his hands and clothes stained with blood*). What do you wish? I have just committed the murder which you commanded. What I foresaw took place. The proprietor of the horses would not deliver them up, and I extended him lifeless with a blow of my club; his blood sprinkled me all over. "I will demand vengeance from above," said he, and his mouth closed forever.

RODOLPHE. And you relate these horrors to me?—You throw all this blame on my heart?—Peter! Peter! your conduct is more strange from day to day! I begin to believe that your wife was right.

PETER. You may believe what you please; it concerns me little: destiny has made me your slave; I must implicitly obey you. Give me better commissions, I will execute better work. You must see whether you will use the horses or not.

RODOLPHE. Now, the murder is committed.—Now, the blood of the innocent demands vengeance.—Go and wash yourself; I cannot bear the sight of blood.

When Peter left the room, the conscience of Rodolphe strongly upbraided him, and loaded him with cruel reproaches; but as the voice of love rose stronger in his favour, conscience was soon silenced.

RODOLPHE (*to Peter on entering*). What a long while you are!

PETER. Human blood is not easily washed off!!!

RODOLPHE. Silence! I have things of the greatest importance to communicate to you. You must carry off Jane, conduct her to Marseilles, and from thence to Italy. I will follow you, and appear to force you to return her. You must guess, without my explaining them to you, the reasons which induce me to employ this stratagem.

PETER. Yes, I can guess; it is most admirably planned.

RODOLPHE. In order to execute it I must have another ship. Must you steal that also?

PETER. I must, if you order.

RODOLPHE. Then steal—kill whom you like, provided that I attain my ends. Is the first vessel equipped?

PETER. It is! it is ready to sail whenever you please.

RODOPLHE. Prepare the second without delay: tell the sailors I am their master, and that they are to obey my orders.

PETER. I will do so.

RODOLPHE. I expect you tomorrow morning at the dawn of the day.

As soon as the sun began to tinge the summit of the mountains, Peter was punctually by Rodolphe's bedside.

PETER. Horses and ships are ready. What more am I to
do?

RODOLPHE. Jane is going to take an airing on the river-
side; you must there lay in wait. Contrive that many witnesses
should be present; but fascinate their eyes to such a degree, as
to prevent them from discovering the road you have taken.

PETER. I will do as you desire.

RODOLPHE. When you are on the sea, how shall I find
your ship?

PETER. The same wind which fills my sails will also fill
yours; and, moreover, I am always at your command by means
of the book.

RODOLPHE. Then make haste, and fulfil your mission.
But do not frighten the poor girl too much; do not deprive her
of every ray of hope; do not kill her with fear.

PETER. Rely on my delicacy.

Peter left the hotel, and Rodolphe anxiously expected the
event. Towards mid-day a report was spread, that the Lady
Jane had been carried off by a monstrous Giant. The royal
family, and the whole court were in a state of dreadful alarm.
All the knights that were present, mounted their horses and
followed the road which the Giant seemed to have taken. They
swore never to return without having discovered the Giant,
and delivered Jane. In order to avert every suspicion, Rodolphe
presented himself at the palace, endeavoured to console the
father, and promised to become the liberator of his daughter.
"I swear," said the old Count of Ponthieu, in the excess of his
grief, "to give her to him who shall return her to me uninjured,
if only a knight."

Cheered by this assurance, Rodolphe returned to his hotel,
found Sir Bruno in the outer court, and entrusted to his care

his arms and costly wardrobe. This knight was very poor, and had for some time followed Rodolphe, and subsisted on his liberalities. Rodolphe had the greatest confidence in him.

"You shall soon hear from me," said he to him; mounted his horses, and galloped towards Marseilles.

He was the only knight that took that road; the general rumour was, that the Giant had fled towards the confines of Spain, with his precious treasure, and that he was some Moor of distinction.

CHAP. VI.

WHEN arrived at the port of Marseilles, Rodolphe, anxious to possess Jane, sought his ship in vain. He saw several, but none that were freighted for him to Italy; the greatest part had their merchandize on board, and the others were destined for other countries. Rodolphe had left Sens with such precipitation, that he had forgot the little knapsack given him by Peter, and consequently the book. He perceived this only at that moment, and cursed his own giddiness. He was on the point of returning, when a ship entered the port in full sail. "That is perhaps my ship," said he, jumping into a boat, and ordering the man to row towards it. "What passengers have you?" said he, to the captain, when on board; "how long do you stay here, and whither are you going when you leave Marseilles."

CAPTAIN. I come from Egypt; I have with me but one passenger, a pilgrim, who intends disembarking here. I am going to purchase some provisions, and immediately set sail for my native country, Italy.

RODOLPHE. Buy them speedily, and transport me to Italy; I will pay for the freight of the whole vessel.

CAPTAIN. It is lucky for us both that we have met. Your time is precious; I am in want of money; the wind is favourable; my vessel is a good sailor; we shall be able to depart in two hours hence.

Rodolphe firmly believed this to be the ship promised him by Peter, and recommended the Captain to use the utmost diligence. "Who is that pilgrim?" added he; "is she beautiful?"

CAPTAIN. Like an angel! as beautiful as the Virgin Mary, and as pious! She has never ceased, during the whole passage, to fast, to pray, and to kneel before the crucifix. She is now rendering thanks to the eternal Giver of all, for having safely conducted her to this port. Descend into the cabin if you wish to see her. During that time, I will arrange my affairs.

Rodolphe descended; and, to his utter confusion, beheld Euphrosina.

RODOLPHE (*trembling, and in the greatest astonishment*). Euphrosina!——

EUPHROSINA (*looks at him, falls backwards on the chair, then rises again, and embraces him*). Almighty God, thou hast favourably heard my prayers! O my mother, your prediction is accomplished! I have found him, I have found the beloved of my heart, the father of the child I bear! I will persuade him by my love, by my prayers! He cannot resist the tears of an unfortunate woman; he will listen to the voice of nature; he will become the husband of the mother, and the father of the child.

RODOLPHE (*overcome by her caresses, and pressing her closely to his bosom*). Euphrosina! My Euphrosina! I have then found you!

A silent transport, a celestial ecstasy seized the lovers; and they experienced those emotions which can only be felt, but never described. Rodolphe looked down on the countenance of Euphrosina, where languor and sufferings were visibly depicted; she raised her eyes to those of Rodolphe, in which shone the fire of love. They remained for some moments in this attitude; but Rodolphe, the inconstant Rodolphe, satiated with silent voluptuousness, soon recollected the object of his journey—the beautiful Jane. He compared that rose in full bloom with the one before him, withering and nearly perishing. The comparison could not be borne, but yet a latent spark of pity rose in his almost callous bosom: he wished to put an end to this painful sensation, by leaving the faded charms of her whom he had seduced; he unclasped his arms, and exclaimed in an hypocritical tone: "Euphrosina, I do not merit such goodness, such love! I am as unworthy of it as of your pardon. Learn to know me, to hate me! I betrayed you; I delivered you into the hands of the sultan. Fly an ungrateful perfidious wretch, who, far from deserving your love, is not worthy of one of your looks."

EUPHROSINA (*following him*). Stay!—Oh, stay!—I forgive all!—I would wish to see your crimes re-doubled, to enhance the value of my forgiveness. Pardon is an appendage of true love. I will not leave you. Think, Rodolphe, that a sinner demands a husband at your hands; (*lowering her eyes, and blushing.*) The child which I bear cannot come into this world without finding a father.

RODOLPHE (*embarrassed*). I have sinned too much, you cannot forgive me.

He endeavoured to conceal his embarrassment by averting his looks. Euphrosina preserved a deep silence; *she* expected, alas! to see her generosity repaid by an act of tenderness. Rodolphe, in order to break this cruel constraint, asked her the following question: "How did you escape the hands of the tyrant, and discover my retreat?"

EUPHROSINA. The infinity of the Deity would be necessary faithfully to depict my situation at our separation, as my grief was unbounded. But I have forgiven you all, I have forgotten all and will not mention it. When I found myself again in the power of the sultan, a mortal disease attacked my weak frame. I should never have returned to the land of the living, had not my mother come to my aid. I was already in the agony of death, already a cold sweat spread over my forehead, when she presented herself before my bed. "Sinful and dishonoured daughter," said she; "you do not merit my compassion, and much less my assistance; but for the sake of the child, which you unknowingly bear, I will have pity on you; I will save you, to save the innocent creature. Take this and drink." At these words, she gave me a draft which I swallowed, and soon afterwards fell asleep. My sleep must have resembled death so exactly, that the sultan and his physicians imagined that I was really dead; for, on awaking, I found myself in a sepulchral vault, covered with flowers, and embalmed with precious essences. My mother stood before me. "Follow me," said she. I tremblingly obeyed. She conducted me to this ship, and before this altar. "Repent of your faults," continued she, addressing herself to me; "fervently implore pardon for them. He who took upon himself the sins of mankind, will also take yours upon him. This ship will conduct you to the coast of France; there you will find your seducer. If his soul is not engaged by some new object, if you succeed in re gaining his affection, he will become the father of your child, and your husband; you will save his soul and your honour; you will offer a sacrifice for the criminal, and you will be blessed on this earth. But if he resists your love, if he will not listen to your sighs, if he will not present you his hand before the altar, oh! you will then be miserable indeed! Repent, mortify yourself until the Ruler of all the creation is pleased to put an end to your sufferings, and calls you to his bosom. I shall then see you again!" She disappeared, and my heart was filled with happy presentiments. "He will have pity on me, and save his soul and my honour!" This was the only thought which occupied my mind during the whole of the passage, and to which my prayers were incessantly directed day and night. Rodolphe! Rodolphe! turn your eyes to me—cast a look on your victim. (*She falls on her knees.*) Consider me as suppliant at your feet. I have given you all; I lavished on you my only treasure. I demand but one favour; to return me to my honour, and to give a father to this child. Will you abandon me? Will you leave me without listening to my complaint? Speak, Rodolphe, end my dreadful incertitude.

RODOLPHE. No! No!

EUPHROSINA (*rising with precipitation and clinging to his neck*). No? No? O repeat, repeat again that divine word! How it comforts my soul! *No!* did you say? If you knew what an infinite power I find in that single word, you would repeat it a thousand times. Beloved of my heart, I cannot find words to express my generosity. New creator of life, heighten my bliss, complete your work; say, will you become my husband, and the father of your child?

RODOLPHE. I will! I will!

EUPHROSINA (*transported with joy*). You will? You will? (*Not being able to continue, she placed one hand on her face and the other on her heart, and at last exclaimed with ecstasy*): You will?

RODOLPHE. Yes; I will, but——

EUPHROSINA (*closing his mouth*). Oh! no *buts!* A *but* is a horrible shoal at sea! See, Rodolphe! your Euphrosina is lost in the transports of her joy; the storm will clash her against the rock, and she will be lost forever.

RODOLPHE. No, my sweet friend; believe my word. But listen first, and then judge. Since I left you I have resided at the court of France. I joined the tournament. A Giant, whose cavern I suppose to be in some desert, or in some rocky island, appeared at that feast, and carried off the youngest daughter of the Count Ponthieu. All the knights assured the desolate father that they would conquer the monster, and return his daughter, or die in the attempt. I am one of those who took the oath, and am seeking the unfortunate maiden. An idle report conducted me to Marseilles; and I just heard that he fled to the confines of Spain. Yesterday, he was not far from this place, and I must not delay one moment if I wish to attain the ravisher, and deprive him of his prey.

EUPHROSINA. The oath of a knight is sacred. But are the duties of a husband and a father less so? Are they not even more important? I fear I am sacrificed; that other victim is perhaps pure and innocent! Her situation is terrible, if she is in danger of losing all in one moment! Haste! Rodolphe! hasten to save her innocence: she who lost hers can alone appreciate its value. Haste; and when you return her to her father, and when he, in the excess of his joy, offers you the hand of his daughter as a reward, remember that you have already a spouse; that you are already a father. I will await you herein a convent; I will pray to God; I will pray to him incessantly to accompany you, to guard you in every danger, and to return you to my arms.

RODOLPHE. I shall return! I shall return! Adieu! my dearest friend! rely on my promise; I will certainly return, and that soon. (*He then embraced her hastily and was retiring*).

EUPHROSINA (*stopping him*). You are leaving me without knowing whither I retire, without conducting me thither? Oh! Rodolphe! if you—if really—Come hither! Behold this image of Christ! If you should not return, know, that if he has promised to take upon himself the sins of mankind, he is also to appear one day to judge the living and the dead. I shall add but a few words more: lead me to a convent; tell the nuns that I am your wife, in order, that if you should not fulfil your promise, I may not die with shame, added to pain, when I give birth to your child. (*Rodolphe attempts to speak.*)—Say not a word, but lead me to the convent.

The knight, on the way, renewed a thousand times his promise to return, and marry her at the expiration of a month at most. But Euphrosina answered him not; a profound grief had overcome her soul. She suffered herself to be placed with resignation into the hands of the nuns, who willingly received her, as Rodolphe threw several hands-full of gold into the poor's box. When he retired, Euphrosina gave vent to an exclamation of grief; she embraced him in sobbing, and said, "In one month or never." Her lover immediately left the house of God.

CHAP. VII.

ODOLPHE had no sooner repassed the threshold of the
convent, than he repressed the importunate emotions of
his heart. He forgot the unfortunate Euphrosina, and such
was the perverseness of his nature, that he thought only of
the beautiful Jane; for the principles of honour and religion
had long been banished. His heart, a prey to every voluptuous
passion, resembled a deserted field, where nothing but thorns
and thistles vegetate.

He consulted with himself what he was now to do. He was
convinced that the mother of Euphrosina had deprived him of
the vessel destined for him by his friend, Peter, and that, perhaps, this very friend was again fallen into her snares, and that
she retained him prisoner with the Lady Jane. But, in order
to ascertain this more fully, the only thing he could do was to
return to Sens to fetch his knapsack, to open his book, and if
Peter appeared, to demand explanations and advice of him. He
hired fresh horses, hurried on day and night, and arrived late
on the third evening at his inn. He had left his wallet hanging
over his bed before his departure, but he could no longer find
it. All his effects were packed up; he forced open the trunks,
turned them over, and could nowhere discover his precious
treasure. He called the servants whom he had left at Sens, and
one of them instantly made his appearance.

RODOLPHE. Who has taken the little knapsack which
hung here above my bed when I left Sens?

SERVANT. Indeed, my lord, I know not.

RODOLPHE. Who, among you, packed up all my things?

SERVANT. The fortunate Sir Bruno.

RODOLPHE. Where is he? And why do you call him fortunate?

SERVANT. Is he not so indeed, he who (his nobility aside) was just as miserable as one of us, and will receive tomorrow, with the title of count, the hand of the beautiful Jane, youngest daughter of the Count of Ponthieu.

RODOLPHE. How is it possible? No; it cannot be.

SERVANT. May I die on the spot, my Lord, if I deceive you. Go to court, and inform yourself of the truth. Immediately after having packed up your things, he ordered a horse to be saddled for him, departed, and returned the next day with the countess. He had found the Giant in a forest, deprived him of his prey, and brought her back to the court. If his joy was great, his reward was still greater; the count has given him his daughter.

RODOLPHE. Impossible! Impossible—And yet—yet—O horrible light!—How does the afflicted Jane behave? What says she?

SERVANT. Some of your squires, who assisted yesterday at the betrothing, said, that she wept and appeared very melancholy. I can easily believe it, for Sir Bruno is not a handsome man; he is rough in his manners, and has not received the education of a knight, much less that of a courtier. That tender flower will fade and die away in the hands of such an adventurer. Everybody pities her for becoming the victim of a hasty oath of her father, while her sisters wear crowns.

Rodolphe, overcome with fear and surprise, took off his armour, put on a mantle, and flew to court where, to complete his astonishment, the whole was confirmed to him. Although he ardently desired to see Bruno, Jane, or at least her father, it was not possible that day. Not even one member of the royal family was visible; they were assembled in the interior of the palace, where the contract of marriage of the new count was preparing. Rodolphe returned to his hotel, a prey to the most infuriated passion. "The fellow has taken possession of my knapsack," exclaimed he; "I will demand it of him! I will challenge him!—But will he not vanquish me? Will he not kill me with the assistance of his new slave?"

Rodolphe reflected and consulted with himself, but he perceived no hope, no resource. The idea that the beautiful, the charming Jane, was to fall to the lot of another, was horrible to him; but a more horrible idea was that of being abandoned by Peter; obliged to renounce the voluptuous enjoyments which he had anticipated, and be reduced to consume the remainder of his life in a lonely obscurity, with the languishing and faded Euphrosina. He had, until then, enjoyed everything which could charm his senses; and now he was forced to stifle all his desires, and be reduced to eternal privations. In his despair he flung himself on his bed, and sought repose; consolation, and hope—but he sought them in vain. The hour of midnight found him still sleepless, and Peter presented himself when he least expected it.

PETER. A faithful servant does not forget an old master and though he cannot any longer be of service to him he still continues to enquire after him from time to time.

RODOLPHE. O! Peter, my faithful, my only friend! take pity on my sufferings; save me, save Jane!

PETER. Your wishes are very reasonable, and I should be exceedingly happy in being able to satisfy them; but you are yourself the only author of your misfortune: either you placed too much confidence in a traitor, or you did not sufficiently value my present——

RODOLPHE. Alas! I was in too great a haste to follow you, and forgot the wallet, which Bruno (as I suppose) found.

PETER. Certainly he found it, and thereby rendered me his slave. Just as I was crossing a forest with my prey, the book called me; I hid Jane in a cavern, the opening of which I enchanted. I thought you had opened the book, and were in want of my services; but it was Sir Bruno, who had, for the sake of curiosity, been prying into your knapsack; and who, to your future detriment, had opened the book to the left, without knowing what he was about. He was thunderstruck when he saw me, and trembled in every joint when I asked what he wished; but he soon recovered from his fright:—"Are you not the Giant that carried off the Countess of Ponthieu?" said he to me. "I am." "And where is she?" "I have concealed her in a cavern." He continued his questions, and as he held the book open in his hand, I was forced to tell him everything, even to reveal the virtue of the book. He immediately determined to possess the treasure which he so little expected; he performed what you intended to do; he delivered Jane, and will marry her tomorrow. I saw you crossing the gallery of the palace this evening, and determined to convince you of my innocence, and to take leave of you.

RODOLPHE. What?—You?—abandon me?—you—refuse to save me?

PETER. I am the slave of the book; he who possesses it has an unbounded power over me; my services are exclusively consecrated to its possessor.

RODOLPHE. In that case, evil to Rodolphe! evil to the beautiful Jane! Go; leave me, witness not my despair, nor relate it to your new master—go, curse him in my name.

PETER. Adieu! return to your castle, and endeavour to live happy.

RODOLPHE. Peter! Peter! can you then not assist me? Stay and answer me this one question: what does Jane? does she love the traitor?

PETER. She hates him more than death; she loves you passionately; she will be as miserable in his arms, as she would have been happy in yours.

RODOLPHE (*rising from his bed*). Yes! I will tear her from him, although I should suffer in hell to all eternity!

PETER (*returning*). If you—but no; you would not, you could not!

RODOLPHE. Speak; are there any means? I will fulfil any condition, however terrible.

PETER. If you despise your salvation; if you wish to enjoy yourself in this world; if you wish to await unthinkingly the end of this life, and the beginning of the next, I know an expedient.

RODOLPHE. Oh! speak, explain it quickly.

PETER. You know me to be a spirit; and you could not but imagine that I was an envoy of Beelzebub. It is no longer time to dissemble; I own it to you. You ought long since to have been convinced that I only served your passions: if, therefore, you have made up your mind to procure every terrestrial enjoyment, to relish exclusively all earthly delights, and all the voluptuousness which it is possible for man to obtain, listen to my advice. Here is a club; strike seven times in the air, and seven times on the earth, pronounce seven times the name of Beelzebub, and Beelzebub will appear to you. He will return you your knapsack, as it is in his power; he will again submit me to your orders; and you will obtain Jane, and everything else that you may possibly desire, if you sign, and give to the demon a contract by which you forfeit your soul unto him. (*Rodolphe recoils with horror.*) But if this appears too dangerous to you, if it frightens you, return us quick as possible to Marseilles, offer your hand to the melancholy Euphrosina, swear eternal fidelity to her, and keep your oath; pray, fast, chastise your body; and, perhaps, you will one day have sufficiently atoned for your faults (or rather crimes) in this world, to receive in that to come the due reward of your sincere repentance. Adieu!

Peter left the club on the floor, and disappeared

CHAP. VIII.

THE heart of Rodolphe had now been long undermined by vice in its most insinuating form, and scarcely even remembered that virtue and religion which had been instilled into his mind, when yet under the guidance of his pious mother, these sentiments now rose in arms against the dreadful idea of renouncing to that salvation his Redeemer had so dearly bought by his cross and passion; he trembled, he recoiled with horror, and passed a sleepless night, as his conscience and his passions predominated by turns.

At break of day, he proceeded to the palace; firmly resolved to revenge himself on the traitor Bruno: he found him walking in the gallery, meditating on his approaching bliss. Rodolphe attempted to draw his sword, and bury it in the body of the perfidious wretch; but his strength abandoned him: it was impossible for him even to draw the sword from the scabbard. He endeavoured, however, to overwhelm him with imprecations: his tongue became embarrassed, he stammered, and finished by complimenting the author of his sufferings on his marriage. Bruno thanked him, promised never to forget his liberalities, and passed into the apartment of his bride.

Rodolphe, confounded, returned to his inn; ordered his horse to be saddled, and departed for Marseilles; but he had not proceeded one league, before an invincible passion forced him to retrace his steps. In crossing the town, he met the procession of the newly-married couple returning to the castle. Indissoluble bonds had united them forever: Jane was dressed in white; her pale countenance resembled that of an angel; a cloud seemed to obscure her formerly bright eyes. Rodolphe dashed his spurs into his horses' sides, galloped to his hotel, entered his chamber, seized the redoubtable club, trembled, and threw it far away.

He now only wished to see Jane, and depict to her the excess of his passion. He dressed himself pompously, and directed his steps, towards the evening, to the palace. The great esteem which his valour had acquired was evident, in the distinguished reception he met with. His turn came to dance the dance of honour with the young spouse. Jane trembled when he seized her hand, looked up to him in a languishing manner, and immediately cast her eyes on the ground, to hide a tear which had unconsciously escaped her. Rodolphe perceived this and it caused a burning fire to run through all his veins. "I wish it had pleased God," said he to her during the dance, "that I had been the happy mortal."

"I wish to God!" replied the unfortunate and fell nearly senseless into his arms.

"Deplorable victim," he whispered to her, "I will save you, or die in the attempt." A look of gratitude, announcing the impossibility of her deliverance, was her only answer.

When the ball was finished, Rodolphe returned home burning with rage in his heart. He sought the club, which he had thrown away with such horror; struck the air seven times, seven times the earth, and pronounced seven times the name of Beelzebub. Instantly, a person dressed in gold, ornamented with diamonds and pearls, entered the chamber; he had a roll of parchment under his arm, and a pencil in his hand. Sweet perfumes were diffused throughout the whole apartment.

BEELZEBUB. What do you wish?

RODOLPHE. What you ought to know. Save Jane—fulfil all my wishes, and I will——

BEELZEBUB. Well, continue! And you will for that forfeit, by writing, your soul unto me?—Is it not so?

RODOLPHE (*hiding his face*). Yes;—it is!

BEELZEBUB (*seated at a table*). Then, I will draw up the covenant. It will be clear and concise. (*Writes.*)—In how many years?

RODOLPHE. In——in forty years.

BEELZEBUB (*rolling up his parchment, and bursting into a laugh*). In forty years? The least of my demons would not accord you such a long period, much less their chief. My dear fellow, merchandise is not so rare; I can have it at a very reasonable price. A thousand years ago, I would have accorded you what you ask, but not now. Luxury and pleasures are good purveyors; they furnish me abundantly. War, the right of the strongest, enriches me also; and I shall in future be much better off than now. In five centuries, I shall have souls for nothing. Men will then no longer believe in God, and will deliver themselves into the claws of my demons. (*Retiring*)—Now consider.

RODOLPHE. Stay—explain—how many years will you accord me?

BEELZEBUB. Why should I stay to haggle. Although I was once a Jew, I do not like to make too bountiful purchases. I will give you ten years—not a day more or less; and I would not even give you that, if I had not laid a wager on your account.

RODOLPHE. Grant me at least three—nay, two years more.

BEELZEBUB. Well, in order to prove to you that Beelzebub although a devil, is not interested, I will consent. (*He returns to the table and writes.*) In twelve years, at this very hour.—Done.—Sign: give me your left hand. (*He scratches the thumb.*) Sign with your blood; for blood is ineffaceable, either by fire or water. (*Rodolphe signs in trembling. Beelzebub looks at the signature, and continues.*) It is not legible; but the intention is better than the writing. You may ask what you please, and it shall be granted. I shall see you again in twelve years. I will come and fetch you myself. Go on as you have began; practice every vice, that you may one day be of some service to me.

He disappeared; leaving after him a smoke and the insupportable odour of sulphur, which forced Rodolphe to leave the apartment.

"'Tis done," said he, when recovering his senses; "irrevocably done. I will—I will enjoy myself as long as it is in my power."

He endeavoured by such reflections to appease his conscience, and throw off the burden which oppressed his heart. When he returned to his room, he saw the little knapsack hanging near his bed; he opened the book to the left, and Peter came running in.

RODOLPHE. Save Jane.

PETER (*bustling*). How soon?—In how many minutes?—In how many seconds?—And whither shall I conduct her?

RODOLPHE. As soon as possible, and bring her hither.

Peter disappeared, and returned some minutes after with the beautiful Jane, in a state of insensibility; he laid her on Rodolphe's bed. "Give her some assistance," said he, "and I will hasten to amuse those who are pursuing me, and prevent them from disturbing you."

The endeavours of the knight to recover Jane from her swoon were long unsuccessful: at last she opened her eyes.

JANE. Where am I?

RODOLPHE. Under the protection of him who promised to save you, and has kept his word.

JANE. What! You? Yes, you are the knight of Westerbourg!—I thank you, generous knight!—You have saved my
soul. I had decided to destroy myself, rather than share the
couch of that hideous monster. An inflexible father closed
his ears to my complaints; I was sacrificed: the only refuge
I could find was in death. Complete your work—conduct
me to your country—place me in a convent where I may
bemoan my hard destiny, and sanctify my life.

Rodolphe promised everything; but he secretly rejoiced
at the victory which he hoped to gain over the virtue of his
victim.

CHAP. IX.

WHEN Jane recovered sufficiently to reflect on her situation, she trembled at the idea of being discovered in the inn, and conducted to the arms of the odious Bruno. But Rodolphe assured her, upon his life and honour, that she had nothing to fear. She blushed, and declared that it was not decorous to be with a stranger at that hour of night. In order to calm her fears and scruples, the hypocritical Rodolphe promised with a modest air to leave the room, and guard the door himself. "Repose yourself," said he; "I will take proper means to ensure success to our flight." He retired, and called Peter.

RODOLPHE. Where have you been?

PETER. I have been taking every possible means to fascinate my pursuers. All the knights are seeking me in the fields with torches. I was continually before them, and leaped over the hedges and ditches. Two of the most venturesome followed me, and have broken their necks. I hope I have procured Beelzebub some new subjects, for their sins were of the blackest nature. I endeavoured also to excite Count Bruno to follow me; but he would not attempt the leap, although much grieved at the loss of his spouse. At last, I entered a wood, where they are wasting their time in seeking me.

RODOLPHE. Are you henceforth my slave only? Will you not be my friend?

PETER. I will be your friend, your slave, your adviser, your faithful assistant. I will assume all these shapes, and you can equally profit by my power in any one of them. You acted very wisely; it is an admirable thing to have twelve years of illimited enjoyment. Thus enjoy yourself, friend, and do not think of the future. How has Jane received you?

RODOLPHE. She is gratitude itself towards her liberator; but——

PETER. My friend—leave all *buts*, they only disturb our pleasures. You have triumphed over the great *but*,—what shall we become in the next world? Resist also the little *buts*.

RODOLPHE. Yes, I must repeat it—*but* it will be difficult for me to triumph over Jane. She is more chaste than a nun, more modest than a German!

PETER. Oh! pray be silent, I beg you! Has she no desires—has she no senses? The senses, my friend, are real famished monsters; they devour everything that is presented to them. Take the most simple and sober people: they will not immediately seize those dishes with which they are not acquainted, or which are forbidden to them; but make them fast, and let them see how other people relish them; excite their appetite, they will soon endeavour to taste, and will finish by relishing them, in proportion with the time you have kept them away.

Peter entertained his master with other reflections of the same nature. It was decided, that he should assume the figure of one of the servants of Rodolphe, and always accompany him.

In order to return safe to Germany, for Rodolphe had determined to bend his course thither, Peter proposed that Jane should travel with them in man's clothes. "Thus disguised," added he, "she will habituate herself to act and think more freely; the modesty of a woman often disappears with her dress."

In order to propose this affair to Jane, and enforce its necessity, Rodolphe entered her chambers at an early hour. She was sleeping on his bed: her body was so enfeebled by grief and despair, that her lassitude had overcome her apprehensions. She had resigned herself to the soft impulse of nature. In order to breathe more freely, and to alleviate her respiration, she had unbuttoned her collar, and detached the golden clasps of her robe. Her bosom discovered itself unveiled to the eager looks of Rodolphe. Ravishing image!—even an innocent eye could not have withdrawn itself from such a sight, much less a voluptuous one: the long tresses of her hair descended on a neck, which rivalled the dazzling whiteness of a swan. Rodolphe enjoyed this intoxicating view until the beauty awoke, and rose, alarmed, to fasten her vestments, while a deep blush was diffused over her whole countenance. The knight then made her the proposition of changing her dress, as Peter had advised; and as Jane was aware of the necessity of this disguise, he easily prevailed over all her objections. "When am I to be ready?" asked Jane.

"I had fixed the time of our departure in half an hour," returned Rodolphe; "but I will wait two, three hours, if such is your desire; for you are the absolute mistress of my servants and myself." She assured him that she would not abuse either his generosity or patience; and it was arranged that Rodolphe should fetch her at the expiration of an hour.

Rodolphe proceeded to the castle, testified most lively regrets for a loss which he had been informed some few moments before, and took leave of the court. He was thanked for his condolence: his precipitate departure was deplored; and he was assured, that if he would but stay one half day more, he would see Jane return in triumph with her ravisher in chains.

"The knights of all the orders," said Prince Charles, "are in pursuit of the Giant. We have just received intelligence, that they have encompassed a forest into which he had retired with her, and that they only awaited the broad daylight to enter the forest and search the cavern."

Rodolphe wished success to such promising hopes, and retired.

CHAP. X.

WHEN returned to his hotel, Rodolphe found Jane dressed in her new accoutrements: the timid looks which she cast on her lover, on herself, and on the attendants—the awkward but amiable manner with which she wore her doublet and sword, added much to her native charms. She filled the situation of a page; and not one of his people suspected the disguise, for they all slept at the time that Jane was carried off, and had not yet even heard of that event.

Our travellers arrived at Marseilles unsuspected. Before they entered the town, Rodolphe made a rapid progress on the heart of Jane, on her modesty, and on her innocence. She listened to the knight without disgust, when he painted his love in the most glowing colours: she did not avert her eyes when he looked at her; and she did no longer repel him, when, in the excess of his passion, he clasped her in his nervous arms, pressed her to his heart, and imprinted a kiss on her coral lips. She loved him before; and loved him much more when she compared *his* noble figure with the disgusting Bruno; and the gratitude with which her deliverance had inspired her, favoured the corrupting views of Rodolphe. When shame and virtue condemned her, gratitude exclaimed—"Be not ungrateful to your deliverer! he has saved you from infinite sufferings; he has saved you from death! Return love for love!"

Gratitude is certainly a noble virtue; but it often becomes, in the heart of an unexperienced young woman, the very principle of vice. If her seducer renders her an important service, she will be ready to accord him everything, to sacrifice both innocence and virtue to him; because the cunning hypocrite only demands the slight remuneration of a kiss, and because the heart of his victim imagines she can never sufficiently repay his kindnesses. Numbers have fallen into those scarce visible snares and have lost, in an excess of virtue, their honour and repose.

Dear children, beware:—may the example of Jane prove a lesson to you:—do not listen to the man, who, even in jest, demands a kiss for any service whatever. He is like the fisherman, who offers but worms to the credulous inhabitants of the waves; they hasten to seize it, and are caught by the perfidious hook.

Rodolphe traversed the town without thinking of Euphrosina, (for he breathed, he existed for Jane alone)—without even recalling to his mind the innumerable sufferings of that unfortunate. He passed before the monastery, in which she anxiously awaited his return. The clattering of the horses drew her from her usual impassibility; her window looked into the street; she precipitately opened it, and recognised Rodolphe. At his approach, a torrent of joy overwhelmed her heart; but an inexpressible pain succeeded, when she perceived that he paid no attention to her, that he listened not to her voice, and continued his journey as a stranger. "He abandons me!" exclaimed she. "He abandons you!" answered her soul, and the infant which she bore. She fell senseless on the ground. A mortal fever usurped its empire over her feeble body, and the remainder of her strength. She died without bidding farewell to her dear Rodolphe: she died before she gave birth to her child—before Rodolphe reached the shores of Italy.

The travellers arrived at the port, and a vessel was ready to receive them. It was provided with all the conveniences possible, but had only one cabin. This was elegantly fitted up, while all the other places were obscure and dirty. Rodolphe entered that cabin with Jane. No one followed them; and the knight received the first of all the kisses which Jane gave to *him*; she gave it him in the joy of seeing her deliverance nearly achieved. As soon as the vessel had quitted the port, and was in full sail, the cunning Peter, who had accompanied Rodolphe as a servant, entered.

PETER. Master, where am I to prepare your bed, and that of this young gentleman?

RODOLPHE. I will sleep here; and you will prepare another room, the best in the ship, for my page.

PETER. If you do not permit him to pass the night in this room, he will be obliged to sleep with your servants; for, although this ship is very large, this is the only good cabin in the whole.

Rodolphe guessed the artifice of his friend, and seconded it. He offered to give up the room to Jane, but she would not consent. This little alteration of generosity was terminated by their deciding to place the bed of Jane in that same apartment.

"You have vanquished!" whispered Peter to the delighted Rodolphe, and retired.

Jane blushed; she was seized with a violent agitation: "You will not abuse the excess of my confidence?" said she to Rodolphe; "nor abuse your hospitality by playing the part of a corrupter." Rodolphe promised everything, approved everything and demanded only her love, and innocent proofs of her attachment. The first, the second, and the third night, were passed in perfect tranquillity. The danger of Jane augmented with her security. On the fourth night, Rodolphe hazarded solicitations; the fifth, he became more pressing; but Jane steadfastly resisted. On the sixth night, he renewed his prayers, and vanquished the innocence and modesty of the most beautiful woman of her age. Jane deeply repented her weakness, and left her seducer. During the whole of the voyage, she refused to accord him the slightest mark of affection; she slept no longer in his room; she ate no more at his table; but mixed with the servants, who treated her with the greatest respect. At the end of the passage, when the travellers had disembarked, she approached and addressed him thus.

JANE. You have rendered me miserable in this life, and perhaps in that to come. Be generous now, and suffer me to depart.

RODOPLHE. Go!—poor unfortunate! If I could repair my fault, if I could return what I have deprived you of, I would willingly sacrifice my life.

JANE. Do you repent of your crime? You have not committed it voluntarily?

RODOLPHE. I sinned through excess of love. It was love which bore me away in the whirlwind of passions, which mastered my reason: that reason which now exclaims:—"You have conducted yourself basely!—you have outraged the beloved of your heart! Implore not the forgiveness of the offended angel, for you cannot obtain it! Then go whithersoever your fate may call you; and if gold can expiate my horrible attempt, take all I possess."

Jane had granted that for love, which Rodolphe had demanded for luxury; and the greater the efforts she made to hate her seducer, the more she felt her passion increase. Her love became a devouring flame, when she heard that he, like her, had not committed the crime designedly; but that, like her, he had lost himself. She unreservedly pardoned her lover, and fell into his arms. "I will ever remain with you!" were the only words she was capable of uttering.

CHAP. XI.

A VIOLENT love, which has been for some time opposed by obstacles or remorse of conscience, is like an impetuous torrent, which the farmer endeavours to hem by a dyke; it increases to an alarming height, surmounts the barrier, saps its foundations, breaks forth with unbounded fury, and ravages all the surrounding country. This, Jane experienced: she had long withstood the torrent; but, incapable of further resistance, she abandoned herself to the arms of her lover. She forgot her birth, her virtue, her honour; her love only ceased with her last breath. No woman ever loved Rodolphe so ardently, so tenderly, so exclusively, and never held him so long within the bounds of fidelity.

When he entered his paternal castle, Jane embraced her dear Rodolphe; and, thanks to the assistance of his friend, Peter, he soon changed this solitude into a paradise. He almost every day gave splendid feasts, unknown until then in Germany, and which would have exhausted the treasures of a Crœsus. Numerous guests, parasites, and vile flatterers, arrived at the castle of Rodolphe; courted his favour, and lived at his table during whole months. He thought himself happy in this perpetual tumult, and delighted in the praises bestowed on him. He gave himself up to every vice; pride and ambition became his ruling passions. When he wished to satisfy them, the most odious means were employed by him. He drove away the nobles that surrounded him, took possession of their castles, and forced free men to bear his yoke. Monasteries and even towns humbly implored his patronage; He became the terror of the country: virtue fled far away, for it could not flatter, truth retired from his castle, for it could not deceive; innocence was banished to distant countries, for he protected debauchery alone. I should never conclude, if I were to enumerate all the excesses into which vice hurried him. Murder accompanied by the most atrocious barbarities, often stained his hands. Not one day passed, at the expiration of which he could not say, "I have done no ill."

The whole country felt the weight of the yoke of Rodolphe. Several barons determined to break it and declared war against him; but, as he possessed immense riches, which he profusely showered on his flatterers, he had formed a numerous party, and always frustrated the cries of innocence and justice.

Jane, who loved Rodolphe alone and who enjoyed happiness but in his arms, often cast looks of compassion on these scenes of horror—often relieved the sufferings of the unfortunate, and poured a healing balm into their wounds. But she had not sufficient courage to give salutary advice to her lover, and to turn him from the perverse path he was following. When, after several days' absence, Rodolphe returned all covered with blood, he had but to cast on her a tender look, or gently embrace her, in order to stifle in her every subject of discontentment.

He had presented Jane as his wife to all the knights, and she was respected as such by them. The great riches of Rodolphe were attributed to this alliance; and he was esteemed happy in the possession of such a treasure. She had already presented him with two children, whose beauty equalled her own, and whose looks partook of the nobleness and pride of their father.

CHAP. XII.

TEN years were elapsed since the return of Rodolphe into his country, and he had squandered them in the rapid torrent of every vile enjoyment; when, one day, he left Jane and her children alone, and departed for the chase. Towards midday, the Abbess of the Convent of St. Bernard, situated in the jurisdiction of Rodolphe, and honoured with his patronage, was announced:—"I come," said she, "to ask yourself and your lord to pay us a visit. We shall celebrate the day after tomorrow, the anniversary of our holy founder. We have three novices, who are that day to pronounce their vows. They are sisters, and of a very ancient family; but, as orphans, they beg you to represent their father and mother at that ceremony."

Jane, who well knew that Rodolphe did not relish such ceremonies, promised to go, and to engage the knight to accompany her, provided he returned before the day from the chase, which was, however, very doubtful. The Abbess retired, fraught with hope. Rodolphe returned the next morning, and was informed by Jane of the invitation of the Abbess, which he accepted, contrary to her expectation. "I will go," said he, "and give the nuns such a feast as they shall remember to the end of their lives."

The day of the ceremony arrived, and Rodolphe, surrounded by all that was pompous and splendid, entered the Temple of God, which he had not placed his foot in for upwards of ten years. But he did not enter to pray, and repent of his sins. He considered the church as a hall of pleasure; and while the priest was officiating, he enjoyed the curiosity of the congregation, who forgot the Creator to admire the vain magnificence of a mortal. The spiritual brides advanced, clad in white robes, symbols of innocence, and their foreheads bound with the bridal band. The two first pronounced their vows with courage and resolution; the third hesitated, and trembled. They were all three beautiful; but the last was more than beautiful. Covetousness, which had only slumbered, awoke afresh in the heart of Rodolphe. The desire of change soon gained the victory. "I will deliver you," said he to himself; "you were not created to chant hymns—you were formed to breathe the language of love in the arms of man."

He did not partake of the splendid banquet which his liberality had prepared; he only distributed rich presents to the sister nuns, pressed the hand of the youngest, and left the convent, alone, for one of his castles in the forest. Peter had not accompanied him to the church; he called him by the means of his book, which he carefully preserved in his knapsack.

RODOLPHE. Where have you been?

PETER. To the treasury of the Indian Caliph: I have brought some gold and diamonds for you, in order to have it ready in case of necessity; for your prodigalities have brought you into such discredit in Germany that I could not raise one hundred florins for you.

RODOLPHE. Preserve those riches until they are wanted. I have been charmed with the youngest of the nuns, who this day renounced her vows at the Convent of St. Bernard; I will make her break that vow, and endeavour to make her acquainted with other sentiments than those of a recluse. Conduct her this evening to my room.

PETER. Master, that is not possible; I cannot cross any sacred threshold—I cannot approach any convent or church, as our entrances into such places is interdicted.

RODOLPHE. If *you* cannot, your chief can.

PETER. No more than I. Ask any other thing; but for that, impossible!

RODOLPHE. I demand it, and insist upon a punctual execution.

PETER. Of a thing which is not in the power of a demon.

RODOLPHE. In that case, the contract which I signed for Beelzebub is null and void:—"You can demand whatever you please, and it shall be accorded to you." Those were his words, and I insist on their fulfilment.

PETER. If he promised, he will keep his word. You can but summons him, and he will answer for himself.

RODOLPHE. I will call him; he shall return my contract, or satisfy my demand. This condition is of the utmost important and I will not give it up.

Rodolphe took the club, and Beelzebub presented himself; dressed in a coat of a fiery colour, was lame, and held a roll of parchment under his left arm.

BEELZEBUB. Well, how do you do, Rodolphe?—You seem discontented! Are you satiated with enjoyments?—Are you desirous of seeing the conclusion of the contract before the time we agreed on?

RODOLPHE. Not at all; I only request you to answer my question.

BEELZEBUB. Well, speak!

RODOLPHE. Did you not promise to accomplish all my wishes?

BEELZEBUB. I did.

RODOLPHE. Then keep your promise, and bring hither the nun.

BEELZEBUB. I cannot.

RODOLPHE. Then return me my contract.

BEELZEBUB. That is equally impossible:—read, and be convinced. (*He unrolls the parchment, and reads.*) "Except the violation of a church, of a convent, or any other consecrated place." Well, will you any longer insist on your demand?

RODOLPHE. You have deceived me.

BEELZEBUB. But it is written and signed; it is your fault, if you did not read and examine the act: but compose yourself, what is often impossible to a demon is possible to man. You shall not want good counsels. What joy in hell if you succeed in seducing a sacred sheep, and exposing her to the temptations of the world? Enjoyments easily obtained are insipid; hunger seasons the dish; an obstinate combat alone renders a victory glorious. Courage! search the knapsack of your friend, perhaps you will find some assistance. I wish you happiness; if you succeed, I will reward you below.

Beelzebub disappeared, and Rodolphe searched the knapsack, which he always carried with him. Besides the book, he found a rope-ladder, and a key.

RODOLPHE. Can these objects serve my purpose?

PETER. Certainly;—the key opens every lock, and this rope-ladder will descend to the earth when applied to the highest windows.

RODOLPHE. These instruments are well imagined for carrying off a nun! I will make the attempt. Your chief is right! Hunger seasons the dish, and the obstinacy of the fight makes the glory of the victory. At the rising of the sun, I shall go to the convent, inform myself of the cell of the nun, and commence my expedition.

CHAP. XIII.

RODOLPHE, firm to his resolution, proceeded early to the convent, was introduced to the Abbess, and promised to be in future the benefactor of her house. The Abbess, honoured by this visit, received her guest in the best manner she could. During the dinner, vocal music was performed in an adjoining apartment by a chorus of young singers; and, soon after, the enchanting and penetrating melody of a single voice, accompanied by a harp, was heard. Rodolphe was in ecstasy. "Who sings so sweetly?" said he; "who can create such ravishing tones?—is it an angel or a mortal?"

ABBESS. It is the youngest of your three spiritual daughters, to whom your generosity made such splendid presents: she is sufficiently accomplished in every degree to make the happiness of a husband; but, educated in the fear of God, she has preferred to consecrate her talents to Heaven.

RODOLPHE. May I not see that angel?—may I not thank her myself?—may I not recompense her for the exquisite moments which I have passed in hearing her?

ABBESS. I would willingly grant your novel request, but our austere rule forbid it: my sisters cannot see a stranger, after having once pronounced their vows.

RODOLPHE. But I am her spiritual father.

ABBESS. I should be obliged to conceal her forever from your eyes, if you were even her real father; such is the will of our founder. This young lady has renounced her parents in this world, and must henceforth occupy herself with her divine spouse alone. I myself ought not to have received you, were it not a duty incumbent on my situation, which exempts me from this law, and permits me to receive as well as pay visits.

RODOLPHE. You are too severe, and too scrupulous. Will you not then permit me to send my daughters, from time to time, proofs of my attachment?

ABBESS. They do not value either gold or precious objects; but holy images, calculated to entertain the ardour of pious meditations, are objects they can receive.

RODOLPHE. Where are my children lodged?

ABBESS. On the second floor, near each other, numbers 7, 8, and 9.

RODOLPHE. And the beautiful singer?

ABBESS. Number 9.

Rodolphe, instructed in all he wished to know, liberally rewarded the Abbess, and retired as soon as he could. "I shall soon," said he, on the road—"I shall soon possess the ravishing singer—the angelic siren! I will teach her more soft impressions, and I shall enjoy in her arms all the voluptuousness of love. I have long abstained from it. Always at the side of Jane, like a real husband; it is more than a century since I have relished the exquisite pleasure of change. I will fly from flower to flower, like the inconstant bee, and enjoy their nectar while I am yet on this earth. My life will but conclude too soon; let me pass it in pleasure, and gently glide to the end of my career."

He was occupied with these reflections when night set in, to conceal the wicked actions of mankind. At midnight, he approached the convent with the key in his hand. Peter held the horses at some distance. It seemed to Rodolphe as if all Nature was asleep but himself; a profound silence reigned around. He gently, but not without agitation, opened one of the sequestered doors of the convent: the bars gave way, and he entered the sanctuary which he was about to profane. He sought the staircase with precaution, paying great attention not to be mistaken. Having mounted two stairs, he believed himself to be on the second story, and proceeded along the corridor. He examined every door with a small dark lantern, and soon discovered number 9. The door was half open: the nun believing herself to be in security, had neglected to shut it; she was praying after her mortifications. Rodolphe opened the door wider, and saw, by the faint glimmering of a lamp a figure kneeling devoutly at the upper end of the cell. He immediately seized her with his nervous arms, closed her month with a handkerchief, and carried her off irresistibly. He soon bore her, in a senseless state, to the spot where Peter was keeping the horses, placed her before him, and they galloped off as fast as their steeds could bear them.

CHAP. XIV.

THE first signs of approaching day were perceptible, before they reached the castle in the forest. "Let us rest in this wood," said Rodolphe; and, in entering it, they descended. The nun had again fallen into that deadly sleep, out of which she had only awoke by intervals on the road. Rodolphe laid her gently on the thick grass, and Peter ran to fetch some water to sprinkle on her face. The black veil which covered her head was undone, but not taken off. When Peter returned, Rodolphe gently raised it. "See," said he, turning to his confidant, "behold this celestial figure, and judge whether such a beauty is not worth carrying off."

They both hastened to admire her charms: the veil was thrown off—Rodolphe remained so confounded, and Peter so astonished, that they could not pronounce one word. They sometimes looked at each other, and then at the nun. They had flattered themselves to behold a model of beauty, and they saw only the hideous image of suffering and misery. Projecting bones, and a deadly yellow skin, composed a figure which perfectly resembled death; while the eyes, sunk in their sockets, completed the hideous spectacle. Peter first recovered his speech: he thought his master had mistaken, and dragged a skeleton from her tomb.

"There is some enchantment!" said Rodolphe. He rubbed his eyes in vain—in vain he turned them again on the object of his surprise; it continued to remain the figure of death, and its hideousness augmented every moment.

While he endeavoured to explain this mystery, the deadly figure began to move; she opened her dying eyes, and fixed them on Rodolphe. "Is it you?—is it you?" said she, in a hollow voice. At these words she rose, and presented her wan hand to Rodolphe, whose limbs trembled beneath him.

RODOLPHE. Do you know me?

NUN. I know you!—(*with pain.*) I know him whose image incessantly fleeted before my eyes, accompanied me to the chorus, and was beside me when I prostrated myself before the altar.

RODOLPHE. Who are you then?—What is your name?

NUN. It is then true that you do not know me? Pity does then not inspire you in my favour?—(*she falls back.*) Oh! horrible truth! You do not know Clara?

RODOLPHE. You, Clara?—(*retiring with horror.*) Impossible!

CLARA. Yes; I am yet, I am always your Clara. Even in this dress, my feeble heart has never ceased to beat for you. Oh! if you knew—if I could describe my sufferings, my anguish, the perpetual solicitude which you caused me, you would feel some compassion, you would allow me the favour I so ardently desired, of dying in your arms!

RODOLPHE. How did you escape from the tower? How did you enter this monastery?

CLARA (*her hand on her bosom*). The joy of seeing you once more before my end deprives me of speech. Oh!—I feel—I feel! the hour of my death approaches: (*with painful convulsions*)—I cannot continue: (*assembling all her strength*)—I expected you in the tower during two years. I prayed for you and myself; I often repented of my crime, and committed it again; for it was impossible for me to forget your image; I was more attached to you than my Saviour. One day, however, I expressed the ardent desire of devoting my life to the Lord in heaven; I took the resolution if ever I became free, of consecrating myself to him in a cloister. The tower instantly opened, and I was conducted by unknown guards to the convent, from which you carried me off this night. I was received with kindness; and I took the oath of living chaste forever. I kept it in words and actions, but not in thoughts. My heart was devoted to you—to you alone! Grief and regrets sapped my feeble body; I became a skeleton!—I implored divine mercy—it is come—I die content as I have seen you once more!—O may my image, the image of my agony, be ever present in your mind! May it ever recall to you the power of death! May you repent of the sins you have committed in this world—that one day—one day we might meet again (*with redoubled efforts*)—Give me your hand! (*he gives his hand*)—Adieu, Rodolphe! think of death; (*she lays down*)—reconcile yourself with God. Honour my remains; and let this, my last hour, never be erased from your mind.

At these words, the anguish of death seized her: she made some useless efforts to speak; and died, according to her last wish in the arms of Rodolphe. He remained some moments deeply moved; his eyes fixed on the pale corpse. "Why did I not end like you?" was all be could think, and all he could say.

Peter awakened him from this reverie. "Master," said he, "leave the dead in repose, and rejoice with the living; come, let us continue our road. Tomorrow brings another day, which will be followed by another night; and that night we will fetch the beautiful nun, in whose arms you will forget Clara."

RODOLPHE. I shall never forget her.

They mounted their horses, arrived at the castle, and, thanks to Peter, the day was not closed before Rodolphe had forgotten that Clara was no more—that she had recommended him to honour her remains. Her body was found by some peasants, who immediately informed the Abbess of the circumstance. It was carried away, and buried the day after with all possible secrecy, because the sisters had remarked in her some signs of absence of mind; and they supposed that, in an excess more violent than she had hitherto experienced, she had found the door open, fled into the forest, and ended her life without the assistance of a priest, and without receiving the holy viaticum.

The very day of the burial of Clara, Rodolphe, accompanied by Peter, returned to the convent. They examined how it was possible he could have made such a fatal mistake. He desired to ascertain whether the suspicious Abbess had purposely deceived him, or whether he was to attribute his error to the natural situation of the building. They were soon convinced that the latter circumstance was the true cause, and saw plainly that the convent being built on a declivity, had three stories at the lower end, and only two at the back; and Rodolphe, who had entered the convent at the lower end thought himself on the second floor, when he was only on the first. This would have deterred him from continuing his criminal enterprise, if he had not been so profoundly plunged in vice; and if his long series of crimes had not closed the openings of his heart forever against the voice of repentance.

CHAP. XV.

AS soon as the nuns, fatigued with singing their psalms, had returned to their cells, and extinguished their lights one after the other; as soon as the convent was buried in a profound silence, Rodolphe opened the gate nearest the mountain, ascended to the second floor, ascended to the second floor, approached the cell marked number 9, and found the object of his researches. The young Mary, an angel of beauty, was sitting at a table, writing by the light of a feeble lamp. Alarmed by the noise, she rose—saw Rodolphe—recoiled trembling, and seized the corner of the table with her left hand. She endeavoured to speak, but the words became unintelligible sounds on her tremulous lips. Rodolphe was overcome by the all-powerful regard of love;—he hesitated, and knew not whether he was to enjoy the enchanting aspect, or boldly seize on his prey. Mary, however, soon recovered from her astonishment.

MARY. What do you wish?—How did you enter my cell at this hour? (*Rodolphe cannot answer.*)—Did Ivan send you?

RODOLPHE (*profiting by the mistake*). I come from him.

MARY. Are you his confidant?

RODOLPHE. His intimate friend.

MARY. Are you commissioned to end my sufferings—to drag me from this horrible prison?

RODOLPHE. Yes; the horses are ready:—follow me!

MARY. And why did he not come himself? As he assured me he would, if possible, in his last letter.

RODOLPHE. Because——

MARY. Oh! inform me of the reason for that change! Does illness detain him? Can he not support the pain of losing me? It is then not without reason that he wrote to me: "Be assured that I will deliver you; and if the loss of my strength will not permit me to do it myself, I will send one of my friends conduct you to my death-bed." Oh! say, are his fears realised?

RODOLPHE. He is not so ill as you imagine: it is true that he is confined to his bed in my castle, where he awaits you; but your presence will restore him to life; do not deprive him of it any longer; come, I will conduct you to him in safety. Do you not know me?

MARY. If I recollect right, I have seen you before; you are come to console me in my affliction! Are you not the rich and powerful Rodolphe of Westerbourg?

RODOLPHE. The very same.

MARY. And you take pity on us? You are come——

RODOLPHE. To deliver my unfortunate daughter. I yesterday met your friend rambling in the forest; I invited him to my castle, and assisted him as much as was in my power. His heart soon opened: he discovered his designs to me; and, as he was too weak to execute them himself, I proffered my services. I have faithfully fulfilled my promise; now keep yours, and follow me.

Mary, reassured by this discourse, kissed the hand of Rodolphe, and suffered him to imprint paternal kisses on her forehead. "I am ready to follow you," said she at last; "my sisters will mourn, and curse their departed companion; but it is impossible to fulfil vows so austere: my heart is entirely devoted to Ivan."

He offered his arm, and they descended to the gate of the convent. Rodolphe was astonished to find it closed. In vain he sought his key in the knapsack, for he had forgot to draw it out of the lock when he opened the door outside; and the wind, or perhaps, as Mary conjectured, the porter had shut it. They remained a long while in this strange perplexity, and endeavoured to open the door without success. Mary begged Rodolphe to follow her: she returned to her cell, and offered to hide him under her bed. Before he accepted this last resource, he took the book and opened it; but Peter did not appear. When he replaced it in the knapsack, his hand felt the rope-ladder, and he pulled it out. The countenance of Mary beamed with joy. "That is what we want!" said she, and helped Rodolphe to fasten the ladder to the window. The knight descended first; Mary followed: he received her in his arms, and carried her rapidly to the horses. His first care was to apprise Peter of the mistake of Mary; and the latter answered so correctly to all the questions of the innocent victim, that she doubted not of soon seeing her lover, and already believed herself in his arms.

"Is that castle the term of our journey?" said she, in a transport of joy, to Rodolphe, when she saw the battlements rising above the dark firs.

"Yes," answered he.

"O then conduct me to my friend!—partake of our rejoicings, and may they reward you for your goodness!"

She continued to discourse in this strain, until she arrived at the gate. She ascended into the hall. "Where is he?—Where shall I see him?" was the only question she uttered.

RODOLPHE. I will go and see how he is. I must prepare him for your reception; a sudden surprise might be mortal to him. (*He leaves the apartment, and returns a little while after.*) You cannot see him yet; he is sleeping. His nurse told me he had, after my departure, been attack by a violent fever, which rendered him delirious for some moments. The fever abated, and he must now enjoy his repose.

MARY. Oh! Let me see him sleep! I will not awake him, although I so ardently wish to embrace him.—I will remain by his bedside, and will be content to allay with my breath the heat of his fever.

RODOLPHE. The moment he would awake, would be the moment of his death. Wait with patience, my dear Mary, and relate to me how you became acquainted with the cause of your ardent love, and strong attachment for him. Your lover was not in a state to satisfy my curiosity—reward my trouble by the recital.

MARY. With all my heart. But I can scarcely depict our sufferings, when joy entirely occupies my mind: you must be contented with the little I can collect in my memory at this moment. His father was the knight of Sehellheim: my father's name was Hallbron. They had jointly inherited the Castle of Lauterbourg, on the border of the Rhine, and both resided in it. We were children then: innocence and joy presided over our amusements, when our fathers proceeded to Palestine to fight for the cause of Christianity. As we grew up, love, the most tender love, inspired our hearts by degrees. I cannot myself define the first origin of that inclination. A message arrived from our fathers in Palestine: they were in want of money to carry on the war. Our mothers mortgaged the castle to the Abbess of St. Bernard; and we willingly consented, for the glory of God. But what was my horror!—what was that of Ivan, on hearing that he was to be the bearer of the gold, and that he was to display his valour against the Saracens! The idea of our separation was terrible; we bid each other adieu with tears. The pleasure and gaiety of my heart departed with him. Soon after, our mothers entered the convent with us. At the expiration of two years, we were informed that our fathers, my lover, and a thousand other German nobles had perished by the plague. This news was a death-blow for my mother. I was myself at the gates of death, and I owed my recovery to my youth. We were orphans, without fortunes: the Abbess offered us the veil; my sisters joyfully accepted the proposition, and I myself consented to take it, as I supposed Ivan was dead, and with him the happiness of my life. We pronounced, as you know, our irrevocable vows some days ago. The day after, as I was praying in the chapel, I looked through the iron gate, and I thought I saw Ivan on his knees before me; I looked a second time, and fell senseless to the ground. During the night, I heard some moanings under my window, which I opened, and saw him again. He told me he had a letter to give me; I pulled it up by means of a piece of thread, and desired him to return the next night. He informed me that he had come to marry me—that he had courageously fought the Infidels—that he had resisted the attacks of the plague, but that he was reduced to the greatest despair, as I was lost to him. "Take pity on your Ivan," said he, at the end of his letter; "leave your prison. We will go to a distant land—to a desert—and be happy." I answered, "Yes; I will follow you—I will follow you; for I declared, I would consecrate myself to God, only in case you should no longer exist." The following days were employed in seeking the means of arranging our flight; and we should perhaps not have been able to accomplish it for a long time, perhaps we should even have given it up, had you not had compassion on our sufferings.—But he has slept enough now—let us go and awake him. Believe me, his joy on seeing me will be as efficacious as sleep.

RODOLPHE. Stay one moment, my dear Mary, only one moment. What would you say if your Ivan was not here?——

MARY. What!—is he dead?—

RODOLPHE. Permit me to continue. What! if I had only profited by your mistake to carry you off from the convent?—if I had attempted this only because I was charmed with your beauty, and determined to rescue you from slavery?—to offer you my heart?—to place my treasures at your feet?

MARY. Impossible! impossible!—Then I should abhor you—curse you—for having blasted all my hopes—then——Oh! it cannot be!

RODOLPHE. But nothing is more true. Be indulgent and just, my dear Mary; forget the languishing Ivan, in the arms of the ardent Rodolphe. Believe that he is dead, and live happy with me; believe, as you said yourself, that he was not capable of saving you. I—I have saved you; broken your chains; be grateful, and return my love.

MARY. May God help him if you speak the truth! alas! alas! take pity on me; return me my lover. It is in vain you speak thus—I can love but him—him alone in this world.

RODOLPHE. Give vent to your complaints; your pain will be the sooner alleviated. If you knew the whole extent, the ardour of my love, if——

MARY. O cease, I conjure you! God of Heaven, I cannot believe it! Is it true that he is not here? Have you then so cruelly deceived my hopes?—Is he not here? Did he not send you to deliver me?

RODOLPHE. I do not even know the knight, and have never seen him. I resolved to save you the moment I saw your celestial figure in the church; the divine charm of your voice completed the victory. Believe me, I love you tenderly, more passionately than your knight

MARY. Poor Mary! you have offended God, and this is his punishment. (*She runs to Rodolphe and clasps him in her arms.*) My father! oh, my father!—Take pity on your unfortunate child—close not your ears against her complaints—I fall on my knees: I will not quit them until you restore me my Ivan.

RODOLPHE (*raises her up*). Come into my arms, beautiful Mary! How happy I am in yours.

MARY (*thrusting him away*). And you can thus deride my sufferings?—You can thus insult my tears? Monster—is your heart inflexible to my sighs? I am lost!—God punishes me!

RODOLPHE. Anger heightens your charms, but time will calm it. Think of the part you will take: I will leave you; solitude is necessary to your reflections.

Rodolphe left the room, and called his friend Peter.

RODOLPHE. Do you know the whole adventure?

PETER. I do.

RODOLPHE. What must I do?

PETER. You must not lose courage, and profit by every circumstance.

RODOLPHE. Then, be once more my friend, and advise me.

PETER. Her heart is entirely devoted to her lover; it is the only point by which she can be attacked; propose her the alternative of seeing Ivan die, or resigning herself to your wishes. I bet she will choose the latter and think she commits an act of heroism in saving what is most dear to her.

RODOLPHE. Well; let us try, and see whether you are a good prophet. Precaution is necessary, but such a victory is well worth some trouble. Where shall we find the knight?

PETER. He is retired to the hermit, in the forest of Rheinthal. He is there meditating on plans to save Mary; he is very ill and weak; if this had not been the case, you would have found him last night beneath the window of the convent.

RODOLPHE. Bring him hither in chains.

PETER. I obey your orders.

CHAP. XVI.

RODOLPHE had scarce given the order before Peter returned.

RODOLPHE. Have you executed my desire?

PETER. I have; and placed the knight in the tower, until I learnt your further commands concerning him.

RODOLPHE. How does he look there?

PETER. He seems like a dove whose companion has been taken away, that strikes the cage with its beak, feebly agitates its wings, and coos in a melancholy tone. He imagines that his communication with Mary has been discovered, and that he is in the power of the Abbess. He has several times repeated the words, "Save her, and make me endure a twofold pain."

RODOLPHE. I am impatient to observe the effects of this intelligence on Mary.

He entered the chamber in which he had left her and said: "Well, my amiable Mary, have you duly considered?"

MARY. Change my heart, change my sentiments, change the whole of my being, then I will fulfil your desires; but if you cannot create for me another soul, your word are eternally lost on me.

RODOLPHE. A happy chance has placed your lover in my power.

MARY. Him?

RODOLPHE. Yes; himself. Do you see that tower? Do you see its iron door? There he lives, and there he will live in chains, until your heart, your sentiments, your very being are changed. If I am not happy, he shall be much less so. The day of my happiness shall be the day of his deliverance; the instant of my triumph, that of his liberty. Well, Mary, you shall have one hour for reflection? I will willing grant it you; but remember that Ivan is languishing in a dungeon, that I am not accustomed to long delays, and that I can take by force what you refuse.

MARY. You would not be so barbarous? No—you speak not the truth, that tower cannot be the residence of innocence.

RODOLPHE. Do you wish to be convinced by ocular evidence? You shall have it. (To Peter, who enters.) Bring the prisoner out of that tower, turn his face towards this window, that Mary may behold it and cease to accuse me of imposition.

Perter executed the order of Rodolphe; Ivan was conducted into the court, and placed opposite the window. His hands and feet were laden with heavy chains, which dragged after him with a horrific noise. Mary, who during that interval had remained in silent expectation, was awakened from her stupor by the clanking of chains; she approached the window, looked into the court, retreated horror-struck, looked once more and exclaimed: "It is him!"—"God of heaven, it is himself," said she again, and fell senseless into the arms of Rodolphe. He basely profited by this occasion, imprinted kisses on her face, and unveiled her bosom with his impure hands. The prompt instinct of modesty soon revived her; she tore herself from his arms, and burst into tears, wrung her hands, and abandoned herself to mortal anguish. Rodolphe suffered her fury to exhale; the complaints of innocence had the same charm for him as the most melodious harp. The wandering of a woman, who in her delirium neglected her person, uncovered it and exposed it to view, was become to his perverted mind a ravishing spectacle;

he satiated his senses, and the fire of voluptuousness kindled the most ardent flames within him. Mary soon exhausted her strength, and fell breathless. She could not prevent the monster from again clasping her in his arms, and kissing her. "Grace! mercy!" was all her agonized voice could pronounce.

RODOLPHE. May I hope? What do you decide?

MARY (*firmly*). To die rather than be yours; to endure the most cruel tortures, rather than consent to grant you one kiss! this is my irrevocable resolution; the resolution which I have taken, in the excess of my grief, and which I will never alter. I conjure you in the name of Heaven kill me; annihilate me, and you will fulfil my most ardent wishes; but spare his life; (*tears roll down her cheeks.*) Take pity on the innocent; is he guilty because Mary loves him with unbounded ardour?

RODOLPHE (*enraged*). He, innocent? Has he not robbed me of your love, and with that love, of my joy and happiness? He shall suffer for it! this hour, this minute shall be the instant of his death, if, before its expiration, you do not promise to be mine; he shall die, and die before your eyes.

MARY. I die for him! death will be pleasing.

RODOLPHE. No, you shall live; I will ravish what you will not grant me. After having dishonoured you, I will drive you away; I will make you a laughing stock of the rabble; a herald shall precede you, and exclaim: "There is the prostitute! there!" Now—choose.

MARY (*with a hollow voice*). Let him die; and may his blood fall on you! (*With a solemn air.*) There is above a Being who protects the innocent, on Him I call, to Him I abandon myself.

RODOLPHE (*choked with rage*). Peter, order the guards to take the prisoner from the tower, to cut him in pieces before this woman. Then return, and hold Mary at the window, that she may behold his sufferings, and hear his cries for mercy.

Peter delivered the orders of Rodolphe, and then dragged Mary to the window. She fixed her haggard looks on the court.

RODOLPHE. It is yet time; hear my last condition: I exact, that you should entirely deliver yourself up to me during three days only; and then he shall be returned to you for life. He shall never know what you have accorded me; I will overwhelm you with riches, I will have you conducted to a strange country; you may there live happy.

MARY. I have nothing to answer.

RODOLPHE (*springs to the window, and orders the guards to open the prison*). Drag him into the court; tear him limb from limb, that she may enjoy the sight she has herself ordered.

The guards obeyed; they brought Ivan out of the tower; he bent beneath their nervous arms; he exclaimed: "Mercy! help!" The swords were raised above his head—he beheld Mary at the window. She was motionless—petrified. Every feature, every muscle of her countenance bore the impression of the most excruciating torments; her heart beat no longer; she was crushed by the band of grief. "Mary," said the young man, "save your Ivan!" His voice drew Mary from her stupefaction!—her heart began to resume its usual functions; her senses returned.

"Stop! stop!" said she.

"Stop!" said Rodolphe, in a voice of thunder.

RODOLPHE (*in a softened voice*). Well, have you resolved?

MARY (*with an august air*). Will he be saved if I fulfil your condition?

RODOLPHE. Yes.

MARY. Will you swear it in my hand?

RODOLPHE. I will.

MARY. Before the face of the Almighty?

RODOLPHE. Before the face of the Almighty.

MARY. Will you forfeit your happiness in the world to come, your eternal salvation, if you do not keep your oath?

RODOLPHE. I will.

MARY. The Lord hears, the Lord sees you; the Lord will judge you. Well, then, silence my conscience! modesty accuse me not; it is for the life of a man. I am yours for three days; but shall I be free with him? May we go wherever we choose?

RODOLPHE. I will keep my oath. (*To the guards in the court.*) Conduct the prisoner to the dungeon, take off his chains, and treat him well.

The guards obeyed; a look of love and expression was all the gratitude Ivan could evince towards Mary.

RODOLPHE. He shall be kept as an hostage for the accomplishment of your promise. If you fulfil it willingly you shall open the prison yourself, and be his deliverer.

It is time to throw a veil on this horrible scene; it must long since long irritated my readers. I would have terminated it, did not my duty as an historian and the object of this work, force me to bring to light the progressive development of human malice, cherished in a perverse heart, to show how it attains the highest pitch, and spurns disdainfully all that opposes its passage.

CHAP. XVII.

IT is with regret I take up again my pen; it is against my inclination that I relate what followed.

Rodolphe gained his execrable victory; he felt not for the sighs of Mary; he wiped away her tears with odious kisses. But such a possession could not afford him a lasting pleasure, and the third day he was already disgusted with his conquest.

"She has but poorly returned my love," said he to Peter; "I will reward her in the same manner. Ivan shall not enjoy the pleasure which she has reserved for him alone. I swore to return him free; but dead or alive, that is as I please."

PETER. Certainly.

RODOLPHE. Then let him be beheaded, and let Mary be conducted to him. She was insensible, she was dead in my arms, and he shall be so in hers.

Peter punctually executed the order of his master. Mary hastily descended, opened the prison-door herself, and beheld the lifeless and headless corpse of Ivan extended before her. Scenes of this nature are above all description. The last excess of torture cannot be expressed, and I therefore shall pass it over.—Peter abandoned Mary to her destiny and returned to his master.

"This picture," said he, "would have delighted Beelzebub himself! it is an action of which he will be jealous."

Rodolphe did not remain long in the castle; some feeble remorse troubled his conscience. He ordered the horses to be saddled, and returned to his usual place of abode.

Perhaps the sequel of this history will inform us, whether Mary recovered from her swoon, or whether she felt the whole extent of her misery.

Contrary to his former expectations, Rodolphe again returned to the seat of his ancestors—it would have been better for him to have abided by his first resolution, when he left it after the death of Agnes. Jane received him with transports of tenderness and affection. She was ignorant that he had spilt innocent blood; she imagined not that the tears of suffering virtue had bedewed his hand. Happy in seeing him return, she soon forgot the grief she had experienced in consequence of the length of his absence. But Rodolphe continued his opprobrious life—enjoyed the present—and never thought of the future.

That same year, Alphonse of Spain was elected Emperor of Germany. He dispatched messengers to invite all the German nobles to his coronation at Aix-la-Chapelle. It was destined to be celebrated with great splendour. He promised to exercise a justice throughout the whole empire, and to abolish the abuses which had crept in during the reigns of his predecessors. Rodolphe, who often felt himself constrained in his castle—who sought every means to banish the lassitude that sometimes overcame him, resolved to proceed to Aix—to dazzle all the princes with his magnificence—and to gratify his ruling passions. Peter was forced to plunder the treasures of the Caliph of India, before he procured a sufficiency to pay for the rich armour—to hire the squires and attendants, and to prepare all with that grandeur his vanity exacted. He left the castle accompanied by the benedictions and tears of Jane. She desired to follow him; but Rodolphe would not permit her, as he was anxious of being at liberty.

One day, as he was crossing the forest of Mayence, he ordered his followers to response during the heat of the day. After a long repast, he lay down under a tree to slumber. Before he fell asleep, a hermit passed by: he wished Rodolphe a good morning, and stood still before him.

HERMIT. Is it not Waldemar that is passing by here? Are you not one of his followers?

RODOLPHE (*rising at the name of Waldemar*). Waldemar? No: I do not belong to him; but I have known him. Is he returned from Palestine? is he to pass here? and whither is he going?

HERMIT. Three years are elapsed since he returned; he brought immense riches with him—he does a great deal of good, and frequently supplies me with the necessaries of life. One of his men told me yesterday, that he was going to the coronation at Aix. I thought it was him, and was going to beg of him.

RODOLPHE. I can give as well as he can. (*He gives him a piece of gold.*) There, take this, and for once procure some pleasure for yourself—rejoice and feast upon it.

HERMIT. I will devote it to God; I will nourish others poorer than myself, and tell them to pray for you. I fly the pleasures of this world in my solitude, in order to be rewarded in that to come.

RODOLPHE. Does Waldemar live near this place?

HERMIT. His castle is situated in this forest, two miles lower down; he bought it of the Baron of Wétéravie for a considerable sum. He is a respectable old man, and blessed by all the country; he is powerful, and yet he is good; he never oppresses the weak, and always assists the unfortunate. He has built, on the bank of the river, a little house, which is as humble as my hermitage. He walks there every evening—he prays to the Lord, and often passes the night there. The indigent and oppressed have free access to him: I have often been to see him—he sometimes kept me for hours together, and related to me, in the most affable manner, the account of the battles he fought in Palestine for the restitution of the holy shrine.

RODOLPHE. If he loves solitude and retirement so much, why does he go to the feasts of the coronation?

HERMIT. He does not go to indulge in vice or vanity; but undertakes this journey with better intentions. The knights of his neighbourhood commit many excesses: they torment the shepherds—sack the towns—and oppress the people. He intends representing these disorders to the new emperor, that he may remedy them, and enable his subjects to cultivate their fields in peace, and enjoy the labour of their hands.

RODOLPHE. You are right—he is a respectable old man; I have long known him; I was his companion in arms in Palestine. I cannot dispense paying him a visit, as I pass so near his castle: await me here; I shall soon return. You shall conduct me to the little house—I will surprise him agreeably, and pass this day in his embraces.

HERMIT. Heaven will recompense you if you afford any pleasure to the old man. I will wait for you here.

Rodolphe ordered his people to unpack his bag, and unsaddle the horses; he then called his friend, Peter.

RODOLPHE. Can you guess?——

PETER. I know all; I can hear at any distance all I wish to hear.

RODOLPHE. Now, what shall I do? The Hermit assured me that he was going to the coronation; and I am lost if he is in possession of the fatal hat!

PETER. That is possible.

RODOLPHE. Then neither you, nor your Beelzebub could save me?

PETER. No, we could not.

RODOLPHE. Then it is in his power to cover me with shame before all the assembled nobles, or at least to poison my enjoyments. One or the other must not go.

PETER. It is natural the old man should be at home.

RODOLPHE. Then you approve my resolution.

PETER. Certainly. Tell the Hermit to conduct you to the little house, and if you should find him, make him pay for all the evil he caused you.

RODOLPHE. You must come with us, to warn me, in case you should feel the influence of the hat.

As soon as the sun declined towards the horizon, Rodolphe and Peter, accompanied by the Hermit, descended through the forest to the castle of Waldemar;—the old Hermit endeavoured to shorten the road by relating pious histories, which, however, did not edify those perverse men. The sun set in all its splendour at the moment they were passing the residence of Waldemar. Peter approached Rodolphe:—"I feel the influence of the hat," said he, "it extends over the whole castle—it is hidden there. Advance boldly to the cottage, and if you find the old man, do as you please."

The little solitude of Waldemar soon appeared in view. It was romantically but agreeably situated in a valley opening towards the river. Several lofty trees surrounded it; and a winding path, bordered by sweet briars and other shrubs, led down to it.

RODOLPHE (*to the Hermit and Peter*). I will go alone to cause him the greater surprise. Await me in this arbour on the left.

HERMIT. I envy you that pleasure; follow this path; it will conduct you to the house. You will certainly find the knight, for I see the door is open.

Rodolphe followed the peaceful path. At every winding was the statue of a saint with a praying desk—but the murderer did not pray, and continued unmoved. He soon arrived—found the house open—entered; and saw Waldemar, bareheaded, kneeling before an altar. So fervent were his prayers, that he did not hear footsteps of Rodolphe.

RODOLPHE. Waldemar?——

WALDEMAR (*rising, and looking at Rodolphe*). What do you wish, Sir Knight?

RODOLPHE. I come to cast up accounts with you—I come to demand satisfaction for the evil you have done me. Do you not know me?

WALDEMAR. Are you not Rodolphe?

RODOLPHE. I am.

WALDEMAR. Then you are welcome: if the torments of your mind harass you, if remorse lacerates your conscience, come and join me; Heaven will hear you, as it has heard me. You come here to seek a satisfaction, with which you find me just occupied. I every day demand pardon of the Almighty for having caused the death of Agnes, for having pursued you with an inveterate hatred. The Lord has heard me; peace dwells within my bosom; forgive me, and I shall die content.

RODOLPHE. Never!—I will treat you as you treated me; I will render measure for measure; I must have other satisfaction but that which you propose;—you must die.

WALDEMAR. What, you would murder an unprotected old man?—Why must I die?

RODOLPHE. You best know why you must die; the hat no longer protects you.

WALDEMAR. Am I not under the protection of God?

RODOLPHE. He judges all according to their actions. (*He plunges a dagger into Waldemar's heart*).

WALDEMAR (*dying*). He will judge us!—he will judge us!

Without waiting any longer, Rodolphe retraced his steps; found his companions laying on the grass—"Let us depart," said he, in haste.

HERMIT. Why do you return so soon?

RODOLPHE. The knight is ill; he sleeps; and I would not disturb him.

PETER. Does he sleep soundly?

RODOLPHE. Yes, very.

They continued their road; and as they were passing by a hedge, Rodolphe drew a club from it, and struck violently behind him.

PETER. What are you doing?

RODOLPHE. I am guarding against indiscretions; the Hermit might have betrayed me.

PETER (*looking at the Hermit lying lifeless on the ground*). He also sleeps well; he will tell no one whither he conducted us.

RODOLPHE. Carry him to the cottage, place the dagger, which is in the heart of Waldemar, in his hand, and we shall thus avert every suspicion.

PETER. Excellent; you must soon instruct me: the disciple honours the master.

CHAP. XVIII.

RODOLPHE proceeded on his road the next morning, loaded with a double murder; but he felt not the burden, and rejoiced at having freed himself of a dangerous enemy. Arrived at Aix-la-Chapelle, he attracted the attention of the whole town. The report of his extraordinary magnificence, of his unbounded liberality, soon reached the court. His figure, which had preserved all its primitive beauty, was the object of admiration amongst the ladies, and of envy amongst the knights. The coronation was celebrated; Rodolphe added much to its splendour; he followed the monarch in the train of the nobles, and gained the prize at the tournament, given in honour of the new emperor, in despite of the efforts of his valiant opponents.

He was seated at the banquet beside the emperor; princes and counts all drank to the health of Rodolphe. Suddenly, a tumult was audible in the outer hall; the people forced the guard, entered the banqueting-room, and all crowded round Rodolphe. A pale hand stretched over his shoulder, and placed before him a covered dish. "Victor in the tournament," said a voice in his ear; "seducer of innocence! murderer of young women! murderer of old men! eat, and be satiated!" He turned, and beheld Mary and the Hermit behind him; he became pale as death; and all the assistants, astonished by this singular address, fixed their eyes on him.

MARY. Well, Rodolphe, you will not touch the dish I have brought you from so far? Endeavour to taste it!

He pushed off the cover, and the head of Ivan, already disfigured by putrefaction, displayed its menacing teeth. At this horrid spectacle, the emperor and empress rose from their seats, and all the guests followed their example: Rodolphe alone remained immovable.

EMPEROR. What means this apparition? Nun, why do you interrupt our festivity by such horrors.

MARY. He has merited it—merited it a thousand times. (*Prostrating herself at the feet of the Emperor.*)—I demand vengeance and justice.

RODOLPHE. Sire, she is mad.

MARY. No, I am not mad: it is true that the excess of my pain deprived me of my reason; but the desire of vengeance returned it to me! Here are my witnesses.

Rodolphe turned again and saw the men whom he had commissioned to guard Mary; and who, touched with compassion for her misfortunes, had betrayed their master's cause.

Mary then related to the Emperor the infamous attempt committed by Rodolphe; she openly declared everything; she owned herself criminal, but demanded vengeance on the murder of Ivan. When she had completed her tale; the Hermit advanced. His grey hairs, his bloody wound, testified in his favour: he depicted the horrid assassination of Waldemar. "They thought me dead," said he, "but I already recovered my senses when his servant dragged me to the cottage. He placed the dagger in my band, to dishonour me even after my death. I soon regained my strength, and was enabled to publish his crime. I was directed to the tribunal of Spires, which sent me to your majesty. O Emperor, I met this nun on the road; she charitably bound up my wound, and I endeavoured to console her soul. I join my prayers to hers, to demand justice on that murderer."

At these words, a mournful silence pervaded the whole assembly; all eyes were fixed on the Emperor, all ears awaited his judgement. He cast a look of compassion on the accusers, and a look of anger on the criminal. "Evil!" exclaimed he, "to him who could have committed such a crime!"—"Evil! evil! be to him!" re-echoed all the vaulted roofs of the palace. "Evil unto him!" repeated all the streets of the town.

"It is painful," continued the Emperor, "to commence my reign with a punishment, but the enormity of the crime demands an example. I have sworn to God to protect innocence, and to avenge murder: I must keep my oath. Nobles of the empire, it is for you to judge; I resign the privilege of according grace on this occasion. If you find him criminal, judge him according to the laws. Guards conduct him to prison."

While Rodolphe passed along the streets, joy gleamed in every countenance; everybody was delighted to have an Emperor who testified so lively a sense of justice. Rodolphe resembled a man disturbed by frightful dreams, and who endeavours in vain to awake. He already approached the dungeon prepared to receive him, when a troop of horsemen galloped along the street, dispersed the people, and the soldiers surrounded the prisoner, and disappeared with him. The walls of the town were already far behind them when Rodolphe recovered his senses; he recognised Peter at the head of the party, and called him.

PETER. Master, the peril was great this day: I had no time to lose to save you from the scaffold.

RODOLPHE. It seems as if I dreamt; I cannot explain to myself what has been going forward for this hour. But, although you are my liberator, I have some grounds of displeasure. Why did you not warn me? Why did you not suffer me to be overwhelmed with eternal shame?

PETER. You demand things that are impossible; I can satisfy your wishes, but I cannot avert the consequences. I can second, I can even commit a murder in your name; but I cannot prevent evil from rewarding evil. If you set a house on fire, you cannot be astonished to see the flames burst through the roof; and if you commit a murder, you must expect to hear your name pronounced with horror.

RODOLPHE. What shall I now become?

PETER. They will seek you, and will not find you; you will be put to the ban of the empire, but no one will pursue you. During that time, you will live quietly in your castle, and deride all this. Perhaps even some pious ecclesiastic will excommunicate you; but what is that to you? you can have no care for a soul no longer your own.

RODOLPHE. My reputation, my honour is lost. Before, everybody esteemed me; now, I shall be despised: knights gloried in sitting at my table, in joining in my banquets; but now they will pass my castle, without stopping, and abandon me to a solitude, which will now be more insupportable than ever. Can you not recover my honour? O Peter! have you no balm to cure this wound?

PETER. I have. No one will esteem or honour you; but they will fear you, and flatter you; nuns will bless you as you pass, and implore your protection when you approach their monastery. What signifies whether those demonstrations proceed from the heart, provided you attain your ends? Do not anticipate evil; occupy yourself with the present and you will not fear the future.

Peter endeavoured by these, and other discourses of the like nature, to console Rodolphe, who sometimes approved, and sometimes rejected them. It was not remorse which tormented his mind; but the regret of having lost his honour and his reputation. The idea of the impossibility of ever recovering them, roused his anger. He would not become better, he would not do good; but he would have the appearance of doing so; and it was an infernal torture for him that Mary had unmasked him before all the nobility of Germany.

The nearer he approached his castle, the more his ill-humour augmented; and it attained its highest pitch when he clearly saw he was detested; when he heard himself termed the murderer of nuns, the assassin of old men. He found his castle deserted; Jane came not to greet his arrival; his children came not to embrace him. "Where is Jane?" said he, to the only servant whom he perceived. "Where are my children?"

SERVANT. When the account of your horrible transactions reached this place, your wife fled with her children to a monastery in the neighbourhood. Her servants and your own dispersed, as there was no one to pay or nourish them, because they thought you had been sent to the scaffold. I remained alone here, to guard what belongs to you, and to return it to anyone who might justly claim it.

RODOLPHE. Well, Peter, how do you like this commencement?

PETER. I say it will pass like a storm. (*To the servant.*) Go, old man; go and assemble the servants; announce the return of your master; all that has been reported is a falsehood.

SERVANT. How happy for you, and us all, if it be thus.

RODOLPHE. Here I am, abandoned by everybody! That horrid "evil" pronounced over me at the coronation, still sounds in my ears.

PETER. Compose yourself: you want society? Well, you shall be as much amused and as joyful as you can possibly wish. I will prepare everything to receive your friends.

Rodolphe placed himself at the window, and saw, with satisfaction, his servants assemble by degrees, and return to the castle. At the setting of the sun some strangers entered—thirteen in number: they came, as they reported, from the borders of the Danube, and demanded hospitality: Rodolphe welcomed them, and resumed his usual gaiety in their company. He passed the night in drinking, and retired to rest quite intoxicated. When he awoke the sun was already risen. Desirous of again seeing his dear Jane, he called the old servant.

RODOLPHE. Take a horse, and go to the convent, to which my wife is retired: tell her I am returned, and that I expect her with my children.

SERVANT. With pleasure. Oh! how delightful it will be to live in the castle, when she once more presides in it!

The servant departed, and Rodolphe passed the time in conversation with Peter, who consoled him, and promised him new enjoyments. It was near twelve, and Rodolphe was waiting dinner, when the servant returned alone: "Jane will not return," said he. "Yesterday she pronounced her vows in the convent. It was with difficulty I could obtain permission to see her. She sends you her greeting, and conjures you to repent of your scandalous life, to enter a convent as she has done, that she may once more see you in another world."

RODOLPHE. And where are my children?

SERVANT. A servant has wages, and a faithful spouses merits them in a much higher degree. She has taken her children, in compensation for the loss of her honour and reputation; she has placed them under the protection of a devout man, who is to educate them in the fear of the Lord; you are never to know their abode, for fear they should follow your example and perish like you. And I also, my lord, must leave you—I will retire to some solitude to serve God; for I cannot live any longer in this cast.

RODOLPHE. How! You leave me?

SERVANT. I must: one foot is already in the grave; I must think of my salvation, and I should endanger it too much by remaining here; I should become, against my will, an instrument of vice. When, in your childhood, I rocked you in my arms, and saw you grow up in honour and virtue, I said to myself:—"He will nourish you, he will recompense you for the long services you accorded to his father!" But it has happened otherwise. Man proposes, and God disposes. My lord, save your soul! for as to your reputation, it is irrevocably lost. I will pray for you. Think of your end. (*He retires slowly*).

RODOLPHE (*looking after him*). Yes, certainly, of my own end. I have, like you, one foot in the grave. Peter, how long is it since the contract was signed?

PETER. What are you occupying yourself with such paltry things? You are losing your time. Enjoy yourself as long as you can.

RODOLPHE (*showing his empty hand*). There, take that.

PETER. Leave me alone; I will undertake to procure you amusement. Do not give yourself up to melancholy: you shall amuse yourself this day: I have invited your neighbours, they are all coming.

RODOLPHE. They will not come; or if they do come, it will be only to take leave of me, as my old servant did. And Jane has also abandoned me! Jane, for whom I became what you now see me.

PETER. Forget her, as she has forgotten you. There are other women in the world. Let us see—we will find more than we want.

Peter employed many arguments to tranquilize his master, and to resolve his doubts. Rodolphe expected his guests with impatience; they came. They were acquaintances of the neighbourhood; they congratulated him on his return; recalled to their minds, in their long compliments, the joyous evenings they had spent in his company, and avoided mentioning the sinister report, which had already spread over the whole country. Peter hastened to fill their cups, and gaiety soon usurped its empire over the company. Rodolphe buried his grief in wine, spared not his bottle, and was soon the most joyous of the society. Thus passed this evening; and thus passed many more. Peter brought plenty of company, and Rodolphe gave himself entirely up to the pleasure of emptying his cups. He rarely fasted, and never left his castle. He knew not what was passing, and his friends never announced anything disagreeable. If, sometimes, his conscience was troubled; if he was tormented by the fear of futurity, he called for wine, and drowned his importunate reflections in that liquor.

CHAP. XIX.

LREADY the dreary winter began to lay waste the fertile fields, the sharp north-east wind covered the windows of the gothic castle with hoar frost, when, one evening, Rodolphe having ordered more wine to enliven his company, the usual guests being assembled, the trampling of horses was heard in the court-yard, and soon after steps on the stairs. The guests started, looked at each other, and asked who could be coming so late? "Whoever it be," said Rodolphe, "he is welcome, and shall drink with us." The door opened—an old and respectable priest appeared. In his left hand he held a lighted taper, a crucifix in his right hand.

"Good spirits praise the Lord," said he; "evil spirits fly before his almighty name." Suddenly, all the guests disappeared, with Peter and the servants, and all the lights were extinguished, except the taper of the priest before whom stood Rodolphe quite stupefied.

PRIEST. You are then among the living? you are not a spirit?

RODOLPHE. Venerable old man, why do you ask me that question?

PRIEST. Because I find you in the company of demons.

RODOLPHE. Demons?—I am astounded: They are acquaintances of the neighbourhood, who come to see me every evening.

PRIEST. Then why did they fly? why did they disappear when I saluted them?

RODOLPHE. I know not.

PRIEST. Unfortunate! wandering, perhaps even lost child! It is time to open your eyes. May Heaven bless the steps I have taken, at the earnest supplications of Jane, my penitent! Your friends are demons; you have formed a criminal union with them. Be sincere, and confess your sins.

RODOLPHE. Yes; I am connected with them.

PRIEST. I will endeavour to save you. For these five months you have been reported as dead in the whole country. Not a living creature was thought to inhabit the castle. It is generally believed that the devil carried you off, and tore you to pieces in the air the day after your departure from Aix-la-Chapelle; and that since that time your castle has been his habitation. I have often seen the windows suddenly illuminated—I have often heard a noise resembling that made by a company of drinkers, and I could not doubt but that it was a deception of the demon, when I saw fiery dragons creep along the roof, and precipitate themselves from the battlements. Several persons have, it is true, seen you during the day, looking out of the window or walking in the garden; but they avoided you, and feared to speak to you. Jane, who is at present a penitent in tears, conjured me, yesterday, to enter the castle and ascertain the truth; to provide myself with sacred objects, to banish the spirits and to save you, if you were yet in their company. Prophetic mind, your presentiment was but too true! God has, perhaps, thereby reserved me the happiness of bringing back a sheep to the fold. O how great will be her joy! for the Lord himself said, "There is more rejoicing in heaven over one sinner that repenteth, than over ninety and nine just men." My son, will you follow me?

RODOLPHE (*trembling*). I will.

PRIEST. Will you repent of your criminal life, return to virtue? abjure your alliance with Satan? And renew it with God?

RODOLPHE. I will.

PRIEST. May the mercy of Heaven be granted you! And I will not cease to pray until that moment.

RODOLPHE. Do you then think that I can be saved?

PRIEST. Place your confidence in God, nothing is impossible to him.

RODOLPHE. But you do not know all, you believe me only to be a drunkard, a robber, and a murderer: I am more than that, for near eleven years my soul has been engaged to the demon. I sold it him in the delirium of a fiery passion; he has in his possession the contract, signed with my blood; at the expiration of the next year, he will come and claim his property.

PRIEST. Miserable wretch! you sold what the Lord had redeemed with his blood? Yes, unfortunate, you are fallen into a deep abyss; I deplore your fall, and my hand cannot attain you. But religion, may even now show you a path that leads to heaven.

The Priest prostrated himself on the floor; he prayed long, and in a low voice, then rose again, and began the exorcism. I dare not transcribe the powerful expressions with which he commanded Satan to appear. While he pronounced them the lightnings flashed, the thunders roared, the earth quaked, the walls tottered, the roof of the castle threatened to sink; but the Priest continued the conjuration; in vain horrific phantoms crossed the room, with a dreadful noise; in vain the winds roared, and raised the vestments of the exorcist. When he had concluded, Beelzebub, trembling, and with downcast looks, appeared from beneath the floor. He held a roll of parchment in his hand, and the Priest stretched forth his arm on Rodolphe.

BEELZEBUB. Elect of the Lord, what are your commands?

PRIEST. Thou lion, that prowlest in the dark to surprise mankind, return thy prey.

BEELZEBUB. I only took what he offered me: I have punctually fulfilled the conditions of the contract, and I hope that he will keep his word.

PRIEST. Behold him living; he is yet in the power of Him who created, and condemned thee. He repents; he is desirous of quitting the broad road leading to hell; to follow the narrow path that will conduct to him to heaven; and I will be his guide.

BEELZEBUB. Who shall warrant his resolution?

PRIEST. Himself.

BEELZEBUB. And if he breaks his word?—If he deceives you as he has deceived me?

PRIEST. Then God will judge him, and not I.

BEELZEBUB (*placing the contract at the feet of the Priest*). Then I will demand my right, and the fulfilment of his promise.

PRIEST. Retire—retire.

BEELZEBUB. Who will restore what I have stolen for him?

PRIEST. He will employ all he yet possesses thereunto, and pay those with prayers whom he cannot otherwise satisfy.

BEELZEBUB. Who will dry the tears of injured innocence?

PRIEST. His repentance.

BEELZEBUB. Who will avenge the blood he has spilt?

PRIEST. His penitence.

BEELZEBUB. How shall he be judged?

PRIEST. By his future actions.

Beelzebub disappeared in howling; and Rodolphe, profoundly touched, fell on his knees before his deliverer. He testified the most lively gratitude, promised seriously to convert himself, and was conducted to a monastery. He was there received with compassion, instructed in all the forms of penitence, and shown the true road to salvation.

The Abbot took upon himself the office of disposing of his temporal goods, and returned all that could be restored with the greatest integrity. He went himself to Worms, where the court then was; related to the Emperor the horrid history of

Rodolphe, implored mercy for the criminal, and obtained it under the condition that he should, by sincere repentance and good deeds, expiate the blood of his victims, and dry the tears of innocence. The ban of the Empire was lifted, and Rodolphe re-established in the society of men.

In order to satisfy as soon as possible the decision of the Emperor, and to appease the souls of the dead, the Abbot sold all the possessions of Rodolphe. With the produce, a new church was to be built for the nuns, who had already pardoned him; and a convent, erected in honour of St. Barbara, the inhabitants of which were to sing every day, a "De profundis," and perform a solemn service for the repose of those whose death he had caused. Nothing remained of his great riches; they were consecrated to the last obole—to pious benefactions

At first, his zeal was lively; his piety very constant; he fervently prayed to God, whom he had so horribly outraged, whom he had so often offended. Priests and laymen were edified with his conversion. They firmly believed that he would become an apostle of the miraculous reign of the Almighty; but, unfortunately, this was not the case. His mind was too firmly riveted to the enjoyments of this earth; his passions only slumbered in his heart; and soon awoke with violence. He endeavoured to resist them; but the monotonous life of the cloister, his daily prayers, his daily mortifications, soon overcame his resolution of devoting the remainder of his days to God. Sometimes, but rarely, his repentance partook of a profound sentiment of his crimes; but, in general, it was only a forced penitence; it was only that fear which he felt in the world when wine did not dim his senses. But the cause did no longer exist, and the contract of Beelzebub had been publicly burnt in the convent. He was re-established in his alliance with God and men. He had nothing more to fear, but on the contrary, much to hope. His youth was indeed passed—but he was only forty-one years of age, and could, therefore, promise to himself twenty years of enjoyment. Luxury, honours, and the pleasures of the senses, were not the objects of his wishes; he ambitioned only domestic felicity, the happiness of a private life, with a beautiful and virtuous spouse, and a circle of faithful friends. That was the enjoyment with which he flattered himself in his hours of sleep and watchfulness. He proposed to serve God in the world as well as in the convent, and never again to fall into the dreadful sins of his past life.

CHAP. XX.

WHEN enlivening spring returned to open every heart; when the trees began to assume their verdure; when all Nature began to animate itself; when Rodolphe heard the birds celebrating their loves in their musical strains; when he saw them fluttering about and enjoying their existence, his mind was every day more and more charmed with the images that surrounded him; he could no longer resist the voice of liberty; he resolved to quit his prison and rejoice with the rest of Nature. In order not to afflict his benefactors, he had recourse to hypocrisy, and concealed from them his true motive.

One day he approached the father Abbot, and begged an audience. "Before I gave myself up to my great disorders," said he, "I vowed to the Lord to go to Palestine to visit his tomb, and to offer my prayers on the very spot where he suffered. I had totally forgotten my oath, and now it weighs heavy my conscience. Permit me, father, to fulfil my first vow before I entirely consecrate myself to the Lord. I will return in three years, and will bring you his benediction from the Holy Land,"

A pilgrimage to the tomb of Christ, was, in those days, the most meritorious work which man could accomplish. The resolution of Rodolphe very much delighted the old Abbot. "Go, my son; go in peace—be constant in your repentance—in your penitence, and you will return with the blessing of God." He then gave Rodolphe two pieces of gold, and added—"Use them only in the last extremity. Your merit will be greater, if during the whole of your voyage you can live on alms; and if, at your arrival, you consecrate this gold to the Lord."

As joyous as a bird, whose cage has been opened by a chance, Rodolphe for the first time left the convent and hastened his steps to abandon more speedily a prison, in which he languished during several months. When he no longer perceived its turrets, he laid down on the border of the Rhine. The lordly river gently glided along, and softly caressed the mossy bank when agitated by the east wind; troops of little fishes came into the basin, formed by the waves in this place, amused themselves in the rays of the sun, and seized the flowers which Rodolphe threw into the water. On the left hand he beheld a great plain, on which were men and animals, some negligently enjoying their existence, and others occupied in tilling the earth—presenting an agreeable contrast of labour and leisure. The lark twittered above his head, and other little birds enlivened the surrounding bushes by their warbling. He remained in his reclined position for some moments, and seemed for the first time to delight in the spectacle of Nature; even the humming of the bee appeared to him a melodious sound. When satiated with these enchanting objects, he seized his staff and continued his road.

But his heart soon saddened—every living being abandoned itself to joy; and found a friend to whom they communicated their happiness: he alone was lonely—he had none to rejoice with, none to partake in his grief. It is a horrid destiny for man to see himself abandoned by all his fellow-creatures; to wander in the regions of Nature without finding a being to whom he may say, "*my friend*." To such a traveller, every unpleasant circumstance, every misfortune is redoubled, because no one pities him—no one pours a salutary balm on his wounds. Such a child of misery finds no pleasure, because he is deprived of the only source from which mortals can derive it—because he is not expected by a person, to whom he has devoted his sentiments, with whom he can empty and fill again the cup of happiness. He who has never experienced this melancholy sensation—he who has never been acquainted with its effects, can form no idea of it.

Fraught with these thoughts, Rodolphe entered the great road. He had other subjects of grief besides this; he had till then existed in plenty; he had been rich and powerful; he had enjoyed every convenience of life, and every means of allaying his pains. Now he was poor and destitute of everything. His whole fortune consisted in two pieces of gold, which he was not even to touch; he was hungry and thereby forced to beg; he blushed with shame at the *idea* of seeing himself in the attitude of a suppliant. "What shall I do," said he, "when it is a reality?"

The sun had just attained the horizon, when he arrived before a cottage. He knocked, after much hesitation. A young girl, simply, poorly, but cleanly dressed, opened the door. She was plaiting her hair, and had suspended her toilet to open to Rodolphe; her large blue eyes smiled with benignity.

MAIDEN. Enter, good pilgrim; if you wish to sleep here, my mother will procure you to eat and drink.

Rodolphe gave her his hand, without answering a word.

MAIDEN (*smiling*). Why are your eyes thus fixed on me?

RODOLPHE. I admire in you the almighty power of God.

MAIDEN. If I am so well, I must thank Him alone. Enter; you are tired, and it must be very uncomfortable for you to stand.

Rodolphe entered the cottage, and found it as clean, but as poor as its inhabitants.

MAIDEN. Now, sit down. (*Rodolphe still looking on her intently*).

MAIDEN (*smiling*). The power of Heaven is very evident in me by your looks.

RODOLPHE. Young woman, you are beautiful!

MAIDEN. The son of my neighbour tells me so every day; it is a pity I cannot say as much of him.

RODOLPHE. I wish you a husband who can appreciate your beauty.

MAIDEN. The Lord reward you for your wish! (The mother enters the cottage.) Mother, I've invited a guest; I hope you will welcome him.

MOTHER. Certainly. Whence are you, good pilgrim?

RODOLPHE. A vow which I have made conducts me to Palestine.

MOTHER. May God grant you strength to accomplish your vow. Many go thither, but few ever return. My husband went there twelve years since with the troops of the Emperor. If you should meet him, salute him for me, and tell him that his wife is in great trouble—that she awaits him with the greatest impatience. Oh! my good sir, without that girl, I should have died with hunger long since.

RODOLPHE. I envy you, good mother, in the possession of such a daughter.

MOTHER. She is not my daughter: I took her into my house ten years ago, when her mother died in our neighbour-hood, and she now amply repays my trouble.

RODOLPHE. You are then very poor?

MOTHER. I have this house, two goats, and two sheep. If I was not so old and infirm, I could gain my livelihood; but now my Agnes works for me.

RODOLPHE (*trembling*). Agnes!

MOTHER. Why are you so frightened?

RODOLPHE. I also knew an Agnes.

MOTHER. O Lord, there are so many Agnes' in this world; but certainly there are few equal to mine.

During this conversation the inhabitants of the hut had prepared the repast. Rodolphe, to whom the enjoyments of a rural life were unknown, soon resumed his gaiety; he experienced new emotions on casting his eyes on the young and beautiful peasant. He placed himself at the table beside her; he ate with her out of the same bason, of the milk which her hands had prepared; and asked her, in the most passionate manner, whether she could love a man like him? She answered with much ingenuity: "Yes;" and added, "that of all the men she had seen, none had pleased her so much as himself. If you were to take off that frock, and let the ringlets of your beautiful hair fall on your shoulders, you would look very well—you would look like a knight." He conversed with her till the night was far advanced; and when he quitted her, to seek repose on his couch of straw, he felt that he was deeply in love with her.

"If I had only five hundred pieces of gold," said he, "I would marry that girl—go to a foreign country, and live happy." The day following, when he seized his staff, and stretched forth his hand to bid her adieu, she shed abundant tears.

RODOLPHE. Why do you weep, my amiable child?

AGNES. Because you will never return, and I should like to see you again.

RODOLPHE: (*Joyfully*). You shall see me again: yes, you shall see me again!

AGNES. In that case you must return very soon—for, in two months, my mother intends marrying me to George, the son of our neighbour.

RODOLPHE (*to the old woman*). Do not do that my good mother, but await my return.

He placed the two pieces of gold in her hand, and disappeared as soon as possible; for he could never have left the cottage, had he not taken the resolution of departing so suddenly.

CHAP. XXI.

RODOLPHE arrived at the summit of a hill which over-looked the cottage, turned round and beheld Agnes at the door; she wished him, by signs, a happy journey and speedy return. The knight reposed himself on the soft grass, in order to listen to the arguments of his heart and his reason. He had soon done with the first. Filled with the idea of the young peasant, his only desire was to possess her; and he was determined to marry. But with his reason, the argument was longer.—"You can very well marry her," said it; "and even your conscience would have nothing to reproach you. But how will you support your wife and yourself? Will you work with her?"—"Yes;" answered his heart, without hesitation.—"But can you work?" said he, to himself. "Will not a burden, which you are unaccustomed to bear, soon oppress you? Will it not be the torment of your life? Will it not subvert all your pleasures? Can you enjoy any happiness, when you return to your house, harassed with fatigue, dripping with sweat, and finding your wife groaning beneath the weight of her misery? When you are forced to refuse her most ardent desires, for want of means to satisfy them? Or would you only enjoy her charms, and rob her of her innocence, the only treasure in her possession; and again fall into that criminal life, from which you receded only by a miracle?"

His conscience and his very heart revolted at this idea; he loved the young woman as he had never loved before. He desired to render her happy, to be happy with her, to live and die in her arms. "Will you return to the convent" continued his reason, "confess your situation to the father Abbot, and entreat him to build one tower less, and restore you some part of your riches to nourish Agnes and yourself." "But the insensible priest will not consent," retorted his heart; "he has devoted you to Heaven, and will not suffer you to enter the world again. He will imagine that you are falling into your old errors, imprison you, and thus deprive you of every hope of ever seeing Agnes again." "Or will you," said he, at last, "call your friend, Peter, order him to empty the treasure of some Pagan prince, and bring you as much gold as will suffice for the remainder of your life? Good deeds can counterbalance such sins, if it be a sin to deprive an Infidel of his superfluity, and thus prevent them from persecuting the Christians."

His heart seconded this proposition, but his conscience strongly opposed it.

Rodolphe had the little knapsack with him. During his retreat, he had left it in a corner of the cell, without paying the least attention to it. At his departure, he found it convenient for his journey, and placed in it several necessary articles. Whether he had accidentally, or intentionally forgotten to empty it before he left, is what I cannot determine; it sufficed that he had it with him. In crossing a desert tract he put his hand into it, felt the book, and brought it forth. He instantly recollected that if he opened it to the right, the mother of Euphrosina would present herself. She had always given him good advice, of which he was now in want; he was on the point of opening the hook, when his heart opposed him, and recalled to mind the evils which she had accumulated upon his head. "She is like the Abbot," exclaimed he, "who interdicts every degree of pleasure, and orders only mortifications." His memory retraced all that had passed, and he placed the book in his knapsack.

Hunger forced him to walk faster; he was wandering in a wood, and could discover no outlet; and, when night surprised him, he had neither eaten nor appeased his burning thirst with one drop of water. He lay down under a tree; his extreme fatigue prevented him from sleeping, and hunger became more and more urgent. "If, in this extremity," said he, "I take the only path which remains to me, the Father Abbot himself could not condemn me." He seized the book, and opened it to the left. Peter immediately presented himself, laid a club on the ground, and disappeared without giving him time to speak. Rodolphe understood the meaning of this; the well known club possessed those marks, indelibly fixed on his heart; he tremblingly took it up—shuddered at the past—surveyed the fatal talisman; laid it down—and again—and again reviewed it; but, at length, overcome both with fatigue and hunger, he almost unknowingly laid himself down to sleep.

The next morning, he endeavoured eagerly to find a passage out of the forest, but he only entangled himself more and more in its intricacies; he fell exhausted to the ground. The idea of dying, after having seen the beautiful Agnes, after having promised himself to live with her in a supreme felicity! of dying when she expected his return, overcame him. The pressing wants of his body triumphed over the resolution of his mind. He had scarce sufficient strength to take the book and open it. Peter, when he placed the club at his feet, and disappeared, as suddenly appeared.

"Merciless wretch!" said Rodolphe, "give me only a drop of water." But Peter was deaf. The knight in despair, at last took the club, and after long hesitation, performed the conjuration. Beelzebub appeared to him as the first time.

BEELZEBUB. What, you wish to deceive me a second time?

RODOLPHE. Give me some water, and we will converse afterwards.

BEELZEBUB. Hypocrite! You have recourse to me in the last stage of necessity? But I shall take better precautions in future. I will not perform the least service for you before I have your signature.

RODOLPHE. I will not sign, whatever be the consequence.

BEELZEBUB. Come, let us see; I could demand a renewal of the old contract; but, as you return to me. I will accord you a delay of twelve years more.

RODOLPHE. I cannot; I cannot.

BEELZEBUB. I give you twenty years; I will give you thirty. It is the longest period to which you can aspire, and then I am not certain that you will not escape me in the last month.

Rodolphe, exhausted, at last gave his signature, and Beelzebub disappeared; suddenly a magnificent table rose from the ground, with Peter beside it, ready to obey his orders. He ate with appetite; and, after the repast, he consulted with his reason. "You have signed again," said he, "and you have renewed your alliance with Satan; but thirty years is a very long term; there will be a change from this time till then. The cloister has nothing terrible for a man satiated with life; why it is a repose for his body. Before the expiration of the term, I go to a monastery, repent sincerely, and I am then certain of salvation at the expiration of my career. Moreover, during that interval, I will not charge my conscience with any crime; but only order Peter to bring me some gold; then discard him; marry my mistress, enjoy with her a peaceable felicity, and begin a meritorious and edifying life."

His conscience seconded this resolution, and his heart adopted it without hesitation.

RODOLPHE. Peter?

PETER. How happy I am to hear your voice, my dear master! What are your wishes?

RODOLPHE. Go to India, take ten thousand pieces from the treasure of the caliph, and bring them hither.

PETER. Must I not procure horses first?

RODOLPHE. That you may kill the proprietor in my name, and under my responsibility? No! no! Execute my orders, and leave the rest to me.

PETER. As if the caliph stationed no guard at his treasury gate?

RODOLPHE. You can deceive them, but you shall not kill them. Make haste, for I am in a hurry.

Peter left the forest, and soon after brought the money his master demanded.

PETER. Now, how shall I carry it? You see I must have horses.

RODOLPHE. Carry it on your back, and lead me out of the forest.

PETER. You convert me into a beast of burden; but as I have before observed, a faithful servant never abandons his master.

Peter marched on; and Rodolphe perceived, to his utter astonishment, that a hundred steps would have led him out of the forest; that there were some cottages in the neighbourhood, and that if he had persisted in his resolution, he would have extricated himself from his embarrassments, without again becoming the property of Beelzebub.

He bought two horses, hired a servant, and discharged Peter. "If I am in want of your services I will call you. You can seek another master; for now you would only be wearied in my service."

CHAP. XXII.

RODOLPHE followed the great road to the first town, and there exchanged his pilgrim's dress for that of a simple knight.

As he was going to leave the inn to rejoin Agnes, he met a gentleman of Thuringia, who offered to sell his castle and estates, and sacrifice his patrimony, to the pleasure of going to Palestine. Rodolphe sought what the other wished to dispose of; he promised to visit the castle before the expiration of one month, and to purchase it if it answered his expectations.

As he was anticipating his future bliss, his vanity suddenly recalled to his mind that Agnes was not of a noble family, and he could boast of no quarterly bearings by an union with her.

But his love soon triumphed over these objections. He desired repose, and peaceable felicity alone had charms for him. The storm of passions, which had formerly so violently agitated his bosom, had subsided; his only wish was to seek tranquillity, and share it with the only object which could enhance its value. "I shall never," said he, "find a person comparable to Agnes in the most exalted stations of life."

His heart was occupied with her alone; he retraced in his imagination the amiable simplicity with which she received him in the cottage; he beheld her standing before him, with her eyes cast down and streaming with tears, when he beheld her. "Sweet creature," said he again, "you expect me, but do not imagine that I am so near you."

When he discovered the hill upon which he had stood to deliberate with his conscience, he spurred his horse, and soon attained it. But what a horrid spectacle presented itself! A thick smoke was diffused over the whole plain; and he perceived black vestiges of a conflagration in those fields where peace had so lately dwelt. When the wind dispersed the smoke, he discerned the inhabitants clasping their hands, and uttering mournful cries, which the zephyr wafted to his ear. He flew to the plain, and sought the cottage of Agnes; his heart soon indicated the spot where it had stood—but the flames had consumed it. Not far from thence, the lifeless corpse of her mother was exposed to view by the barbarous ruffians who had massacred her—blood still distilled from her wounds, and demanded vengeance of Heaven. Rodolphe endeavoured long, but in vain, to discover the cause of this disaster—mangled and inanimated bodies bestrewed the plain in every direction, and the survivors fled him in terror. At length he approached an old peasant, whose age prevented his escape.

RODOLPHE. Hear me, good old man; I come not to injure you—I come to offer my services, if it be not too late.

OLD MAN. Oh! if you do not live in the society of those monsters; if you are an honourable knight, the Lord reward your good intention,

RODOLPHE. Inform me of what has passed. Who are the authors of this horrid disaster?

OLD MAN. Robbers, noble lord, robbers! They have long infested the forest of Mayence, and devastated the whole neighbourhood. They surprised us some few hours ago—deprived us of all our cattle—of all we possessed: they set fire to our cottages; killed many of our neighbours; and seized many more. Few have escaped bondage or death.

RODOLPHE. Could you give me any information concerning the young woman who resided with her mother in that isolated cottage?

OLD MAN. Was she called Agnes?

RODOLPHE. The very same.

OLD MAN. I am ignorant of her fate; perhaps she has fallen a victim to the fury of the robbers; or, what is more likely, they have carried her off; for when I returned from the field, I saw several of our maidens linked together, and driven before their oppressor, like a herd of cattle. O, my good lord, Agnes was a very beautiful girl, and her mother was a very excellent woman. I was their near neighbour. Some days ago a pilgrim of distinction came to their cottage and gave her, at his departure, two pieces of gold. Her joy was extreme; she immediately purchased a cow, and begged me to partake of its first milk. At this repast we repeatedly blessed the unknown benefactor. But the robbers have deprived her of everything. Perhaps she is herself wandering like me in search of her child.

Rodolphe was often on the point of interrupting the old man; but how could he stop that flow of words which relieved the anguish of his heart? He at length ceased, to the great satisfaction of the knight, who trembled for the fate of his Agnes, and thought only of the means of discovering her. He begged the old man to assemble some of the inhabitants, and three of them agreed in the assertion that Agnes was amongst the number of the young females that were driven away. Rodolphe trembled with fear at this intelligence. The only object of his wishes was to rescue his mistress from these ravishers. He bestowed a handful of gold on the assistants, and departed accompanied by their benedictions. The only expedient which was left was to call Peter—and Peter appeared.

"That's the way," said he, when Rodolphe had related the whole to him; "that is the way things turn out when an old and faithful servant is discarded, and told to seek another place. I being averse to indolence, entered this morning the service of the captain of robbers, and assisted him in his expedition. This would not have been the case if you had not dismissed me— you would have spared yourself and Agnes many sufferings."

RODOLPHE. What! you committed that atrocity?—You robbed the innocent and massacred the aged? Away!—out of my sight; for I will have nothing in common with you.

PETER. As you please—but permit me to inform you that the captain is pleased with your mistress. He has given her this day for reflection; and if she will not willingly accept his propositions, he will ravish what she refuses.—Adieu!

RODOLPHE. Ah, traitor! hasten to deliver her, and conduct her hither immediately.

PETER. That is impossible—I cannot undo what I have done; all that remains in my power is to give you advice, in consideration of our old acquaintance—but you may be sure to deliver her, if you will await me here until the evening. Agnes is concealed in a cavern in the centre of the forest. The cavern is surrounded by rocks, which are separated by deep chasms, through the openings of which a man can descend to the den itself. When night has spread its dark shades—when the robbers are fallen asleep, or have departed on some new expedition, I will fetch you, and conduct you to the chasm. Then you can yourself save Agnes, and thus redouble the love she bears you. I will await your return, and prepare everything for your speedy flight

RODOLPHE. Will you answer for the life and security of Agnes?

PETER. I will.

RODOLPHE. Then make haste, for I shall expect you here.

PETER. Am I to continue in the service of the thieves, or seek another master?

RODOLPHE. Neither—you shall serve me alone.

That day was the longest of Rodolphe's life.—The desire of delivering his mistress occupied his mind exclusively, and he felt not the calls of Nature. He continually cast his eyes towards the sun and accused its sloth. The so much wished for night at length appeared, and his impatience redoubled at the tardy approach of Peter. He came, however, at the close of day—conducted his master to the aperture in the rock, and Rodolphe descended with precipitation. He soon discovered the pale reflection of a lamp, which he approached, and found Agnes on her knees, with dishevelled hair, praying to Heaven to deliver her. When she perceived the knight, she rose in terror, fled to the uttermost part of the cave, and seized a large stone.

AGNES. Bold intruder! approach me not, if you fear death!

RODOLPHE (*in a soft tone*). Agnes! O my Agnes! do you not recognize in me the pilgrim who promised you to return? Not finding you in your cottage, he has penetrated through the rocks to deliver all he holds most dear upon earth.

AGNES (*dropping the stone*). I recognize your voice. And you also are one of the robbers? you are one of their companions?

RODOLPHE. No: give me your hand fearlessly. I will restore you to liberty; and you can then judge whether you will proceed any farther under the guidance of your liberator.

AGNES. It is impossible not to believe you, and I will confidently follow you.

Rodolphe conducted her without danger through the rocks, and found. Peter at the entrance. "Lead on," said Rodolphe. Peter walked on, and the lovers followed with silent emotion. When arrived at the border of the forest, they found three horses ready saddled. Agnes thanked Rodolphe for this precaution, for she could walk no longer.

"I have stolen them," whispered Peter to Rodolphe, who was busily employed about Agnes.

RODOLPHE. Very well.

PETER. I killed the proprietor.

RODOLPHE. Be silent.

PETER. Am I to follow you in a visible form?

"Yes," replied Rodolphe, for he dreaded some new danger, to which he was not willing to expose his mistress.

At the break of day they arrived at the town which Rodolphe had left the day before. He conducted Agnes to the inn, and procured her decent clothing. He then informed her, that notwithstanding his claims to knighthood, he would marry her if she would follow him to Thuringia, and live retired.

Agnes, educated in a village, and perceiving no difference between herself and a knight, accepted the proposition. She loved Rodolphe—she had never seen his equal in beauty, and her heart was strongly chained to him. Her mother was dead, and she had not one friend or protector in the whole world; she was delighted that Rodolphe offered to be both. "Permit me to hope," said she, with an enchanting look, "that my poverty, that my misfortune, will never abase me in your eyes; my love shall equal my gratitude. I will respect you as my benefactor—as my father; and love you with ever renewed tenderness as my husband."

It had been easy for this consummate seducer to attack the innocence of an inexperienced country girl, but he wished no longer to deceive; he had promised himself domestic bliss in her arms, and he earnestly sought it. A discreet, respectuous love filled his bosom. He was so content in her possession, that he imagined himself to be partaking of the joys of heaven. He discharged Peter, for fear he should be forced to disclose his intentions to him, and he should prevent him from marrying Agnes. The next day he went in quest of a priest to unite them. He soon found one, and begged so earnestly, that he surmounted every difficulty, and the lovers received that same day the nuptial benediction. Agnes, overcome with love and gratitude, sunk into the arms of Rodolphe, calling him her husband, and Rodolphe imagined he had attained the highest pitch of felicity.

They soon departed and arrived at Thuringia. The castle delighted Rodolphe, as it stood isolated according to his wishes. Built on a height, it overlooked all its dependencies; he beheld all his vassals fearlessly cultivating their fields, and quietly keeping their flocks under his powerful protection. The joy of Rodolphe was increased by that of Agnes; she traversed the different apartments with the swiftness of a young fawn; found everything magnificent; embraced her husband with transport, and incessantly discovered new subjects of admiration.

Rodolphe willingly paid the sum demanded, and received the homage of all the inhabitants of his dominions. He passed two months in peace and bliss: he had never been so happy, and had never enjoyed life so well. His pleasures were pure, as Agnes was their source; she was his inseparable companion; she followed him to the chase, and, always returned first to prepare some refreshments for him when he had ended his day's sport.

CHAP. XXIII.

AGNES, a few months after her marriage, suddenly fell into a profound melancholy. Her gaiety disappeared, her cheeks lost their colour. She walked alone, plunged in deep reveries, and was thrilled with horror when Rodolphe came to drag her thence. He entreated her to reveal the cause of her grief; but Agnes was silent, and endeavoured to appease him by constrained embraces. One evening, after having supped rather later than usual, when Rodolphe took her hand to go to her chamber, she shuddered and begged him to remain a little longer. He forced her away, and insisted on knowing the cause of this singular terror. At last she informed him, with excessive agitation, that for some nights passed a white figure had approached her bed, roused her from her sleep, and beckoned her to follow, accompanying the movement of her hand, sometimes with threats, and sometimes with endearing caresses.

RODOLPHE. Did you ever speak to the figure?

AGNES. Never; my terror closed my mouth. I once attempted to awake you; but her menaces, followed by friendly signs, soon deterred me.

RODOLPHE. If she should again appear to you, awake me. But I will watch this night in order to afford you some rest.

He had scarce uttered the sentence, when a tremendous knock on the gate resounded through the castle. Agnes threw herself on the bosom of Rodolphe, when the door of the chamber opened, and the white figure, decked with black crape, glided before him. "Rodolphe, save yourself," said she, in a lamentable voice: "Save yourself Rodolphe, or you are lost." He remained petrified with astonishment, on recognizing, in this phantom, his former Agnes. It was in that very attire that he had found her on the scaffold, on that day he had in vain hastened to her assistance. He had not yet fully recovered his senses, when other figures advanced towards him holding each other by their hands. He recognized in them, Regina, Clara, Euphrosina, and Jane.

"The hour is come!" said they, unanimously. "The hour is come! Save yourself!"

"The hour is come?" asked Rodolphe, slowly.

He immediately cast a rapid glance on his past life, and shuddered on recollecting that twelve years before, at that very hour, he had signed his first contract with Satan. Agnes fell insensible at his feet, he spurned her from him, seized a light and attempted to call Peter; but the book fell from his hands. Suddenly a tremendous tempest arose in and about the castle. Rodolphe was enveloped in total, impenetrable darkness. In vain he sought the window, it had disappeared from his eyes. As suddenly the obscurity was dispelled, and a shower of fire seemed falling from heaven. The doors and windows were forcibly torn open; the floor rocked, the flame glided along the walls, and thousands of monsters surrounded the knight. A tremendous crash shook the castle to its very foundation. Beelzebub, habited in a fiery vestment, appeared before him. He was followed by a long train in the same dress, and Peter, clad in the armour of an old knight, closed the procession.

BEELZEBUB (*to Rodolphe*). Are you prepared?

RODOLPHE. I?—how's this?—not one year is elapsed, and you granted me thirty?

BEELZEBUB. I have deceived you, as you deceived me. You have renewed the first contract. Read, and be silent. The hour is at hand—I come to fetch you.

RODOLPHE. Horrible! Horrible!—You cannot avail yourself of this treachery. I have repented of my past sins.

BEELZEBUB. You lie.—Accuser—What are the crimes of Rodolphe?—How many innocent maidens has he seduced?

PETER (*advancing, and placing his lance before Rodolphe*). He has seduced six women, and is living with a seventh in the ties of a criminal union.

BEELZEBUB. Name those whom he seduced, and how they died.

PETER. The first was named Regina; he carried her off from the castle of her father; she committed suicide after the loss of her honour. I, myself, in the form of a friend, augmented her despair, and placed a poignard in her hands.

BEELZEBUB. Continue.

PETER. The second was named Agnes; he committed adultery with her; she bore him an illegitimate child, and perished on a scaffold. Clara died of grief, Euphrosina of despair. With this last victim, perished an infant, of which he refused to be the father. Jane ended her life the day before yesterday. Sorrow consumed them, and her father could not survive the loss of his daughter. Mary put an end to her existence by the cord, on hearing that the ravisher of her innocence, the murderer of her lover, had obtained pardon from the Emperor. Agnes awake! (*Peter raises Agnes, who recovers from her swoon, and looks around her with dismay.*) The woman, whom he has married, is his daughter; she is the child of Agnes. When she came into this world, I placed her in the hands of a shepherdess, who educated her until the age of seven. After the death of this nurse, she found a mother in the good old woman, with whom she lived when Rodolphe first beheld her; and with this child, conceived in sin, born in sin, he is now living in the bonds of an incestuous union, and daily accumulating forfeits on his head.

RODOLPHE. Horrible and unheard of crimes. (*Agnes falls to the ground*).

PETER. The horror of her crime has deprived her of life; thus the eventful number is accomplished—seven are now dead by his hands.

BEELZEBUB. Continue. How many murders has he committed?

PETER. Exactly seventy; some by my means, some by others, and his own hands have been imbued.

BEELZEBUB. What are his other crimes?

PETER. He has sold his soul; perjured himself; stolen immense sums of money, and lived by plunder. He has enslaved free men, and persecuted just ones.

BEELZEBUB. Enough! enough! How dried the tears of innocence?—How expiated the atrocious murders? How restituted stolen property?—And how has he restored the reputation of innocence?

PETER. He played the part of an hypocrite for some months; fasted, prayed, and repented; sacrificed his stolen goods, to reconcile himself with God; and then he both robbed and assassinated again.

BEELZEBUB. He must, therefore, endure in the other world a chastisement for those crimes which he did not expiate in this.—Avengers, fulfil your duty.

The demons approached the speechless Rodolphe; Death already claimed his due; the torments of hell seemed to have possessed his soul. He mechanically seized the book laying near him, and opened it to the right; suddenly, a piercing voice pronounced the following words:—"Unfortunate son of my descendants, you call me too late; the sentence is executing; I can no longer save you. (*To Peter.*) Husband, forever reproved, you triumph! We shall never see each other again!"

The infernal monsters made the apartment resound with a loud burst of laughter, while Rodolphe lay insensible; the avenging spirits seized him, and agitated him violently to recall him to life. They dashed him with such force against the wall, that his blood and brains besmattered the surrounding objects. They flew away, bearing him with them, and uttering terrific cries; the air became darkened with the vapour arising from their bodies, and their black wings infused terror in the shrieking owl.

The remaining inhabitants of the castle precipitately fled on hearing this fearful uproar, and beheld the horrid spectacle at a distance. The castle remained uninhabited, no one ventured into it; the winds whistled through the doors and windows, and made a tremendous noise during the night. In this state of affairs, the body of Agnes became so infectious, which remained without sepulture, that it attracted various birds of prey, who flew round the castle with frightful shrieks, and superstition mistook them for demons.

CHAP. XXIV.

THE past event was circulated through the country, and the account soon reached the convent which Rodolphe had inhabited. It was reported that an unknown knight had arrived with his wife in Thuringia, that he had bought a castle, in which he had led, during several months, a peaceful and retired life; but that on the night of St. John, the devil had fetched him away, and torn him limb from limb in the air. This recital attracted the attention of the convent; priests and laymen recollected, that the term of the contract, which had been burned in the monastery, was to expire on that very night. The abbot collected further information, and some persons presented themselves, who attested to their having heard that Rodolphe was in treaty about a castle with a gentleman of Thuringia. This was enough to convince him, that the person carried off by the devil in that country, was no other than Rodolphe himself.

For the greater certainty, and in order to ascertain whether he had really married, and whence came his wife, the abbot permitted the priest who had directed the conscience of Rodolphe during his retreat to go to Thuringia, and make those inquiries which were essential, in the village belonging to the castle. He arrived, one fine summer's evening, at the foot of the hill on which it was situated. As he was preparing to ascend, some inhabitants of the neighbouring huts conjured him to abandon his project; they imagined him to be a stranger, who was not acquainted with the past events, and related to him the whole history. They described the knight in a manner to confirm his suspicions, and redouble his anxiety. He reassured these good people exceedingly, when he informed them, that being an anointed of the Lord, he had nothing to fear from the power or malice of the demon. They suffered him, therefore, to continue, more particularly when he assured them he would drive away the evil spirits by his exorcisms, and restore peace to the country.

He ascended to the castle; his steps resounded in the deserted apartments which he traversed; where he found proofs of the precipitate flight of the inhabitants. Clothing and other objects dispersed here and there, some thrown away in haste, others prepared for use. He penetrated into the interior, and at last entered the apartment of Rodolphe. He was struck by an infectious exhalation of a sepulchral odour: he approached the body of Agnes; putrefaction had already disfigured her features. "Whoever you may have been," said the priest, with a sigh, "poor creature, I bemoan your untimely fate. Perhaps you died with fear, when your husband was torn from your side. May God have mercy upon *your* soul; I will bury your body, and consecrate the ground in which you will sleep until the day of judgment." He searched every corner, without finding any object to satisfy his curiosity. Just as he was leaving the apartment, to enter another, he perceived a book on the bed of Rodolphe, which he placed under his arm, and walked on to the next room, to examine its contents. He naturally opened the book to the right, and was contemplating its strange characters with astonishment, when he felt something gently tap him on the shoulder. He turned round, and beheld before him a woman in a very ancient dress.

SPIRIT. Priest of the Eternal, what do you wish?

PRIEST (*retiring*). I did not call you.

SPIRIT. You called me unknowingly, by virtue of that book.

PRIEST. Are you a good spirit?

SPIRIT. Yes; and sigh for my deliverance.

PRIEST. I will procure it for you, if it is within the limits of my power.

SPIRIT. You can do it: destroy that book, and I shall enjoy the company of the blessed, of which I have, alas! been deprived for these five hundred years. As a reward for your good intention, and for what you will perform towards my deliverance, I will satisfy your laudable curiosity; I will relate to you all you wish to know.

PRIEST. Speak, if what you have to say may at some future period prove useful to posterity.

SPIRIT. Listen and judge. I was born at the beginning of the ninth century, during the reign of the pious Lewis. The Knight of Tauenstaf, my father, educated me in the principles of virtue. The nuns, with whom I passed the greatest part of my youth, instructed me in the knowledge of God, and how to honour and observe his holy commandments. When I had attained the age of sixteen, I was betrothed to Peter of Westerbourg, one of the most distinguished knights of that time. He possessed great flocks, and a numerous train of servants. The whole country feared him, for he was powerful. He wore clothes bordered with pearls, and he surpassed princes in magnificence. I was called the happy Mathilda; and I rejoiced in the possession of the affection of the noblest knight of the country. I returned thanks to Heaven for my bliss, for I loved him with all the tenderness I was mistress of; and, at the expiration of one year, I became his wife. He conducted me to his manor, and paid homage to me with all his vassals. During eight years I lived happy in his arms, and his love was exclusively devoted to me. I had given him four sons and three daughters, when I was attacked by an illness which confined me during two months to a bed of suffering; from that moment the love of my husband was averted from me forever. For some time he respected me as his wife, and the mother of his children; but even this outward respect was soon effaced, and there was not a maid-servant which was not more honoured by him than his spouse. In vain I shed tears—in vain I sighed; my parents beheld my sufferings, and, not being able to offer me any assistance, died of grief. He often called me an old witch in the presence of the servants, reproached me with the insignificance of my marriage portion, and disdainfully drove me from one apartment to another. I fled, and sought an asylum in the convent in which I had passed the early part of my life. The pious abbess never ceased to console me, but she engaged me patiently to await happier days, and sent me back to endure new hardships. My husband did not blush to bring young peasant girls, when he returned from the chase, to embrace them before me, and even conduct them to his bed. He forced me to nurse a child which one of them gave him, making me thus the servant of the usurper of my rights; I tacitly obeyed his slightest commands, to avert a torrent of abuse and imprecations. Thus, during ten years of continued sufferings, I shed more tears than could be counted with numbers. I was the only person in the castle that offered up prayers to Heaven; my husband never thought of God; and the servants soon followed the horrid example of their master, who was perpetually intoxicated when he retired; he threw himself on his couch, swearing and blaspheming, and rose in the morning but to recommence. During ten years he never placed his foot in the house of the Lord—during ten years not one mass was said in the castle-chapel. The clergy fled our mansion as a place of abomination; and when I wished to pray to the Lord, I was constrained to do so clandestinely, not to give him an opportunity of deriding my piety. One day, as I returned with my children from this holy exercise, I perceived him standing at the top of the stairs; his arms were crossed, and he seemed plunged in a deep reverie. I endeavoured to pass unobserved by him; but he gently seized my hand, and asked me whence I came. I dared not tell an untruth in the presence of the children, and said, "I have been in the chapel." He turned his back upon me, and said with an oath, "that neither your prayers, nor those of your children can save me."

From that time he became melancholy; often sighed aloud, and sometimes rested his eyes, swelled with tears, on the fruits of our union. Then, again, he seemed to forget his griefs, and passed whole days at table with his companions; he possessed incredible treasures, kept the most sumptuous table, and still his riches augmented. This enigma was inexplicable to me and every body else. When he was alone his melancholy returned; and redoubled, when suddenly a strange and unknown knight, clad in black armour, began to visit him. They often remained together for hours, in a chamber which no one dared approach. I was often tempted to listen to their conversation; but I was averted from my intention, by the fear of acting with impropriety. But, as the sadness of my husband augmented, in proportion with the frequency of the visits of the knight, I surmounted all my scruples, and hid myself one day, before his arrival, in a chamber only separated from that of my husband by a slight boarding. I did not wait long before they arrived, and shook hands. "Have you brought the sum?" said my husband to the knight.

KNIGHT. I have—but I do not see that you will be able to use it, for the term is to expire to night, and tomorrow you will be no more.

PETER (*sighing*). I amass for my children, and still hope for a prolongation.

KNIGHT. You hope in vain; for this very night, at the hour of twelve, we are coming to fetch you.

PETER. But if I promise to serve you well, to procure you numberless innocent creatures, and souls that are off their guard.

KNIGHT. We keep to the more substantial, and have little confidence in such promises. Have you any other commands?

PETER. None.

KNIGHT (*throwing him a great bag of gold*). You may count the sum during the interval of our separation. I shall come tonight to see you for the last time.

The knight left the room, and was soon followed by my husband. It was lucky for me that they retired so soon, for my strength began to fail, and my knees to tremble under me. I was on the point of fainting. I plainly saw that this knight was Satan himself, and that my husband had formed a treaty with him which was to expire that evening. I trembled for his salvation. In this dreadful state of body and mind, I ran to my chamber, and fervently prayed to God for advice and assistance. Suddenly, I recollected that in the neighbourhood there lived a holy man, who possessed great influence against the powers of Satan; his prayers had delivered many that were possessed, and had driven evil spirits from several houses. It was the only ray of hope which remained; I placed in him my whole confidence. I left the castle to beg him to come to the assistance of my husband. Not knowing the road, I wandered during part of the night in a forest; at length found his cottage, and related, with great perturbation, all my fears, and all I had heard; we then set off together. "Console yourself, my child," said he; "if I find your husband among the living, Satan shall not touch a single hair of his head." As we approached the castle a storm arose, and the hermit hastened his steps. We heard horrible yells, and my astonished eyes beheld a troop of infernal monsters issuing from the windows of the castle, bearing my unfortunate husband in the midst of them, and tearing him in pieces. I fell at the feet of the hermit; he immediately began his exorcisms, and forced the demons to descend towards us. What a horrid spectacle to see those monsters dripping with the blood of my husband; to see them holding part of his body in their claws, and endeavouring to tear it still more! I remained insensible on the ground for a long time. When I opened my eyes, I perceived the holy man beside me, endeavouring to administer assistance to me. From him I learnt the following circumstances:—

The devils, constrained by the power of the exorcist, ceased their operation, and obeyed his command to re-compose the body. They hastily assembled the particles which they found, but could only form the figure of a Dwarf. The soul of my husband, which had not yet fled, took possession of it. But the Dwarf remained almost lifeless from the immense quantity of blood which he had lost. In vain the hermit endeavoured to comfort him; in vain he exhorted him to repent of his sins, to confide in the mercy of the most High: he heard him not; he was a prey to the most cruel sufferings; he cursed me, cursed all his posterity, swore eternal hatred to it, and died without evincing the least sign of contrition. I had him secretly buried, and few only were informed of his terrific end.

Three days after, my husband presented himself in the form of a Dwarf, at the hour of midnight, before my bed. "I am damned," said he to me; "Satan has ordered me to wander in this degraded form, until I have fulfilled the oath I took at my death—until my seductions have drawn one of my descendants into hell, and rendered him miserable to all eternity. You must do all in your power to oppose this decree, for the torments of hell are insupportable!—I can warn you today, but tomorrow I shall be forced to obey all the orders of Beelzebub. My power extends only to my male descendants; I can only exert this power when they have attained their twenty-fourth year, and are yet in a single state. I must then induce them to the seduction of six women, and to the contraction of a criminal union with the seventh. They must commit seventy murders before they can entirely be in my possession. I have been forced to disclose these secrets to you; retain them in your mind, and take your measures accordingly, for from this instant my task commences."

If I was afflicted on my own account by such an annunciation, I was much more so on that of my unfortunate race. I sought means to avert all these evils, but only found insufficient ones. The hermit had persuaded me at his departure to give to the poor, or consecrate to God all I might find in my husband's apartment. "They are riches unjustly acquired," said he, "which will bring evil on your descendants."

I found immense sums, but instead of obeying the injunctions of the holy man. I carefully kept them; hoping that by leaving great treasures to my children, I should thereby furnish them the means of resisting the most powerful temptations. With the permission of the emperor, I exchanged all my goods and some gold for an inalienable estate for the eldest of my heirs, under the express condition that he who took possession of it should marry before his twenty-fourth year. I was often tempted to reveal to my family the deplorable end of my husband to warn them from the snares into which he had fallen. But my heart triumphed over my reason, and I thought it barbarous to render odious to my children the memory of the author of their days. I prayed to God to allow me length of days to marry my sons. He accomplished my wishes, and they were all united, before their twenty-fourth year, to those brought up in the fear of the Lord. I died at the age of seventy, and saw too well at the end of my days, how frivolous all my precautions were. When the agony of death was fast approaching, futurity disclosed itself to my weak eyes; I endeavoured to speak to exhort my children, who were gathered around me, but my strength failed, and I was separated from them with a remorseful conscience.

The Almighty weighed my actions, my errors, and my sins. My innocence was not sufficient to admit me immediately into the joys of heaven. I had not returned unjust acquired property—I had not courageously warned my descendants from the dangers which menaced them, in the ever active seductions prepared for them—I had placed greater confidence in gold and temporal goods than in the assistance of the Most High. I was condemned for these faults to wander under the figure of a Dwarf, until my inheritance was restituted or applied to the uses of the church; and until death had seized upon the last branch of my family.—"You knew that you lived in sin—you did not reclaim," said the Lord, with a voice of thunder; "you can no longer relate what you kept secret. You must mourn every time a son is born in the family, for his life will prolong the duration of your trials, and you will tremble for his future destiny. You shall not be able to approach their habitation, for your heart approached not your children. This is your punishment and your penitence; but this is your hope—That the life of man is not eternal; that the most fruitful tree withers in the end; that the will of man is free; and that he can choose both evil and good; that he can resist temptation, or fall into it. You will have the power of protecting your descendants when they freely demand your assistance. There were *you* act, the seducer cannot act; he cannot remain where you are present. It will be permitted to you to appear three times to each of yours sons when his trials are began, and warn him, but mysteriously, as you did during life. During the course of the trials, you shall be enabled once to chain the seducer, when he shall approach the circle of your influence; and only one of your descendants shall be empowered to unchain him. Lastly, if they place their confidence in you, if they desire freely to see you, they may call you, as they may call him. Go, then, suffer and hope. Return when all is fulfilled, when nothing more retains you on earth—when you will have undergone your last penance, and related to a stranger what you criminally secreted from your children. Then your recompense is certain. It will be immense if you keep the greatest part of, or all your descendants from perdition."

When I returned to this globe, my husband had already taken possession of the castle of Westerbourg; he already accompanied his master under his new form, and had rendered himself necessary to them by his brilliant actions against their enemies. He carefully collected all that could lead to temptation, and I all that could avert from it. I established my residence in the mountains far from my heirs, and I invisibly observed his machinations. At first they were not in want of my assistance; they religiously followed my wishes, and did not fall into his snares; but the family multiplied by degrees to such an extent, that the time of my trials was lengthened, and my inspection became much more troublesome. War and the plague made cruel ravages in Germany about this time, and great numbers of my descendants perished. My testament could not escape the destruction of that barbarous century; it fell a prey to the flames which consumed the castle. The few of my heirs who remained, preserved only confused ideas of my last wishes; they were entirely effaced from their memory. It was then the seductions of Little Peter began to operate with greater strength, but my vigilance always defeated them. I educated, in my solitude, pious orphans, and conducted them to the country inhabited by my male descendants: several of them chose them for wives, and lived happy with them: John of Westerbourg now remained alone of all the branches of my posterity, and left an only son, named Rodolphe. This last branch evinced no inclination during his youth towards the fair sex; and attained, notwithstanding all my efforts, his twenty-fourth year in an unmarried state.

Here the Little Woman related all that my readers are already acquainted with, and consoled herself with the hope, that among so many hundreds of her descendants, there was only one who would be deprived of eternal salvation.

CHAP. XXV.

THE priest buried the body of Agnes, burned the book, returned to his convent, and published this miracle. He wrote the history, and transmitted it for the edification of posterity.

More than one hundred years after, a learned abbot presided over the monastery, who brought all the old MSS. forward, and had them examined. Among the number, was this history, which he read, but doubting its truth, and not understanding the true meaning, he communicated it to the most learned men of his time. Several deemed it authentic and incontestable, and praised the Lord for having anciently given certain proofs of the existence and the temptations of the Spirit of Darkness. Others perceived in it a moral allegory. One of these returned it to him, accompanied by notes, in which he endeavoured to prove that this narration, taken in a figurative sense might be of great utility to the faithful, and its publication contribute much to their improvement. We will transcribe some of his notes and explanations without any alteration.

"*Peter,*" said the commentator, "represents the human passions, principally voluptuousness; which incites man to commit every vice, conducts him to the edge of the abyss, and precipitates him in to every misery.

"*Mathilda* is the symbol of religion, which warns men against the snares of error, and indicates the true path to heaven. But as that path is thorny, narrow, and rugged, the traveller encounters difficulties which deter many who strike into a broad road which leads to destruction.

"The *hat* given to Rodolphe represents unmovable faith. No seclusions or dissipations, however brilliant in their appearance, can tempt the possessor to stray from that path which always leads to power and glory.

"Every young lady should wear a *belt* like Euphrosina: it is the belt of modesty. So long as modesty is not attainted, as long even as it is not entirely lost, innocence will surmount danger; it is an impenetrable barrier. Young maidens be modest, and you will always be innocent.

"At first the passions of men are as *Dwarfs*: but, entertained and cherished, they become *Giants*, and nothing then can oppose their progress.

"*Peter* was chained by *Mathilda* to a rock, to prove religion has chains for the passions of man; but there are, unfortunately, too many Rodolphe's who cut these chains.

"The *tower*, the door of which was never to open, represents a monastery; and the *stone*, which the Dwarf throws among the others, denotes that vice can introduce itself in to the convent, and there spread destruction."

The wise abbot was not yet satisfied with these explanations; he had recourse to the records of history. He perceived by the chronicles of the convent, that there effectively existed in that country about the thirteenth century, a person of the name of Rodolphe of Westerbourg, and that the monks had suffered many vexations at his hands. Several centuries before, his ancestors had mortgaged some considerable estates to the convent: Rodolphe claimed and forcibly seized them; when the monks refused to return them, if the conditions of the agreement were not fulfilled. Rodolphe had, as the chronicle expressly mentioned, for his confidant and counsellor, an old Dwarf whom his father had brought from Palestine, and who certainly was not a Christian. He conducted beautiful girls to the castle, and oppressed the monks in every possible manner. He often watched them in the fields, with the servants of Rodolphe, stopped them, bound their hands behind their backs, and sent them back to the convent, having disfigured them by the most atrocious cruelties.

During the government of the Abbot Paul, Rodolphe was first condemned by the sovereign court; and, lastly, by the emperor himself, to return the land to the convent: he was, moreover, forced to roof the principal tower of the edifice, and to banish his Dwarf. Being mortified by this condemnation, he left the country, placing the castle under the care of a steward, who led a most exemplary life, and did much good to the monks. The knight returned some years after with a man of a gigantic stature; the whole country took him to be a magician; but he was more likely to be the chief of a band of robbers. This man brought Rodolphe immense riches. By means of these treasures, and by keeping an open table, Rodolphe gained the attachment of the neighbouring barons, who assisted him in all his undertakings. These associates declared themselves more particularly against the convents, whose cattle, wine, and treasures, they plundered. They demolished a convent of ladies, and carried off several of the nuns. The Giant was always at their head in these horrid expeditions, and was termed the *Devil*. Rodolphe and his accomplices were often cited to appear before the sovereign court but they for a length of time braved its orders.

At last it was no longer safe to travel on the high roads; the whole country implored the assistance of the emperor. This monarch ordered out the imperial banner against Rodolphe. Several commercial towns, and the vassals of the injured convents, united to join the emperor's troops. Several bloody conflicts took place. Rodolphe was vanquished with difficulty, and retired to Thuringia, with several of his partisans. All his possessions were confiscated and given to the church. The chronicle continued to relate that he bought a castle in Thuringia, and married his own daughter, though unknowingly. Being convicted of this incestuous union, he precipitated himself in a fit of rage from his castle, and thus terminated his execrable life.

The curiosity of the abbot was entirely satisfied. He perceived what had given rise to this narrative, and was enabled to distinguish truth from fable. He clearly saw that a pious contemporary had converted the Dwarf and the Giant into a devil; that he had transformed the connexion of Rodolphe with the robbers, into a contract with the demon; and, lastly, that he had interwoven so much of the marvellous with the history, in order to frighten enemies of monks and convents.

FINIS.

A PARTIAL LIST OF SNUGGLY BOOKS

PAUL ALEXIS *Lucie Pellegrin*

G. ALBERT AURIER *Elsewhere and Other Stories*

CHARLES BARBARA *My Lunatic Asylum*

CHARLES BARBARA *Stirring Stories*

S. HENRY BERTHOUD *Misanthropic Tales*

MAY ARMAND BLANC *The Last Rendezvous*

LÉON BLOY *The Desperate Man*

LÉON BLOY *The Tarantulas' Parlor and Other Unkind Tales*

ÉLÉMIR BOURGES *The Twilight of the Gods*

CYRIEL BUYSSE *The Aunts*

JAMES CHAMPAGNE *Harlem Smoke*

FÉLICIEN CHAMPSAUR *The Latin Orgy*

FÉLICIEN CHAMPSAUR *The Emerald Princess and Other Decadent Fantasies*

BRENDAN CONNELL *Clark*

BRENDAN CONNELL *The Metapheromenoi*

BRENDAN CONNELL *Metrophilias*

BRENDAN CONNELL *Unofficial History of Pi Wei*

RAFAELA CONTRERAS *The Turquoise Ring and Other Stories*

DANIEL CORRICK AND JUSTIN ISIS (editors)
  Drowning in Beauty: The Neo-Decadent Anthology

ADOLFO COUVE *When I Think of My Missing Head*

QUENTIN S. CRISP *Aiaigasa*

QUENTIN S. CRISP *Graves*

QUENTIN S. CRISP *The Flowering Hedgerow*

LADY DILKE *The Outcast Spirit and Other Stories*

LUCIE DELARUE-MARDRUS *Amanit*

LUCIE DELARUE-MARDRUS *The Last Siren and Other Stories*

CATHERINE DOUSTEYSSIER-KHOZE *The Beauty of the Death Cap*

ÉDOUARD DUJARDIN *Hauntings*

BERIT ELLINGSEN *Now We Can See the Moon*

ERCKMANN-CHATRIAN *A Malediction*

ALPHONSE ESQUIROS *The Enchanted Castle*

DELPHI FABRICE *The Red Spider*

ENRIQUE GÓMEZ CARRILLO *Sentimental Stories*

EDMOND AND JULES DE GONCOURT *Manette Salomon*